THE END OF

THE END OF

OZ

DANIELLE PAIGE

HARPER
An Imprint of HarperCollinsPublishers

Library of Congress Control Number: 2016961853

ISBN 978-0-06-242377-1

ISBN 978-0-06-266335-1 (special edition)

ISBN 978-0-06-266634-5 (special edition)

ISBN 978-0-06-266023-7 (int. ed.)

Typography by Ray Shappell

Hand lettering by Erin Fitzsimmons

17 18 19 20 21   PC/LSCH   10 9 8 7 6 5 4 3 2 1

❖

First Edition

To my beautiful Munchkins,
thank you for following the Road of Yellow Brick with me.

To my family, Mommy, Daddy, Andrea, Josh, Sienna, and Fi,
for paving the road with love . . .

And to Faith Vincent,
somewhere over the rainbow . . .

ONE

The first time I flew, it was under very different circumstances. That time, my trailer had been picked up by a tornado from Flat Hill, Kansas, and dropped into the middle of Oz. Now I was being hoisted up into the sky by a flying Road of Yellow Brick with Nox and my old-enemy-turned-new-friend Madison Pendleton, zipping away from a battle with the Nome King, who'd showed up unexpectedly when Glamora turned out to actually be (mostly) her evil twin sister, Glinda, and had opened a portal back to Kansas. The Nome King wanted to take over all of Oz, and to do it he apparently needed my shoes, which were originally Dorothy's shoes, and which, as far as I knew, weren't turning me evil the way Dorothy's second pair of shoes transformed her into a super-evil bloodthirsty homicidal tyrant.

Okay, so it's kind of complicated. Like, really complicated. Believe me, I know. I'm living it. And right now, Nox, Madison, and I were being carried to who even knows where by the Road of Yellow Brick, which apparently is sort of . . . sentient.

Below us, the fields and villages of Oz were a moonlit patchwork quilt of silvery green and gold. In the far distance, I could see the snowcapped peaks of the Traveling Mountains. And beyond that, I could almost glimpse the sandy dunes of the Deadly Desert.

The air was cool and we were moving fast, but I didn't feel cold. Just tired, and hungry, and worried about what we'd left behind. Mombi's death. The chaos after Ozma's coronation. The Nome King. And Glinda . . .

Mombi was gone. And for all intents and purposes, she had been Nox's mother. And he was acting like it hadn't happened at all.

The bad dream was supposed to be over. I had spent the better part of months plotting Dorothy's death with the Order to try to save the world. But the Order had a very particular recipe for her death. Dorothy couldn't just be killed. I had had to take out the Tin Woodman's inky heart, cut off the Lion's courage (which happened to reside in his tail), and obtain the Scarecrow's brain before I could finally end Dorothy for good. And it was done. Tin, Scare, and the Lion were dead, and I had just watched a palace fall on Dorothy. It was done. Dorothy was dead but my fight was far from over.

"We have to go back," I commanded, thinking of the fight we left behind.

"We can't."

"But Glinda. And Mombi . . . I am so sorry Nox." I climbed closer to him on the road.

"She did her duty. All of the Order knew the risk," he said, but he wasn't looking at me. He was looking at Madison who began screaming her head off as the road hurtled forward into the night.

"What the fuck was that?" Madison yelled.

"Which part?"

She stared at me, her eyes wild. "Where's my kid? What did Assistant Principal Strachan just turn into? Where are we? Who's that?" She pointed at Nox.

"I'm Nox," Nox said unhelpfully. He yawned and carefully sat down, stretching his legs and holding on to the yellow bricks.

"Is he kidding?" Madison whirled toward me, almost losing her balance on the narrow road. "We're, like, flying? On some bricks? I don't know if you noticed but that's not possible? *Where is my kid?*"

"I think Dustin Jr. is safe," I said, picking the easiest question out of her barrage. At least she'd stopped screaming.

"You *think?*"

"His dad caught him," I said. "I'm sure he's fine. And the Nome King is here now. So, um, Kansas is definitely, totally safe."

"What do you mean, *here?* Where is *here?* WHY ARE WE FLYING?"

"You're not going to believe me," I said, "but we're in Oz."

She stared at me. "That's . . . super not funny, Amy. And

what kind of name is *Nox?*"

Nox smiled. "What kind of name is *Madison?*" he echoed.

"I'm not joking about the Oz thing," I interrupted hastily. Madison was looking at Nox sort of like she wanted to eat him. Or murder him. I knew the feeling.

Madison looked around. She looked up. She looked down at the landscape flying by beneath us. She looked like she wanted to start screaming again but was carefully reconsidering wasting that much energy.

She took a deep breath. "Okay, Amy. Cut it. Seriously, what's going on?"

"You're in Oz," Nox said curtly. Madison looked back and forth between the two of us.

"Madison, you're on a flying road," I pointed out. "I know it sounds totally crazy, but Oz is real, and you're in it."

Madison sat down abruptly with a thump. A brick jolted loose from the road and tumbled away. "Careful," I said sharply. "We have no idea if this thing will actually hold together."

She watched the brick fall until we could no longer see it. She looked around: at the pointy silver stars as they flew by, at a hooting night owl as it floated past, staring at us in startled confusion, at the ground far below. She patted the road as if checking whether it was real. And then she pinched herself.

"You're not dreaming," I said gently, sitting down next to her.

"Are you sure?"

"Yeah. I felt like this the first time I came here, too."

"Like the Scarecrow and the Lion and Emerald City and

Munchkins and all of that shit? It's *real?*"

"Yeah," I said. "The Scarecrow and the Lion are dead, though."

She blinked. "Dorothy? Toto?"

"Dorothy is definitely real," Nox said darkly. "Way too real, if you ask me."

"Toto's actually dead, too," I clarified. "He turned into this giant, super-evil monster Toto, and I killed him, and then for a while there were these, like, zombie Toto reproductions? But they . . ."

I trailed off, catching sight of the expression on Mad's face. "Uh, anyway, I don't think we have to worry about them anymore."

"Your research project," Madison said abruptly. "Your whole thing with the archive at the high school. You were—you were *serious*. You thought all that stuff was *real*." She looked down at the countryside flying by below us and swallowed hard. "When you disappeared after the tornado," she said slowly. "You were . . . *here?*"

"Yeah," I said. "I had just as much trouble believing it was real at first, too. I mean, it sounds ridiculous. A tornado picked up my mom's trailer and dumped me here?"

I thought suddenly of Star, my mom's beloved pet rat. Like a lot of other people and things I cared about, she hadn't made it. But she'd been the only thing that kept me going through the early days in Oz—the only connection I had to the world I'd left behind, and the one thing letting me know I wasn't crazy, that what was happening to me was real. Madison had nothing like that. Nothing, anyway, except me.

"It's all crazy, I know. The thing is that Dorothy is—was—actually evil. I mean, Dorothy's dead now, too. But the fight isn't over. We still have to clean up the mess she left behind."

"Is *anyone* not dead? You know what, don't answer that," Madison said. "Okay, so let's say theoretically we're in Oz and I believe you. How do we get home?"

Nox and I exchanged glances. "I don't know," I said.

"You did it before," Madison said expectantly. "You came back to high school." She frowned. "You were here and you went back to *Flat Hill*? What were you thinking?"

"It's really, really complicated," I said. "I went back when the Wizard opened this portal—"

"The Wizard? Like, the actual Wizard of Oz?"

"Yeah, but he's dead, too," Nox said quietly.

Madison looked at both of us again. She was silent for a minute. And then she started to laugh. She laughed so hard she bent over, propping herself up on her hands. I couldn't help it. I started laughing, too. Nox rolled his eyes. Finally Madison sat up, still giggling, and wiped tears from her eyes. She was ready to listen.

I took a deep breath and began. "It all started when a tornado hit Kansas about five minutes after I had wished to be anyplace but home."

TWO

It took a long time to tell Madison the entire history of me and
Oz. No surprise there, considering how much had happened.
Just saying it out loud to someone who wasn't *from* Oz, who had
no idea what passed for normal here, made me realize just how
insane the last few months of my life had been.

And talking about Oz made me realize how much I'd missed
it. Back in Kansas, I'd resigned myself to never being able to
return to Oz. I almost—*almost*—thought I might know what
Dorothy felt like when she had to go back home—and why
she'd wanted so badly to return to Oz. But that was where the
similarity stopped. Dorothy was a killer and I wasn't.

Well, not unless I had to be.

Madison tucked her long blond hair behind her ears in a futile
effort to keep it out of her face, but the breeze fluttered at the
long strands, sending them flying behind her like streamers. I
thought about plucking one of Oz's stars out of the sky to show

to her, but she was freaked out enough already. Oz's weirder wonders could wait.

"So you were in a prison? And some magic dude just showed up? And then a witch appeared?" Madison interrupted my reverie, impatiently waiting for me to finish my story.

"More like a dungeon. The witch was Mombi." I glanced over at Nox, wondering what he was feeling. I was almost certain Mombi was dead, killed by Glamora and the Nome King as she tried to protect us. I had complicated feelings about the old witch—half the time, she'd felt more like my enemy than my friend, and despite all we'd been through together, we'd never been close. Out of all the witches, she'd made it very clear that just because she was formerly Wicked, she didn't consider herself Good. She was gruff and rude and sometimes her words hurt as much as the purple webs she could spin and squeeze around you. But those same qualities made her possibly the fiercest fighter in the Order, so her loss was huge if we were going to right everything that had just gone wrong in Oz. More importantly, she'd raised Nox. If my feelings about her were tangled, his had to be a labyrinth. I moved on quickly to the rest of my story.

In a strange way, it was a relief to talk to someone from the real world—my world—about what I'd been through. Nox understood so much about me, but he was from Oz. To him, learning magic and fighting monsters was just a part of life. Being able to tell someone from Kansas what had happened in Oz felt totally different.

"And then I went back to the Emerald City to fight Dorothy

once and for all," I continued. "But the Wizard was there, too, controlling Dorothy. He was crazy—he wanted to merge Oz and Kansas, he thought they were the same place."

Madison snorted softly.

"Well, in a way they *are* the same place," I amended. "Oz is kind of like—it's like another dimension, laid over the world that we know, if that makes sense. Kansas and Oz overlap. But he was going to destroy them both with his spell. And then his hold over Dorothy broke, and she killed him, and suddenly I wasn't in Oz anymore, I was back in Kansas, stuck there with Gert and Mombi and Glamora with no way to get home—"

I stopped, aware of what I'd just said. *Home.* Was that how I thought of Oz now? What about my mom?

"And then you decided to go back to high school?" Madison prompted, her voice skeptical.

"The witches thought Dorothy's original shoes were somewhere in Flat Hill," I explained. "The ones that took her home the first time she came to Oz."

"That whole thing where you were trying to prove Dorothy was real—that was just a cover for you trying to find some enchanted doodad and get back here?"

"Exactly. And I did find the shoes, in the high school—just where the witches thought they'd be. The shoes brought us all back to Oz. Glinda was moving against the Order without Dorothy—we fought her and thought we'd defeated her, but actually she had just taken over her twin sister's body—"

"Are you serious?" Madison asked in disbelief.

"I know it sounds super-weird. But I'm telling you, things work differently here." I told her about the final battle beneath the Emerald Palace, when I'd defeated Dorothy at last but been unable to kill her. How Nox and I had left her there to die as the palace crumbled around us.

"Whoa," Madison said softly. "That's pretty cold."

Nox looked at her, his eyes narrowing. "Are you listening to anything Amy's telling you? About how *evil* Dorothy is? She *tortured* people to death, Madison. She murdered whole families, whole towns. She—"

"Nox, it's okay," I said gently. "It's just a lot to take in all at once. Remember, it took me a long time to get used to killing people, too. And I'm still not sure it's a good thing I did."

"How did you know Dorothy was dead?" Madison asked. "If you just left her there?"

"She looked pretty dead to me," Nox muttered.

"Wait a minute," Madison said, realizing what I'd just said. "You've killed people? Like . . . not just by accident?"

"Yeah," I said. I couldn't meet her eyes.

"You? Salvation—" Madison stopped herself. "You couldn't even punch me back a few months ago. And now you're like a superhero."

A couple of months ago I would have laughed at the idea of me being the key to saving Oz. It would have seemed to be the most ridiculous idea in the whole wide world. Or at least my world, which was as small as the trailer I grew up in. But time and distance and Oz had changed my mind. I knew now I had a role to play—something bigger than that trailer—bigger than the girl with pink hair and no friends and a deadbeat mom on the other side of the universe or rainbow or whatever. And I knew, too, that I wasn't the girl who left anyone to fight without her. We couldn't turn the road around, but we would have to go back.

"Not exactly . . ."

"Wow," she said. "Okay. Um, am I going to have to kill people? And you still haven't answered my question. How do I get home? How do I get back to my kid? No offense, but this place isn't really my style." She looked around again, and I peered over the side of the road. The landscape below us was completely unfamiliar—sparse, leafless trees sprouted out of the hard, moonlit ground.

"The Witch's Wastelands," Nox said, in answer to my unspoken question. "No one I know has been this close to the edge of Oz."

"Amy," Mad prompted. "I don't need a geography lesson."

I didn't know how to tell her that the questions she'd asked were impossible to answer. So instead, I settled for telling the last part of my story as if she hadn't asked.

"We thought we'd finally saved Oz when Dorothy died," I said. "But when the Nome King showed up—that's the guy who took over Assistant Principal Strachan's body—"

"How many villains *are* there in this stupid world?" Madison asked in disbelief.

"Tell me about it," Nox said.

"Everybody's Wicked," I said. "Here, I mean. Good means

Wicked, and Wicked means Good . . ." Madison was staring at me as if I'd started speaking Sanskrit.

"Like I said, it's complicated," I amended. "We don't know what the Nome King wants, exactly. He definitely wants these."

I pointed to my feet, where Dorothy's shoes, which had turned into sparkly combat boots that fit me perfectly, still glittered.

"And he wants to kill me, too?"

"I don't think that was personal," Nox said. "He wanted to get to Amy. He didn't care about you."

Madison rolled her eyes. "Fine. So I'm not special. Amy's the Chosen One, or whatever. Ames, I'm really starting to like you, but this story is crazy. And, spoiler alert, whatever's going on here is not my problem. So why don't you send me back to Kansas with your little spell or whatever and we'll call it even. I'll tell your mom—well, I'll tell her whatever you want. I'll tell her you're coming home soon if you want me to. But I want to get back to my kid, and my ex-boyfriend, and my life."

"We can't," Nox said. "Amy already told you. We don't know how."

"I know it's all . . . a lot," I said.

Madison sighed. "So the only way for me to get home is to find out where this stupid road is carrying us, take out the demonic dude who possessed Assistant Principal Strachan, help you kill the Good Witch of the South, and figure out a spell that nobody knows yet?" she asked.

"Basically," I said apologetically.

"Fine, sign me up," Madison said briskly. "Do I get to learn magic, too?"

"You can't," Nox said. "Oz's magic corrupts people from your world who use it."

"For some reason, Dorothy's shoes let me use magic again," I explained. "But before I found them, things got . . . bad."

Madison huffed. "I don't believe this crap. All right, fine. At least teach me how to use a knife or something. Sword? Bow and arrow? Battle-ax?"

"That's *The Lord of the Rings*," I said. "Different book. And only dwarves use those."

"You are such a freak," Madison said.

"Takes one to know one," I said.

But we were both smiling.

"Look," Nox said suddenly, pointing over the edge of the road. "I think we're flying over the Deadly Desert."

We crowded next to him, staring down at the vista below us. Madison and I both gasped aloud. I'd assumed that the Deadly Desert was an empty, desolate wasteland. I'd been completely, totally wrong.

At the far edge of the horizon, the sky was lightening with the coming dawn. And far below, the faint illumination hinted at the extraordinary place we were flying over. Huge dunes of multicolored sand stretched as far as I could see in either direction. Directly below us was a cobalt-blue wave of sand. The dune next to it was crimson red, and the one after that a bright, saffron-tinted yellow.

I saw dunes of apple green, sky blue, velvety purple, and brilliant turquoise. Streams of gold, silver, and black sand separated each of the dunes so that the whole landscape was a brilliant, colorful patchwork.

"Sand sailors!" Nox said in awe. I followed his finger and gasped again, this time in delight.

Far below us, jewel-colored lizards with huge, parachute-like wings drifted over the dunes, their tiny scales reflecting the rising sun in fiery, incandescent streaks of color.

"It's beautiful," Madison breathed.

For a moment, the precariousness of our situation fell away, and her face was suffused with wonder.

"It's gorgeous," Nox agreed, but his voice held a hint of sadness. "But as far as anyone in Oz knows, it's lethal. It's impossible to cross on foot. The dunes are constantly shifting, and they swallow anyone who attempts it. No one's ever tried to navigate the Deadly Desert and survived. Not without magic, anyway."

"The Wizard did it," I said, remembering the original story. "Didn't he? In his hot-air balloon? And the fairies, way back in the day."

"So did Dorothy," Nox said darkly.

So that part was true, too. I wished I'd thought to pick up the complete set of Wizard of Oz books back in Kansas. They might have helped solve a few problems. I'd been too busy trying to find the shoes hidden in my high school. But the Dorothy of those books was nothing like the Dorothy I knew.

I thought again about Madison's question. How *did* we know she was dead?

Nox and I both knew how tough Dorothy was—and how hard she was to kill. We'd left her behind when the Emerald Palace collapsed. Was it possible she didn't actually die down there?

No way, I thought to myself. *Nox is right. The whole palace came down on top of her. She's dead.*

She had to be. Because the way Oz villains kept popping up like new heads in a whack-a-mole game, we didn't have time to kill her again if she wasn't.

One of the sand sailors swept down a little too close to the ground, and, in a blink, the sand rose to meet it in a tiny wave. The sand sailor struggled, but it was over in an instant as the desert swallowed it whole. Madison gasped. Nox and I remained silent.

As the sun rose in the sky, the landscape below us grew even more dazzling. Soon the hot morning light beat down on our shoulders. Without shade or shelter, our flight became uncomfortably warm.

Madison pulled off her pink, bedazzled sweatshirt and draped it over her head to ward off the sun. I sweated miserably in the soft gray dress I'd worn to Ozma's coronation. Already, that seemed like a lifetime ago—but it was only yesterday that I'd thought everything was right in Oz again. How quickly things could change here.

"Look," Nox said, pointing again.

"I thought nothing could live in that sand," I said.

Huge, dust-covered worms slid through the sand, lunging upward to chomp down on sand sailors with creepy fang-filled mouths that opened like wounds.

Madison was looking a little pale. "Apparently *they* can," she murmured. "And, uh, guys? Is it just me, or are we sinking?" Madison's voice was strained.

"She's right," Nox said. And she was.

The road was unmistakably slowing down. And it was sinking.

Toward the desert—and the huge, yawning mouths of the sandworms.

"God, this place sucks," Madison muttered under her breath.

"We'll be fine," I said with a confidence I didn't feel.

The road was bucking and twisting as it lurched downward. I squatted down before it could toss me off, clutching tightly to its golden bricks. Madison was clinging tight, too, looking a little green.

"Look! Land!" Nox said, standing up so suddenly he was almost thrown off the writhing road.

I grabbed his ankles as an upheaval nearly sent him over the side. Past the multicolored dunes, I could see what he meant—an expanse of drab, bleak landscape, hilly and worn-down looking, that was a sharp contrast to the bright and lethal Deadly Desert.

But we were falling fast. If we crashed before we made it to the hills, either the sandworms would finish us or the desert itself would.

The worms seemed to sense our predicament and gathered

beneath the road, yawning and snapping their huge teeth. Madison's knuckles were white where she gripped the road and her face was tense with fear, but she didn't say anything.

I felt my boots throb almost reassuringly, but when I reached within myself for my magic, it felt far away, as if I were trying to reach it through a wall of Jell-O. I closed my eyes, trying to summon something. Anything. The barest scrap of magic to keep us safe.

I opened my eyes and saw Nox looking at me. I shook my head. "Nothing," I said. "I can't do anything." From his expression, I knew he'd been trying, too.

"We have to trust the road," he said quietly.

I loved Nox's faith in magic and in Oz. But it didn't look like we were in Oz anymore . . .

Before I could reply, the road plunged suddenly downward.

Madison screamed in terror. The desert was hurtling toward us at a terrifying speed. The worms were just waiting for us to drop within reach of their serrated teeth.

"Amy! Madison! Get up! Run!" Nox yelled, pulling us to our feet.

Instantly, I saw what he meant. There was still a length of road in front of us, and we were almost all the way across the desert. The three of us staggered forward, tripping and stumbling as the road bucked wildly beneath us. I half pulled, half carried Madison forward. Where the desert ended, I could see hard, rocky ground that the sandworms couldn't move through.

But we had to get there first. And it was a long way to safety.

"We're going to have to jump!" Nox shouted.

Solid ground seemed impossibly far. Madison's mouth was moving in a silent prayer—or, knowing her, a curse—but her face was set with determination.

Madison wasn't exactly athletic—I'd never seen her lift anything heavier than a shopping bag until she started carting around Dustin Jr. She took a deep breath, eyed the gap, and jumped.

The nearest of the worms lunged for her—but somehow, impossibly, she cleared the distance, hitting the ground past the edge of the desert and dropping into a roll worthy of an Order trainee. In a flash, she was on her feet and running. The worm turned to us.

"Go!" Nox yelled. "Amy, we have to go, now!"

The road was breaking apart even as I got my footing. Bricks tumbled to the ground, sinking into the shifting sand and swallowed immediately. Nox grabbed my hand and we jumped.

I hit the ground with a thud that knocked the wind out of my lungs. A worm's teeth snapped shut inches from my foot. I rolled out of its way and somersaulted to my feet, grabbing Nox's shoulder and pulling him to safety. The huge worm bellowed in disappointment as both of us took off running after Madison.

But we slowed down as soon as we realized the worms couldn't pursue us on the rocky soil. Madison and I were panting and out of breath, but Nox had barely broken a sweat. Sometimes he drove me nuts. I'd worked my ass off to become as strong as I was, but I still did normal, human things like get sweaty and winded. Nox made even the most impossible feat look easy. It was alternately infuriating and sexy.

He looked up at the sky, where the remains of the road were rising quickly away from us. Crumbling bricks thudded here and there into the swirling sands of the desert, sinking out of sight immediately into the fluid sand.

"Ugh," Madison said. *"Rude."* She glared at the last of the Road of Yellow Brick as it dwindled to a speck on the horizon.

"I don't understand why it took us this far and then just dumped us," I said. "And what happened back there? What went wrong with our magic? Where *are* we?"

Nox was looking at his fingers, wiggling them experimentally. "I think the road is bound to Oz," he said slowly. "It wanted to help us, for whatever reason, and so it took us as far as it could."

"Took us where, though? Is this some part of the mountains? Why couldn't it go any farther?"

Nox shook his head. "Amy, I think the road took us all the way *across* the desert. That's why our magic isn't working. That's why the road collapsed."

"You're saying we aren't in Oz anymore," I said slowly.

He nodded. "We crossed the entire desert. That means we're in Ev. The Nome King's kingdom. I didn't even believe it was real." He snorted softly. "Then again, the Nome King was supposed to be a legend, too."

Ev. The word stirred something in my memory. Something important.

Had Lurline told me about Ev? About the Nome King, and what he wanted?

But whatever the memory was, it was gone.

"I still don't understand what that has to do with our magic," I said. "Or why the road would dump us here." I looked around. "We tried to defeat the Nome King in Oz, but he was too powerful. Maybe there's nothing *in* Oz that can stop him, and that's why the road brought us here," I said thoughtfully. "Maybe Ev's magic is different somehow? Or there's something here we can use to defeat the Nome King?"

"If Ev's magic is different, that would explain why we're having trouble using ours," Nox agreed. "And the road doesn't do anything without a reason. But as far as we know, the Nome King isn't here. The last time we saw him was in Oz."

I sighed. It was a lot to figure out. But there had to be a reason we were here. And if the Nome King was from Ev, that had to be a part of it. It would make sense if the road had brought us here to discover a weapon we could use against him.

"They don't have, like, treasure maps in Oz, do they?" Madison asked. "You know, 'This way to enchanted object that kills evil sorcerer, gets everybody home to safety' type maps?"

Nox rolled his eyes at Madison.

"My magic comes from Oz," Nox said. "I think that's why it's so hard to reach here. Ev must have a different kind of power. The shoes are part of Oz, too. But your magic . . ."

He didn't finish, but I knew what he was thinking. My magic was part Oz, part me. And I was from the Other Place. Which meant that maybe, just maybe, I could find a way to make my own magic work here. If I could somehow bypass the Oz parts—if that was even possible—I could tap directly into the magic that came from *me*.

But if I tried to access it without the shoes, it might also just kill me.

"Why is this place ugly as hell?" Madison asked, looking around. "I thought there were supposed to be, like, singing Muppets or something."

"Munchkins," I said automatically.

Madison was right. If this was Ev, it was a total dump. Dorothy had been draining the magic out of Oz for awhile. The trees had stopped talking and the river was running in reverse. But there was still some magic and color left in Oz.

In Ev it was as if there had never been any color or magic. The landscape was bleak and twisted. The blackened, winding path that stretched away from us was like the Road of Yellow Brick's evil twin sister. In the distance, dilapidated shacks dotted the horizon like scabs. There was nothing green and growing. No water. No sign of life. No flowers.

"If we're in Ev, the road brought us here for a reason," Nox began. "Maybe Amy's right and there's a—"

But he didn't get a chance to finish his sentence. Because right then the Wheelers came.

THREE

DOROTHY

Quelle surprise, bitches! I'm not dead!

Believe me, I'm just as shocked as you are. When the Emerald Palace started crumbling around me and that god-awful Amy Gumm left me to *die,* I thought I was a goner.

There I was, inches from death, abandoned by Amy and her dimwit boy toy—after everything I've done for Oz! These kinds of situations really lead you to face your own mortality, do you know what I mean? Some people say their entire life flashes before their eyes. At the moment the palace fell, I totally expected to die. And I wasn't happy about it, but I've led an exciting and productive life and accomplished a lot. People would definitely remember me after I passed. I had to be content with that.

A huge chunk of the cavern crashed down right next to my head. I closed my eyes and prepared to say good-bye—and then the floor fell out beneath me and I tumbled into the arms of the handsomest man I'd ever seen, just like that.

That was how I met my current fiancé, the Nome King (*so* romantic, don't you think! I couldn't have staged it better myself) although of course I had no idea at that exact moment who he was or how on earth he'd gotten there—in the nick of time, too—or that shortly I'd be planning our wedding. Or that I'd also be working on thwarting an *extremely* diabolical plot against poor little *moi*.

But I'm getting ahead of myself. Back to my rescue.

He gently laid me on a silver sleigh pulled by some of his soldiers. They were all clad in identical black uniforms, and discs of light were embedded in their foreheads. This light lit our way down the tunnel. I couldn't help but wonder if they'd been born that way, or if the Nome King had someone like Scare come up with clever inventions. Instead of running on snow, the sleigh moved across stone, just as smoothly. It was piled high with red velvet blankets and pillows.

My rescuer got into the sleigh next to me and poured some water out of a silver flask onto a soft cloth, dabbing the dust and blood from my face with a featherlight touch. There must have been something special in that water because I felt almost instantly better. His servants took off running, and good thing they did—behind us, the tunnel began to collapse. But luckily his soldiers were as fast as they were strong, and soon we left the destruction behind.

Once we were clear of the palace and farther into the dark tunnel, I looked down and inspected myself. It was worse than I thought—my dress was ruined. I felt every slash in the gingham like a wound to my heart. I also had bruises and cuts. I called on my magic to repair the damage but felt only a faint flicker in response. I must still be too weak from the collapse of the palace. I would have to try again later.

I turned my attention to my rescuer. "Who *are* you?" I asked. Even then I had my suspicions about the identity of my knight in shining bald armor who had whisked me out of danger.

"I am the King of Ev," he told me solemnly. "I had a premonition you might be in danger, dearest Dorothy. I've been digging under the Deadly Desert for years"—I kept mum, but between you and me, he was *not* supposed to be doing that—"trying to reach Oz on a mission of peace."

I raised one eyebrow. Even in my weakened state, I knew the Nome King did not exactly have a reputation as the world's greatest pacifist. But it was like he could read the thought before it even finished crossing my mind.

"I know in the past I haven't always been a perfect ruler," he said quickly. "But things are desperate in Ev, Dorothy, and only Oz can help us. For years, my people have been starving. The earth is barren. The citizens are poor and without hope."

Not my *problem,* I thought.

"You're poor?" I blurted.

"My land is poor in some ways, but rich in others," he replied cryptically.

I cocked my head to the side. I was not a fan of riddles, even though every witch and even the Wizard himself (when he was alive) spouted them on a regular basis, but he had just saved my life, so I kept listening.

He reached into his pocket and then held out his closed fist. When he opened it, it was filled with rubies. Red, like my shoes. I reached for them, but he closed his hand with a chuckle.

He hung his head humbly. "I've made mistakes, Dorothy, and I regret them every day. But I'm reaching out now to try and make amends for the sake of my people."

Who among us hasn't done things she might regret at some point in her life? You might find this hard to believe, but even I wonder sometimes if I always did the best thing for Oz. I, for one, should not have been so kind. I should have killed Ozma and Amy Gumm when I had the chance. If I had just been less merciful, then Tin, Scare, and the Lion might still be alive. My beautiful palace would not have landed on top of me.

It's a natural consequence of being a ruler, of course—you're just responsible for so much. It's impossible to be everything that everyone expects of you. And if sometimes you overreact because of stress or something like that, you know the whole world is watching and judging, even though you're only trying your best.

Where I come from, in Kansas, trying your best is all you can do. But in Oz people expected me to be *perfect*. I immediately understood what the Nome King was saying. He needed someone who'd been there. Who knew how he felt. Only another ruler could sympathize with what he was going through.

"I understand exactly what you mean, Nome King," I said, covering his hand with my own. His skin was cool and smooth as stone.

I don't think I'm imagining things when I say I felt a spark at that very first touch. In all my life I'd never met a man who was my equal. Of course, Tin had been in love with me for ages, but that was just creepy.

It's next to impossible to resist my charms—I'm the prettiest girl in Oz, even battered by a ceiling and covered in dust. So I wasn't surprised to recognize his attraction.

But I was intrigued.

The Nome King clasped his hands together and closed his eyes. I watched curiously as he opened his hands and was delighted to see that he'd turned the small pile of rubies into a delicate bracelet of tiny ruby flowers winding around one another. I inhaled deeply as he slipped it on my wrist.

As his servants carried us forward, the Nome King opened a satchel beautifully crafted out of leather and steel filigree. He offered me a bunch of sunberries and I graciously accepted them, delicately placing each berry inside my ruby-red lips and allowing the bright, flavorful juice to wash the dryness out of my mouth. He watched me eat but took nothing himself. When I was refreshed, he spoke again.

"It goes without saying that you're the true ruler of Oz, Dorothy. Not Ozma," he said. "The people of Oz know it in their hearts."

"I'm so glad you think so," I purred.

I didn't let my anger show, but I was furious with that stupid, awful fairy Ozma. Her and her stupid fairy magic. Always spoiling my fun! Thinking she knew best. Thinking she was the queen of all things magical. If she hadn't meddled and

tried to stop me from learning magic, Auntie Em and Uncle
Henry would still be . . .

I pushed the thought aside and blinked hard to will the image
away. The tornado that carried the house was mine, but I had
been aiming for Ozma. She provoked me. She cost me my only
family. And Amy Gumm had cost me my makeshift one.

The Nome King cleared his throat, reminding me that I
needed to answer him.

"I'm sure Ozma will do just fine," I said coolly.

"Oh, I'm sure," he agreed with a smile. "But you did better,
and you know it. Oz needs you, Dorothy. You have a duty to
fulfill. You have a destiny."

I liked the sound of that. I didn't trust him as far as I could
throw him, but he certainly knew the way to my heart.

"You really think so?"

"I know it." He took my hand, looking deep into my eyes
with his silver gaze, and my heart began to race. He was so handsome, so powerful. I'd heard stories of his magic. His strength.

I felt something. Something almost as warm and glowy as
when my magic coursed through me. It wasn't his looks. It
wasn't even the gorgeous bracelet that now rested on my wrist
(although that didn't hurt). It was that there was no fear in his
eyes when he looked at me. And he was also Wicked. Perhaps
more Wicked than all the Wicked Witches combined. And don't
tell anyone, that was a little hot, too.

"I've seen it, Dorothy," he said in a low, urgent voice. "It's
why I came to rescue you. You must return to the throne in order

for your country to be whole. It would be my honor to help you."

Well, I wasn't expecting *that*. I tried not to let my surprise show. "And in return?" I asked sharply, although I already knew the answer.

"Perhaps a modest exchange between our kingdoms," he suggested.

I looked down at my hands—one of which was still in his.

My manicure had been absolutely ruined by the collapse of the Emerald Palace. My knuckles were bruised and scraped raw. I was exhausted. But I wasn't stupid.

I knew he meant much more than a modest exchange. He meant that if he helped me take control of Oz again, I'd be in debt to Ev—more specifically, to him—forever. But I'd been around the block a few times by that point. Handsome and magical he might be, but the Nome King should have known better than to underestimate *me*.

"Do you really think Oz needs me so badly?" I asked coyly, as if dazzled by his praise. (See into the future? Please. Even Glinda can't do that.)

"I've foreseen it," he intoned solemnly. His voice did send a tiny thrill through me. Even if it wasn't true, it sounded divine.

"I never wanted power," I said, dropping my eyes modestly and looking up at him through my lashes. "I only wanted to do what was right for Oz."

"And that's why you were born to be its leader," he said, bringing my hand to his chest and holding it there.

He didn't seem to have a heartbeat, but we all have our little quirks.

I pretended to think about it. "Glinda will be a problem," I said, as if this had just occurred to me.

"Glinda will come around," he said lightly. "She knows what's best for Oz, just as you do."

I wasn't so sure about that. Glinda had been an absolute pain in my *ass* lately—and attacking the Order without me? As if *she* was the one in charge?

But I reassured myself with the thought that Glinda could hardly rule Oz herself—she was a witch, not a queen—and once I was returned to the throne, I'd see that she was punished for her disobedience. For the good of Oz. The Nome King and I would go over that later.

"Where are you taking me?"

"To Ev, where you can be safe," he said.

I thought about this.

I might be a bitch, but I'm not an idiot. There was something else going on here, something big. The Nome King was *not* rescuing me out of some altruistic desire to see me sitting once more on the throne of Oz. And Oz might be rich where Ev was poor, but that wasn't the only reason he'd rescued me.

No, he was up to something. And I was willing to bet it was something that was going to benefit him, not me.

However, I was alive. And more or less in one piece.

And surrounded by his henchmen, being carried—if not by force, certainly potentially by force—to a country I didn't stand a chance of escaping without help or magic. In short, I wasn't in much of a position to argue with him.

"I've always wanted to see Ev," I lied politely. "You certainly

went to an awful lot of trouble to rescue me, and I haven't properly thanked you at all." I ate another handful of sunberries, too
hungry to remember to chomp on them seductively. Oops.

"It's really nothing at all," the Nome King said. There was a
glint of menace in his eye. But there was something else. He was
attracted to me, too. I smiled back at him radiantly.

Until I knew exactly what his game was, I'd play. I needed to
know what the stakes were before I made any bets. And I needed
to gather my energy.

The Nome King was either a very dangerous friend—or a
very interesting enemy.

"I can't wait until we've arrived," I said. "But now, you must
forgive me . . . I have to rest."

"Of course," he said. The glint in his eye was gone and he
was every bit the solicitous host again. If he'd wanted to harm
me—right then, anyway—I doubted he'd go to all the trouble
of rescuing me just to murder me in his magic sleigh on the way
back to Ev, so I let my eyelids drift closed.

The last thing I heard before I sank into a merciful, much-
needed sleep was the Nome King humming some strange, old
tune under his breath, and the soft hiss of the runners as we flew
forward over the stone.

FOUR

We heard the creatures before we saw them, but we still didn't have time to prepare. From beyond a rocky hillside came a rattly, squeaking din that sounded like a hundred rusty bicycles being ridden through a gravel pit. "What's that noi—" I began, and then they came over the hill. Madison's face went suddenly white.

"Oh my god," she whispered. "I *hated* this movie."

"Which movie?" I had my back to her and was in a fighting stance, ready to defend us with our fists if I had to, but I knew we didn't stand a chance if they attacked. We were too outnumbered, and we didn't have magic.

"*Return to Oz?* It's like showing a little kid *Clockwork Orange*," she said. "Fucked me up for life. Anyway, those are the Wheelers." Her voice was even but I knew she must be terrified. Madison was tough, though. I knew from experience that she didn't flinch when it came to a fight.

"What's a movie?" Nox asked. In all the time we'd spent together talking about Oz's magic, I'd never gotten much of a chance to tell him about the magic in my world. The tiny television back in my trailer in Kansas had been a window to other places, including Oz.

"Forget it," Madison said.

"Well, whatever those things are, get ready to fight," Nox said as the creatures descended on us.

There were at least a dozen of the Wheelers—they moved so fast I lost count—and they were terrifying. They moved on all fours, their limbs stretched out impossibly long and thin. Each of their arms and legs ended in a huge, spiky, and rust-coated wheel that squealed horribly as they circled us. They were dressed in a crazy patchwork of filthy, bloodstained rags and richly embroidered velvet, scraps of metal, beads, and pieces of old-fashioned armor. Their clothes were crusted with old food and bits of meat and other things I didn't want to think about. They smelled like death.

But worst of all, their faces were human—almost. Their skin was leathery and wrinkled, and most of them had terrible scars or open wounds crisscrossing their faces like an insane road map of pain. Their hair was matted. They held dirty, rusty knives in their teeth and jabbed forward with their jaws, thrusting the weapons at us and herding us into a tight bunch. They formed a whirling circle around us—but they didn't touch us. Madison covered her nose and mouth against the stench.

"Stop!" One of the Wheelers called out to the others in a

deep, scratchy voice that made me think of an old man who'd spent his entire life chain-smoking and chugging hard liquor. Immediately the Wheelers screeched to a halt.

The Wheeler who had spoken creaked closer and stared at me. Even though he wasn't carrying a weapon in his teeth like the others, he managed to be even scarier. His face was deeply tanned and covered with a network of old scars. One eye was missing, the socket a mess of bulging scar tissue. His hair hung in lank strands braided with beads and pieces of metal and chunks of bone. He stared at me with his good eye, which was a crazy, piercing blue, and then he smiled, and I saw why he didn't need a knife: his teeth were filed into razor-sharp points.

I heard Madison breathe in hard next to me, but she didn't make a noise. I felt weirdly proud of her.

"Welcome to Ev, honored guests," the Wheeler sneered. His voice sounded like tin cans being dragged behind an old car. "Princess Langwidere requests your most esteem presence at her palace."

At the word *esteem* the other Wheelers began to snicker. "Esteem! Esteem! Princess call guests esteem!" one of them squealed, and the others burst into awful, screeching giggles that sent chills running down my spine.

Langwidere? What kind of name was that—and who on earth was she? Next to me, Nox looked a shade paler. "That's not good," he said in my ear.

"What do you mean?"

"I don't know anything about these Wheelers, but I definitely have heard of Langwidere. And everything I've heard is . . . bad."

He'd spoken quietly, but the Wheelers overheard him anyway. At his words, they hooted and shrieked with laughter. "Little flesh-foot denies his honor!" one of them howled, sending the others into hysterical giggles again.

"Look, knock it off. " Madison stepped forward. Her voice was clear and loud and somehow, even though I knew she must be terrified, she seemed confident. Most of the Wheelers kept laughing but a few stopped and looked at her.

"Are you going to kill us? Because if you aren't, we have business to take care of, so maybe you can leave us alone and get out of here. Right?" She looked at Nox, whose mouth was open in astonishment. "Right?" she said again.

"Uh, right." Nox closed his mouth and looked serious. "Exactly. Yes, what she said."

The Wheelers' laughter died down into the occasional giggle. The leader peered at us again, his beady good eye squinting. A smile played over his cracked lips and he chuckled to himself. "A spicy little flesh-foot!" he cackled, staring at Madison. He creaked forward until his face was inches away from hers but she didn't flinch. He opened his mouth and screamed with laughter.

Even from where I was standing I nearly gagged at the rank, foul stench of his breath. Bits of rotting meat were caught in his jagged teeth. But Madison didn't back down.

"Cool, so you're not going to kill us, am I right?" she said. "Since we're not dead yet, and you guys are just dicking around. How about you let us go then?"

"Princess says to bring you to her unharmed," the Wheeler admitted reluctantly. He was clearly unhappy about those instructions.

"Princess didn't say unharmed! Princess said 'in one piece'! Could be harmed but still one piece!" one of the other Wheelers broke in excitedly, squeaking back and forth on his wheels. The leader cocked his head, considering, and then shook his head no, sending his dirty braids flying.

"You want to argue with Princess, your problem," he said. The other Wheeler abruptly stopped moving and looked alarmed.

"Not arguing with Princess," he said quickly. "Wouldn't, wouldn't."

"We take you to her now," the lead Wheeler said to us.

"We don't want to go with you," Madison said. At that, the Wheelers screeched with laughter again.

"Wants to argue with Princess!" they yelled. "Wants to argue! Little flesh-foot says no to Princess!"

"You don't choose," the Wheelers' leader said to Madison. He lunged forward so fast that she didn't even have time to scream, fastening his serrated teeth in her arm and dragging her toward the nearest Wheeler, who bent down on his elbows. The leader half dragged, half threw Madison on his back and he reared up again with Madison clutching frantically to his embroidered jacket. Blood seamed her shirtsleeve and her face was white and terrified.

"Now you," the leader said to me, his teeth red with Madison's blood. I swallowed hard as another of the Wheelers bent in front of me. The leader bared his teeth and snapped at me as I clambered awkwardly onto the Wheeler's back. Next to me, Nox was doing the same. Up close, the Wheeler smelled even worse. And when I looked down, I saw fleas crawling in his dirty, ragged clothes. I closed my eyes, willing myself not to throw up.

"Now we go," the leader said, and the Wheelers lurched forward across the barren earth.

I'd had a lot of bad journeys in Oz, but riding a Wheeler across the desert definitely took the prize for Most Awful Form of Transportation of All Time. The hot, merciless sun beat down on my back, sucking all the moisture out of my body. The Wheeler's jagged wheels made his gait jolting and uneven, and although I was exhausted, I had to struggle every minute of the ride to cling to his filthy, bony back. I managed to tear off a strip of fabric from the bottom of my dress and toss it to Madison for her wound. She probably needed some kind of shot to ensure it wouldn't get infected but this was the best I could do for now.

As the sun rose higher, the smell got worse. Every time I glanced over at Madison, she looked more and more as though she was about to pass out. Even Nox was turning a distinct shade of sickly green.

The landscape around us wasn't much better. Mostly it was deserted, but here and there we passed tiny villages that looked even worse than I felt: houses with collapsing roofs and crumbling walls, farm animals with ribs that poked horribly out of their fly-dotted hides, poking dispiritedly along the sun-bleached, rocky ground in vain search of food. As we creaked and rumbled by, terrified faces appeared briefly in broken-paned windows and then disappeared again as everyone we passed hid from the Wheelers.

Once, one of the Wheelers broke off from our group, speeding toward a village with a howl of glee, but the leader sharply called him back and he returned reluctantly, still brandishing his knife in his teeth. The leader bit him hard on the ear and he yelped with pain.

"We follow Princess orders!" the leader snarled. "No play today. Serious business." The other Wheeler shot him a murderous look but obeyed. I didn't want to think about what the Wheelers considered "play." The horror in the faces of the people we passed gave me a pretty good idea.

Nox looked at Madison, who was inspecting the bloody cloth around her arm.

"If you expect to make it here, you can't bully your way through it. You need to take our lead."

Madison looked up sharply. "Excuse me, you don't even know me."

"You're the Madison who used to call her 'Salvation Amy.' That Madison? I do know you."

I had forgotten that Nox had not been there for everything that went down in Flat Hill when I'd gone back with the witches. How do I explain how I had made up with Madison? Nox had been in my head during my initiation into the Order, he had felt every humiliation that Madison had dealt me, and judging from his face, he could not reconcile me forgiving her. I could hardly reconcile it myself.

"You weren't there, Nox. A lot happened in Kansas. She risked her life for me," I said.

Nox scowled, unimpressed. "One good thing doesn't erase all the bad," he said.

I loved that he was protective of me. But this was more than that.

"Hey, I know this isn't about her. This is about Mombi, isn't it?"

He looked up at me, surprised. "What are you talking about? She died doing what she loved. Protecting the Order. Protecting Oz."

I took a deep breath. Nox had been raised to protect Oz at any cost. Duty coursed through him and the other witches. But there was more to him, and there was more to Mombi.

"She died protecting what she loved. You."

Nox blinked hard and looked away. I wanted to put my arms around him. To make him give in to what he was feeling. But I couldn't because I was stuck on the back of a disgusting creature.

"Shhh . . ." screeched the Wheeler beneath me, then it raced ahead to stall our talk.

The sun dragged slowly across the sky. I wondered if someone here controlled the time, the way Dorothy had once used the Great Clock. It certainly felt like some sadistic force was making the time pass as slowly as possible, but I suspected it was just the awfulness of the journey that made it seem endless.

I tried to remember everything I knew about Ev. Mombi had told me about the Nome King back when I'd found Dorothy's journal in Kansas. Something about how he'd tried to invade Oz a long time ago, but Ozma defeated him when she was queen the first time around. When he showed up in Kansas, Mombi immediately assumed the worst and thought he might be trying to use me—and he'd basically told me as much when he'd crashed Ozma's coronation party, dragged Madison into Oz, and murdered Mombi with Glinda's help.

I didn't want to think about the last time I'd seen her or the way she'd looked—almost resigned, as if she knew this might be her last fight. She had not given up—she was a fighter. And she had thrown herself into the fray to give me and Nox a chance to escape. But if the Nome King could take out Mombi, the witch with the most Wickedness, that didn't say much for my chances of defeating Ev's most sinister senior citizen on his own turf.

I was pretty sure she'd never said anything about any Princess Langwidere, though. I wished I could ask Nox more about who she was, but I didn't want the Wheelers to overhear our conversation. Instead, I closed my eyes, concentrating on finding the magic within myself. Magic was the only weapon I had left. We had no idea what we were going to be up against with this Langwidere person. I had to be able to use my powers in case I needed them to help save us.

But trying to find my magic felt the same way it had on the road: I could almost feel it, but it was as if I was trying to reach through a wall. My boots throbbed again, but this time it felt like a warning. As if they were telling me to be careful. As if they were letting me know they might not be able to protect me.

"Look," Madison said in a low voice, jerking me out of my thoughts. On the horizon I saw a black smudge that I thought at first was a heat-induced mirage over the shimmering desert. But as we slowly wheeled closer the smudge got bigger and bigger, looming over the landscape like a bad dream.

"What is that?" I asked.

"Princess! Princess!" screamed one of the Wheelers in delight. "Princess soon! Princess treat guests so well!"

They exploded into their awful laughter again and some of them broke off from the group to speed around us in circles, taunting us. "Flesh-feet think they're too good for Wheelers! Wait until Princess cuts off your heads! Then you won't be so smarty-smart! Little witches get Wheeler stitches!"

The Wheeler carrying me grunted and kicked out with one leg at the others. I grabbed his back, afraid of sliding off. I had no doubt that whatever the princess's orders the others wouldn't hesitate to run me over with their spiked wheels if I fell to the ground.

"They're joking, right?" Madison said.

Nox cleared his throat. "That's, um, sort of what she's known for," he said. "Her head collection." Madison's eyes got wide. I wasn't sure I looked any better myself.

Princess Langwidere's palace was close enough that I could make out its details. I liked it a lot better when it was far enough away that I couldn't see the specifics.

It was big, for one thing. Really, really big. But that part wasn't scary at all. What was scary was how it looked: as if the vampire Lestat had barfed up a gaudy cathedral. A forest of spiky turrets and towers bristled out of a massive, hulking body of black stone dotted with thousands of tiny black windows that seemed to suck up the sunlight rather than reflect it. The towers were carved with hundreds of heads and faces, misshapen and deformed. Some of them looked like they were screaming in pain or fear. Others were grinning evilly. One tower flowed into the next like a massive pile of candle drippings.

But the palace wasn't the worst part. The worst part was definitely the road.

As if in twisted mockery of the Road of Yellow Brick, the road to Princess Langwidere's palace was made of crumbling black stone that split into fissures so wide the Wheelers had to creak around them. The road was lined with dozens of spikes. And on every single one was impaled a rotting head.

Madison looked like she was going to throw up. I couldn't decide whether I was more scared or more grossed out. The heads were in varying stages of decomposition. Some of them looked fresh, and others were just skulls with a few dried scraps of flesh and hair still clinging to them.

But as we passed them I sensed something strange. The faint, unmistakable, electric buzz of magic. Maybe I couldn't use it here, but I could sense it. Where was it coming from?

And then I realized: the heads weren't real. They were a

glamour—a powerful one, if they were there all the time, but an illusion all the same. Why would someone go to so much gory trouble to line a road nobody seemed to use? Why would she send her scary minions to collect us if they weren't going to hurt us? None of this made any sense. Who *was* this chick?

I glanced over at Nox, and he met my eyes. He'd noticed it, too. And from the look on his face, he was wondering the same thing.

I didn't have any more time to think about it—we were approaching the castle gate. Like the rest of the palace, it was jagged and misshapen and carved with howling, grimacing faces. Whatever Princess Langwidere's deal, she had a real thing for heads. I hoped that didn't mean ours were on the line.

The gates swung open with a horrible screech as the Wheelers approached. In front of us was a courtyard paved with the same cracked black stone as the road to Langwidere's palace. Walls surrounded us on all sides, pockmarked with windows that stared down at us like lidless eyes. The skin on the back of my neck prickled. It felt like the castle itself was watching us.

The Wheelers dumped us unceremoniously on the hard ground and circled us again, leering and throwing insults. "Say hi-hi to Princess!" the leader shrieked, happy. "We go now to burn and burn!"

"Burn! Burn! Burn!" the others chanted, wheeling back and forth ecstatically. And then, with one final rotation, they were gone, speeding out of the gate in a racket of clattering wheels and screams. The doors slammed behind them. We were alone.

And now we were trapped.

FIVE

DOROTHY

I awoke in the caverns underneath the Emerald Palace. *It was all a dream*, I thought. *I'm dead. I'm underground, and I'm dead.* I blinked sleep away, my vision clearing. Being dead felt pretty much the same as being alive. Actually, being dead felt a lot *better* than being alive had felt ever since that god-awful bitch Amy showed up in Oz. In fact, it was downright comfortable.

Because I was lying in a bed, I realized. A *big* bed. The kind of bed I'd always liked best—satin sheets (black with red trim, very goth, a little tacky, but obviously expensive), a rich velvet coverlet (more black), high enough off the ground to need a little stool to get in and out (also black, filigree, studded with rubies).

Was I in Hell? Was that the reason for the black sheets? Aunt Em and Uncle Henry had always told me I'd end up there if I didn't say my prayers or feed the chickens on time or milk Bessie or follow any of the ten thousand *other* orders they gave me every single day, but they'd turned out to be wrong about a lot of things. They weren't even my parents. I'd never even *known* my parents. It's really a wonder I turned out so well.

I sat up in the giant bed and looked around. I was in a cave, true, but it was looking less and less like the caverns underneath the Emerald City and more and more like somebody's very weird idea of high luxury. It looked like something out of one of those creepy paintings that had hung up in the church Aunt Em used to take me to back in Kansas. You know the kind I mean: devils tormenting sinners with pitchforks, rivers of blood, lots of gore and dismemberment and serpents? Well, imagine if one of those painters began decorating homes, and you'd start to get an idea of the room I was in.

No windows, of course—it was a cave, after all. Lots of velvet drapes and sinister artwork with people engaged in activities that looked either very unpleasant or very indecent. The rest of the furniture in the room matched the four-poster bed and the stool, all of it carved with creepy elf-looking creatures that had to be the Nome King's various ancestors. If *my* family was that ugly, I certainly wouldn't have commemorated it in stone, but to each their own. Everything was studded with more rubies, and I do mean *everything*.

And then I looked up and suddenly the Nome King was looming over me. I made a *very* undignified noise of fright as everything that had just happened came rushing back to me all at once.

Thankfully, it wasn't actually him, and no one was in the room to witness my embarrassment. It was a huge, somber oil portrait, larger than life-size. His pale eyes seemed to be staring right at me in a way that gave me the shivers, but otherwise he looked very handsome. He was wearing his iron crown and regal robes of black velvet. One hand rested on a staff topped with a massive ruby. Serpents, tongues of fire trailing from their fanged mouths, coiled at his feet, looking up at him with what I can only describe as loving expressions.

So I wasn't dead. Score one for Dorothy the Witchslayer: survived Armageddon. (With help.) (But still.) I was obviously in the Nome King's guest bedroom—at least, I could only hope I wasn't in his *actual* bedroom.

Some fresh air would've been nice, but the whole "windowless underground lair" situation suggested I'd have to pass on that particular luxury. And I had to admit, although the Nome King's style was not entirely to my taste, the place was beautiful. Crystals spiked downward from the ceiling, a black fountain burbled black water in one corner, and now I noticed that a huge black wardrobe was tantalizingly half open, revealing a delectable selection of—you guessed it—black-and-red dresses. At least I wouldn't have to worry about whether I matched. I looked down. Someone—I could only hope not the Nome King himself, because that would be a little forward of him—had gently bathed the dust from my skin and dressed me in a scanty negligee made of black lace and silk. A matching robe lay across the end of the bed and I threw it over my shoulders, feeling suddenly vulnerable. I wanted to wear something else, something of my own choosing, so I snapped my fingers to summon a nightgown with a little more coverage.

Nothing happened. I must still be tired from my giant ordeal and the shock of losing my crown. I snapped my fingers again and waited for the answering feeling of magic to flare up within me.

Instead I got what felt like faint, magical heartburn. I tried again. And again. Each time, the response was stronger. But it was nowhere near strong enough.

Was it possible Ev was interfering with my magic? That I was going to have to outwit the Nome King without my power to help me?

Ooooookay. That was a problem. And it was a problem I was going to have to solve very, very soon.

I threw off the covers, staring down at my glittering red heels. Was it something to do with the shoes themselves? That dimwit Amy Gumm had tried to imply that the shoes might be *bad* for me, but that couldn't possibly be the case. The shoes were what had brought me back to Oz. The shoes were a gift from—

Glinda. Who, as it turned out, *might* not have entirely had my best interests at heart. It's not as though I hadn't had my suspicions at times. After all, she was still a witch underneath all that pink and glitter.

But I didn't care. I wanted the shoes working again the way they were supposed to. The way you wanted to keep drowning in the poppy field after the first time you'd passed out there. The way you kept craving more and more power once you'd had your first taste of it. The way some things just got under your skin. Without them I was nothing. Without them I was just little Dorothy Gale, farm girl, eyes on the horizon and up to her ankles in cow shit. I never wanted to be that girl again. And I wasn't going to be.

What was wrong with my magic? And did it have anything to do with the Nome King?

I needed some food and a manicure before I could do any serious thinking. At least, for the time being, I seemed to be safe. Even if I was no closer to figuring out what the Nome King's plan was for me.

I wondered briefly if the Nome King had a handy Jellia Jamb type around; he didn't seem like the kind of fellow who'd be much use in that department. Oh, Jellia. Do you know, after everything she did to me, I sometimes almost miss her? Nobody could apply a topcoat like Jellia. If only she hadn't betrayed me. If only I hadn't had to punish her. I sighed. It's *so* hard to get good help these days.

So here I was, in the bowels of the Nome King's underground lair. No magic. No way back to Oz. Not even a throne. I was Dorothy Gale, Witchslayer. I had an endless supply of gumption. I could survive this. But how?

And then a soft rap sounded at my door. I brightened. Hopefully, this was breakfast. I was starving. I sat up expectantly and called, "Yes?"

The door swung open soundlessly to reveal the Nome King.

"You're awake," he said in that smooth, sinister voice. It wasn't entirely his fault that everything he said came out of his mouth sounding like he was trying to summon a demon from the far reaches of Hell.

From behind him scuttled a stooped, wrinkled servant in a shapeless, sack-like dress that hid everything about her except her earthworm-pale, nearly bald head. She *looked* like a Munchkin, sort of; the world's saddest, shabbiest Munchkin, anyway. In Oz, the Munchkins were always very chipper. Perhaps the Munchkins of Ev were a different breed.

She was holding a silver tray covered with an assortment of cups and plates and steaming dishes. She placed the tray on the bedside table and scooted back into a corner, where she kept her eyes on the intricate red carpet that covered the stone floor. The Nome King beamed downward at me.

"You slept well, I trust? I know it was a difficult journey."

"Great," I said briskly, eyeballing the food. I was *starving*. And I definitely wasn't going up against Ev's biggest evil on an empty stomach.

"Please, help yourself," he purred.

I was hoping for a singing pastry or two, but Ev's typical fare was not quite up to Oz's standards. There was an inky black soup, a little loaf of bread that was distinctly on the dry side, and a big plate of what looked suspiciously like mushrooms. But I was determined to be on my best behavior until I figured out what was going on. Like, for example, whether or not I was an honored guest—or a well-treated prisoner. I nibbled daintily on the loaf of bread, trying not to tear into it the way I wanted to.

"I have left you a servant, as is, I believe, the custom among your kind." He pointed to the scrubby, bald little thing who still waited patiently in the corner, not looking at either of us. "She is a Munchkin," he added. "I thought you might like a touch of home while you stayed with us."

On the one hand, I was touched.

On the other—well, if he wanted me to feel at home, that didn't suggest he had any intention of letting me go anytime soon. I didn't *want* to be at home in Ev. I wanted to go back to Oz. He'd said he could help me. But so far, he hadn't done anything except give me breakfast and a few things to think about.

"That's not a Munchkin," I said before I could stop myself. If I knew anything about Munchkins, it was that they had round, dimpled faces that I alternately wanted to pinch or slap depending on my mood. This creature's face was thin and gaunt. She certainly did not look like she was about to break into song, as Munchkins were annoyingly known to do.

"I assure you she is. I obtained her myself many years ago from Munchkin Country." The Nome King glanced pointedly at the Munchkin, who curtsied several times in a rather frantic manner.

If he was kidnapping Munchkins and rescuing me from crumbling palaces, he could go back and forth between Oz and Ev. Which meant he was the key to my getting home. Or per-haps—even better—the little Munchkin was. If she knew how he'd done it . . .

"What a lovely and thoughtful gift," I said.

"Really, it's nothing. I shall be honored if you will join me this evening for a banquet." He smiled broadly, his silver eyes glittering dangerously. "I simply won't take no for an answer. And I have some information that might be of interest to you, dear Dorothy. I imagine you're having a bit of trouble with your magic shoes?"

"Nonsense," I said briskly.

"My dear, I'm quite aware that you're lying."

I didn't like the sound of that at all. It was almost . . . unfriendly. Besides, how could he possibly tell? I quickly calculated my options. There was no point in lying. Maybe if I played along I could figure out what he was really up to.

I sighed. "Well, I suppose there might be a few *tiny* issues. How did you know?"

"Because I made them." His smile was almost oily.

"You . . . *made* them?" As far as I'd known, Glinda had made the shoes. Certainly she'd been the one to give them to me. How was it possible that he even knew about them? Where had they come from?

"In a sense," he said, with a sharp look, as though he'd just revealed something he hadn't meant to. He seemed to be considering whether to tell me more. "Their original material is from the kingdom of Ev," he said finally.

This was something Glinda had never bothered to mention. If there is a mine full of what my shoes are made of, imagine what I could do with all that magic! *How very, very interesting,* I thought. *How very interesting, indeed.* There was more to the Nome King—and Ev—than met the eye.

"Hmmmm," I said. "I do use them rather a lot, you know."

He smiled. "I'm aware of that, Dorothy. But we have a bargain now. And it's good for you to remember just how much you have to lose if you fail to keep your end of it."

Well. I didn't like that at all. He might be good-looking, but I've never been one for the authoritative kind. Other than myself, obviously.

"I didn't agree to anything," I said, my voice clipped. He raised a hairless eyebrow, and I carefully moderated my tone. "I mean, my lord—you must forgive me, my palace falling down on my head has put me out of sorts—that I don't recall the exact terms of our, um, deal. Something about me helping you in exchange for support regaining the throne? But I feel certain I'd remember if we'd discussed the details."

He smiled at me in amusement, and for the briefest second, I felt like a mouse pinned by a cat. But magic or no, I wasn't Dorothy Gale for nothing, and I wasn't going to let some creepily hot cave dweller put me off my game. I stared him down—and saw a flicker of respect in his eyes.

"Of course, Dorothy," he said smoothly. "Your reputation as a formidable negotiator precedes you. I wouldn't dream of trying to corner you into an agreement—I've overstepped myself. You know how it is when one is so used to dealing with inferiors. It's been a long time since I encountered an equal."

"Oh, I know all about that," I agreed. "I'd be delighted, of course, to join you this evening. And now, if you'll excuse me to my toilette . . . ?"

"But of course," he said smoothly with an ironic little bow. He turned to the door. "For your safety," he added over his shoulder, "I'd recommend you stay in your chamber until then."

"For my safety," I echoed sardonically.

But he'd already shut the door behind him—and as it slammed closed, I heard the unmistakable noise of a bolt sliding home. I wasn't going anywhere until he decided to let me. For now, anyway.

And then it occurred to me: he might have apologized to me, but he'd neatly sidestepped the question of restoring my shoes' power.

It seemed my status leaned significantly toward the "prisoner" side of the equation. But no matter; I was up for the challenge, and the Nome King was an intriguing—and attractive—opponent. Amy was so obvious. So tacky. And ultimately, so boring.

The Nome King was right. It was a treat to face an equal. Even if it was looking more and more like he might be my enemy.

But I'd conquered men before with a single bat of my magically enhanced eyelashes. Or a show of my devastating wit. And if that didn't work, I could spell them into my arms. But my lashes were decidedly magic free right now. Still, I had my looks. If I couldn't talk him into reactivating my shoes' power, maybe I could trick him into it. And he'd be a lot more likely to miss whatever I could cook up if he was distracted by my ravishing beauty.

I yawned and stretched, and the sad little servant who'd

accompanied the Nome King (did he even have a name?) scurried forward.

"Good morning, mistress," it—she—whispered. Up close, she didn't look any more impressive than she had when she'd accompanied the Nome King into my chamber. Her face was seamed with dozens of tiny wrinkles; dark eyes peered nervously out from under her heavy, pale brow. Her larva-white skull was dotted with sparse blond fuzz. Her black robe looked like a potato sack, although at least it was clean. If this was the best Ev could do in the service field, I was totally out.

I looked at her and decided something. The Nome King had a whole castle of servants, but none of them were likely loyal to him for any reason but fear. I had always had three allies at my side—Tin, Scare, and the Lion. I needed some new ones. The Munchkin didn't know it yet, but she was going to be my new best friend.

"Who are you?" I asked imperiously.

"A gift to you, mistress, from His Highness," she whispered.

"Well, obviously," I said, rolling my eyes. "I mean, servant, what is your name?"

"Bupu, mistress."

Even her name was ugly. I sighed, calling on all my reserves of patience and reminding myself that when in Rome, we do as the Romans do, at least until we can fiddle while the city burns. I would have to make the best of a bad situation.

"Are you truly a Munchkin? You don't look like one."

"Yes, mistress," the little creature said, looking despondent.

"What *happened* to you?"

"The Nome King brought me here, mistress. And for a while I had to work in the tunnels. With the Diggers." A shudder rolled through her.

"The Diggers? What are Diggers?"

"His Highness's guards, mistress," she whispered. That was definitely fear.

I sighed. If I was going to make Ev my temporary home, I needed to know what I was in for. This sad little creature was the only source I had. I patted the bed beside me. "Have some porridge," I suggested. "And tell me everything I need to know about these . . . tunnels."

Her eyes went huge and rabbity with terror. "I mustn't touch mistress's food."

"I'm not going to punish you." She was still frozen and staring at me. "I promise. When was the last time you ate?"

She made a weird convulsive movement with her shoulders, somewhere between a shrug and a nod. I filled an empty bowl from the tray and held it out. "I'm serious. Come on."

Her hands were trembling as she reached out and slowly took the bowl. She was obviously expecting it to be some kind of trick. She actually flinched when she touched the bowl with her stubby little hands. I'm all for disciplining one's staff—after all, the devil makes work for idle hands—but the poor creature seemed downright abused. I made a mental note and filed it away. She was obviously powerless, but she knew the palace better than I did—and she doubtless knew plenty more about the

Nome King. If I got her to trust me, who knew what she might be able to do for me.

Bupu wolfed down the unappetizing stuff—at least someone was enjoying it—and didn't put up a fuss when I refilled her bowl. When she'd cleaned up every last drop of porridge, she looked up at me, her eyes shining. "Mistress is very kind," she said, and this time her voice was the tiniest bit stronger than her habitual whisper. I must admit I was touched. I *am* a kind mistress, but it so rarely gets acknowledged.

"Now it's time for you to repay mistress," I said briskly. Instantly, she shrank back in alarm, cowering at my feet. "Calm down, I'm not going to murder you. I just want to know a bit about the palace." She'd gone mute with terror, staring at me with beseeching eyes. This was really going to take some patience. "Gossip?" I suggested. "How things work around here? Who's in charge?"

"His Highness," she babbled immediately. "His Highness, wisest of all kings, noblest of all rulers, bravest of all—"

"Noblest?" I asked, raising an eyebrow. "Of *all*?"

Her eyes got even bigger and she looked frantically around the room as though searching for a way out. "Noblest . . . of all . . . rulers who aren't Dorothy," she finished miserably. I smiled. That was better. But really, the poor thing couldn't help herself. She'd clearly been terrorized. I wasn't going to blame her for not acknowledging my obvious superiority. Perhaps the journey from Oz had addled her head somewhat. *Something* had happened to her in Ev, that was for sure. She was the most decrepit-looking Munchkin I'd ever seen.

"Look, I'm not going to tear you limb from limb for skipping the standard company intro," I said impatiently. "I know the Nome King is the king. It's in his name. I want to know the rest. The good stuff. How the behind the scenes works." I hit on a flash of inspiration. "So I can best please His Majesty this afternoon when I meet with him," I said. "Bupu, I'm just so nervous. The king is so powerful and strong. What will I do if you don't help me?"

To my relief, that worked. I wasn't sure how much more nonsense I could come up with. She nodded eagerly. "I understand now, mistress," she said, her voice a little firmer again. I settled against the pillows. Maybe Bupu could scrounge up some nail polish once she was done filling me in on the palace intrigue.

I wasn't going to hold my breath.

Once she got going—and reassured herself that I really wasn't going to smack her around for talking—she seemed to enjoy herself as she explained the intricacies of the palace hierarchy.

According to Bupu, she wasn't the only Munchkin the Nome King had kidnapped—he preferred them for his household staff. (Interesting.) They were overseen by a senior Munchkin named Esmerelda. Bupu's tone suggested she didn't think much of this Esmerelda character, but she didn't comment. The cave trolls, who were bigger, stronger, and most likely dumber, although Bupu didn't say so, did various labor-intensive tasks, like widening the tunnels, forging weapons, hauling stone and coal, and stoking the huge forges. And the Diggers . . . Bupu trailed off when she got to them, her lower lip trembling.

"The Diggers . . . dig?" I prompted. She nodded mutely. "As well as?" Her shoulders were crawling up her ears again as if she was trying to make herself as small and as invisible as possible.

"Hurt people," she said miserably.

The Diggers must be the Nome King's soldiers with the strange lights in their foreheads. How did he control them? Could they use magic? Were they Nomes, like him, or some other kind of creature? But when I pressed her, she only shook her head, her eyes wild, so I left it alone. I'd have plenty of time to do more research. Now it was time to get dressed.

"You must help me select my court dress," I said imperiously. Another look of terror flitted across her face. "Let me guess," I sighed. "Not a lot of noble ladies in Ev? You're wildly under-qualified for the position of lady's handmaid?"

She stared at me with her big, uncomprehending frog eyes. Not a problem. I'd worked with rough clay before. Give me a couple of days with her, and I'd turn her into the Ming vase of ladies-in-waiting.

"Okay, I'm going to explain how this works," I said. "But first, let's get *you* something better than that awful sack." I hopped out of bed—and then gasped out loud when my feet hit the softly carpeted stone floor

Despite the nice nap, I was a *mess*. My body was bruised and battered. Every part of me ached. It turns out having a palace fall on you is pretty rough on your general health and well-being.

Bupu was at my side immediately, crying "Mistress! Mistress!" in distress. I waved her off.

"I'm fine," I said through gritted teeth, although I had no idea if that was true. The truth was, I could barely even stand up.

"How will mistress be able to walk for the wedding?" Bupu blurted, staring at me. And then she clapped her hands over her mouth and stared at me in horror, her eyes wide.

"Bupu," I said. "*What* wedding are you talking about, exactly?"

Bupu's eyes filled with tears. "I wasn't supposed to say anything," she whispered. "It's not my job to say things. It's my job to watch over you and . . . and . . ." She burst into sobs.

"And . . . ?" I prompted. And then I realized. Of course. "And tell the Nome King what I'm up to?"

She nodded mutely. "Please don't tell," she said. "He'll skin me. He said he'll have the Diggers sk-sk-skin me alive and they'll do it, too, they will, they've done it before!" she babbled, tugging at my hand beseechingly.

"Of course I won't tell on you, darling," I said, my mind racing.

It would be easy enough to feed her information to take back to the Nome King. If I could win her over, I could use her as a double agent. Slowly, the beginnings of a plan began to take shape in my head.

But first, I needed my shoes working again. And more information.

"Bupu, you must be very strong," I said gently. Her shoulders squared up immediately and she looked into my eyes. "I will protect you from the Diggers, I promise. But you have to tell me everything. All right?"

She nodded again, her eyes huge.

"What wedding are you talking about, Bupu? What wedding am I supposed to attend?"

She cocked her head.

"Yours, mistress," she said.

SIX

Nox, Madison, and I didn't have long to wait. At the far end of the courtyard, a section of wall swung inward. It was a door, I realized, effectively camouflaged by being indistinguishable from the stone walls around it. We exchanged nervous glances.

"So, what's the deal with this chick?" I asked Nox.

"To be honest, I wasn't ever sure she was real," Nox said. "We started hearing stories about her right before you showed up in Oz. But like everything in Ev, it's impossible to say what's true and what's just some crazy story. It's not like we have a passenger pigeon service across the Deadly Desert."

"But it's possible to cross, or you wouldn't have heard anything."

"Mombi—" He paused for a second, conflicting emotions battling for supremacy on his face. "There are . . . spells. It's been done at least once."

He wouldn't meet my eyes; he was being deliberately vague. I fought back the urge to hit him. He was always going to be Nox, no matter how I felt about him: refusing to tell me everything until he decided it was time for me to know the whole truth.

"Okay," I said, keeping my voice even. "And obviously the Nome King can go back and forth. That still doesn't cover who Langwidere is."

"Honestly, I'm not sure you want to know," Nox said.

"We're about to go face this bitch in there," Madison interrupted, jabbing her finger at the yawning black doorway, "and homeslice over here is holding back because he thinks his information is too 'scary stories to tell in the dark' for the girls to handle? In case you missed the memo, we're going to find out the truth in about T minus five, so maybe tell us what you know?"

Nox looked at her, startled. Despite the seriousness of our predicament, I had to resist the urge to laugh. Madison clearly had no use for Nox's pretty-boy mystery act.

He shot an apprehensive look at the open doorway and then said, "Supposedly she's into wearing people's heads. She has a . . . collection. Nobody knows what she really looks like."

"Oh," I said. Okay, that was pretty gross.

Incredibly, Madison rolled her eyes in disdain. "That's so *Silence of the Lambs* it can't possibly be real," she said. "Somebody plagiarized that plot point just to scare you. I don't believe it for a second."

"I'm pretty sure they don't have Anthony Hopkins in Oz," I pointed out.

"I'm trying to keep our spirits up. Can you work with me?" Madison snapped.

"Right," I said. "Sorry. So, our options are stay in the court-yard with no food and no water in the middle of a desert and die of dehydration shortly if we don't sunburn to a fiery crisp, or go into Scary Princess Palace and meet an unknown, potentially very gruesome fate with no weapons and possibly no magic."

Nox thought for a minute. "We could wait to see if the Wheel-ers come back," he offered.

"Please tell me this isn't really happening," Madison said to the sky. "Someone? Are you there, God? It's me, Madison."

"I know," I said sympathetically. "It's not . . . ideal."

"Ideal?" Madison snorted. "I'm still not convinced I didn't accidentally smoke some *really* bunk weed. Not that I would do that. I *am* a mother now. But if this is real"—she waved a hand at the creepy courtyard—"we might as well get this part over with, right? Plus, I'm about to drop dead of heatstroke."

"Ladies first," Nox said, ushering me forward with the ghost of a smile.

At that, I *did* sock him in the shoulder, and he flashed me a real grin that made my knees weak. It felt like ten years ago that I'd been kissing him in the Emerald Palace and a flush of heat that had nothing to do with the scorching sunlight rose to my cheeks. He took my hand and squeezed it.

"We got this," I told him, with more confidence than I felt. "It can't be as bad as the Scarecrow's lab."

"It could be worse," Nox said cheerfully.

"Thanks for the encouragement," I said, but I was smiling as we walked toward the doorway. Whatever was waiting for us, we were going to face it together.

Madison was right: the cool, dark corridor might be leading us to our doom, but after the hellish journey across the desert, being out of the sun was a blissful relief. If we got out of here alive, I was never going to take shade for granted again.

I stood blinking for a moment, allowing my eyes to adjust to the sudden change in light. As I got used to the dim corridor, I was able to pick out elaborate, carved murals in the stone walls. Dropping Nox's hand, I stopped to look closer.

They were the stuff of nightmares: multi-limbed demons with white blubbery skin that reminded me of dolphins and oversize heads with bulging black eyes tearing people apart, monsters with three or four or five heads wolfing down human flesh, helpless humans boiling in vats of oil or being tormented on any number of awful devices. Most of the people seemed to be missing their heads, which were carried around instead by the monsters: monsters bowled with them, made necklaces out of them, lounged in huge thrones made of grinning skulls. . . .

"Someone's into Eli Roth," Madison said drily next to me. I raised an eyebrow. "If I'm not being a smartass, I'm going to start screaming my head off," she said. "I'm assuming you prefer me being a smartass."

"Yes," Nox said from up ahead of us. "Definitely go with the smartass route, please. Can we get a move on?"

"Right," I said. We'd have to face this mysterious Princess

Langwidere sooner or later; might as well get it over with now.
Without another word, I followed him down the hallway, doing
my best to ignore the *Saw V* scenery. Madison was a few steps
behind me.

The hallway wound up, down, and around. Here and there it
was lit with torches that burned with a sickly greenish flame that
gave off no heat at all—but when Madison reached out curiously
to touch one, she yanked her hand back with a yelp of pain.

"It burned me," she said, staring at the cold green fire. "But
not like fire. I think it, like, frostbit me."

The light was just enough to make our way by, although in
places it created looming, flickering shadows that moved ominously toward us, until I was jumpy and paranoid, sure that at
any moment something was going to leap out of the dark at us
and tear us to shreds.

Sometimes we passed huge rooms: a banquet hall with a
vaulted, gilt ceiling, curlicues of gold spinning down the walls in
the shape of vines and thorns; a narrow stone table long enough
to seat dozens of people; high-backed wooden chairs carved in
more elaborate, twisted patterns. Rooms that looked like salons,
with sofas covered in black velvet and more gilt, or bedrooms
furnished with looming black wardrobes and shadowy figures
that startled me into frightened silence before I realized they
were just our own reflections peering back at us out of tall,
ornate mirrors. Every room was deserted.

And every room was full of mirrors—and heads. Patterned
into the carpet, carved into the chairs and bedposts, paintings of

heads on the walls, velvet curtains embroidered with heads.

"I have a bad feeling about this," Madison said under her breath as we crept slowly forward.

"Tell me about it," I muttered. Nox held up his hand to hush us. Madison rolled her eyes at him, but he shook his head.

"I can hear something," he hissed.

In the ensuing silence I strained to catch whatever it was he was talking about, and then I heard it, too: a faint scratching, as if a mouse was scrabbling through the walls a hundred yards away. It was coming from up ahead, and I was pretty sure that whatever it was it wasn't a mouse.

Nox jerked his head forward, one eyebrow cocked, and I shrugged. What were we going to do—turn around, try to escape the courtyard, walk back to the Deadly Desert, and hope the Road of Yellow Brick showed up again? As my mom used to say once upon a time, before the pills anyway, there was no way out but through.

My mom—but no. I pushed that thought down as soon as it reared up. I couldn't think about her right now

"Let's do this," I said, and strode forward toward the source of the noise.

The narrow hallway opened up suddenly into a room so enormous I almost tripped in surprise. A vaulted, cathedral-like ceiling soared upward. Huge, black marble columns formed two orderly lines leading to an immense throne at the far end of the room. The floor was polished to a blinding glow but that wasn't the part that made all of us shield our eyes against the sudden, dazzling light: every surface in the room was covered in mirrors. Every wall, every shelf, every corner, every nook and cranny.

As my eyes slowly adjusted to the brilliance, I realized that cunningly placed windows allowed sunlight in at angles that maximized the sparkle. It felt like we were standing inside a giant disco ball with a strobe light going. The effect was disorienting but strangely beautiful—a strange, alternate-world echo of the shifting, sparkling mists at Rainbow Falls. But it was sinister, too: the fragmented mirrors made it look as though our heads were refracted hundreds of times, looking out in disembodied confusion from every angle no matter which way we turned.

The scratching sound was coming from the far end of the room, where a black-clad figure—the only other person in the enormous space—was bent over a table in front of the giant throne. Slowly, cautiously, we walked closer. The figure was a woman. She was wearing a loose, silky, black kimono-type outfit, embroidered with faces in delicate gold thread. Long, glossy black hair spilled down her back.

But her face was hidden behind an eerie, expressionless silver mask.

She had a ledger of some kind in front of her; the scratching was the sound of an old-fashioned quill pen moving across the rough paper as she filled out line after line of numbers, pausing occasionally to dip the nib in a ruby jar of pitch-black ink. She didn't stop writing as we approached her, and she didn't look up, even when the three of us had crossed the entire room and stood in front of her.

I stepped forward. "Hi, I'm Amy Gumm, and this—"

"I know who you are," the woman said shortly, still not looking up. "Wait until I'm done."

Somehow, the mask actually *moved* with her mouth. As if it was a part of her. As if it was her real face.

The three of us exchanged glances. Who was this chick? Langwidere's inexplicably disguised secretary? Was her mission to slay us with rudeness?

I looked down at my glittering boots, wiggling my toes. Madison fidgeted. Only Nox stood straight and still, looking calmly ahead at nothing as if all of this was perfectly ordinary. He'd grown up in Oz; maybe for him, it was.

Finally the woman reached the end of a column and set down her pen. Her hands were beautifully shaped with long, pale, slender fingers. She pushed back her heavy black hair before looking up at us. Behind the mask, I caught a flash of extraordinary green eyes, gold-flecked like a cat's.

"Well, well, well," she said. "Look what the Wheelers dragged in." The mask's silver mouth smiled sardonically.

"We're citizens of Oz," Nox began. "We have no quarrel with your country. The Road of Yellow Brick brought us to—"

"Still lying through your teeth, even after all these years?" the woman asked. "Of course you have a quarrel with this country, Nox."

She said his name like it was a curse word. Nox started.

"How do you know who I am?" he asked cautiously.

"Oh, Nox," she said, her voice like ice. "I know all about you. You might choose not to remember the past, but I don't forget. Anything."

I looked at Nox, but his face was a blank. I knew he was as confused as I was. He'd never been to Ev before; how could he have met this woman? Who on earth was she?

The silver mouth opened wide, and she laughed—a cold, cruel laugh that sent a shiver down my spine.

This was *definitely* not a secretary.

I took a step forward. "Are you Princess Langwidere?" I asked, keeping my voice neutral. "I'm Amy. Amy Gumm. I'm with Nox and um, my friend Madison, and we didn't mean to disturb you at all. In fact, we could totally just, um, leave," I added brightly.

Okay, so maybe I wasn't going to win any awards for diplomatic speeches. But still, I didn't see a reason for this creepy chick to keep laughing at me.

"You're the most recent conquest, I take it?" she said, when she was done chuckling. "You know you're not the last in a *very* long line. Nox is quite the pretty boy, isn't he? Always an eye for the ladies. So troubled and remote. 'Only you can save him,'" she said mockingly.

"Look," Nox said, his teeth gritted. Whoever she was, her barbs had landed. "I don't know who you are, but you should really think about—"

"Oh, Nox," she said. "Has it been so long? Have you *really* forgotten me so easily?"

Suddenly lines began to appear in the sinister mask. One by one, silver sections peeled away from her face like petals of a flower unfurling. As each section opened, the silver disappeared in a puff of gleaming smoke.

Underneath the mask her face was ordinary. Neither pretty nor plain. Something in the middle—a face almost remarkable for how completely *un*remarkable it was. I had the feeling if I glanced away from her I'd immediately forget what she looked like.

There was something almost uncanny about her ordinariness. Something almost . . . enchanted.

But next to me, Nox breathed out hard with a noise of total shock.

"*Lanadel?*" He was staring at her, his mouth actually open. I'd never, in all the time I'd known him, seen him so astonished. I looked back and forth between the two of them.

"Wait, you *know* her?" I asked. The air around her was charged with unmistakable, naked hostility as she stared Nox down, and to my utter surprise, he looked away first, his cheeks flooding with color. As if he was embarrassed—or ashamed.

"Who I used to be doesn't matter anymore," the woman said.

"But you're—you're—" Nox was still trying to get out a sentence.

"Not dead? Not so lucky for you, I'm afraid."

"I didn't—you weren't supposed to—"

"Survive?" She smiled. "I'm so sorry to disappoint you, Nox. Listen, I don't know why the road coughed you up at my doorstep, but this is not a good time to rehash our past."

She stood up and walked away from us, the silky robe clinging to her body. As with her face, there was something almost impossible to pin down about it. She wasn't tall, she wasn't short, she wasn't thin, she wasn't curvy.

Somehow, everything about her avoided description. As if her whole being was a disguise.

"Why are you here?" she asked curtly.

I took a deep breath. I had no idea how Nox knew this woman, and I wasn't entirely sure I wanted to. But I could tell that she was on the verge of doing something bad. To all of us. And I needed us to get out of her palace in one piece. *All* of us.

"We don't know," I said. "The truth is—"

"Amy," Nox said, a warning note in his voice. I knew what he was hinting at. Telling this person everything might be incredibly stupid—especially if she was on the side of the Nome King. But somehow, I didn't think she was. The road had brought us here for a reason. Maybe it had meant for us to meet her. Besides, I was tired of the Wicked way of doing things.

"Nox, no more secrets," I said. I saw something flicker in Langwidere's eyes—something that could have been respect. "Like I said, we don't know why we're here. The road brought us across the Deadly Desert and dumped us."

I quickly explained how we'd ended up running away from Oz, the road whisking us off. I didn't tell her everything, because that would have taken all day. But enough.

She didn't say much while I explained—just stopped me a couple of times to ask more questions about the Nome King. When I told her that the Nome King and Glamora had killed Mombi, her eyes widened, but she didn't comment.

Nox stayed quiet. It felt good to be the one making the decisions. And why shouldn't I? I'd been through as much as he had in the time since I'd met him. I'd trained like crazy and fought like a warrior.

Nox wasn't in charge of me anymore. We were equals.

When I was done talking, she was silent for a long time. Madison had sat down on the hard stone floor and rested her head on her knees. Despite her bravado, it was clear she was overwhelmed. I knew how she felt. And she didn't have the grandmotherly Gert to help her adjust like I'd had. I was tempted to join her. I was exhausted—we all were. But I stood my ground.

"Lanadel," Nox said suddenly. "Langwidere—how did you get here? What are you *doing* here?"

She walked to one of the narrow windows overlooking the wasteland outside. The mirrored walls refracted her every move as if we were in an amusement-park fun house. The effect was spooky and distracting—as she moved it got harder and harder to pin down which image was her and which was her reflection.

"After you and Mombi sent me here to spy, the Nome King captured me," she said. She held up one slender wrist and I saw a thin silver bracelet from which dangled a glittering ruby padlock and key.

Wait a minute. This girl had been in the *Order?* What was going on? I stared at Nox but he shook his head, warning me to stay quiet. Quiet was not exactly something I did well.

"He . . . interrogated me for information about the Order," she continued. Her voice was steady, but I thought about what

I'd seen of "interrogations" in Dorothy's palace, and shuddered. "When he had what he wanted, he turned me into his spy."

"You work for the Nome King?" I interrupted. If that was the case, we were in trouble.

She shrugged. "I stay alive. For now, that means keeping him happy."

"Does he know we're here?" Nox asked.

"Well, *I* haven't told him," she said. "But I wouldn't have to. And he's as connected to the magic of Ev as you are to Oz. If the road brought you here, he probably felt it."

"So we're not safe here?" Madison asked from the floor, lifting her head.

Langwidere glanced at her and smiled without warmth. "In these times? You're not safe anywhere."

Madison stood up and glared at her. "Okay, fine. Then can you just kill us now? Because I'm really tired and I'm pretty sick of listening to people talk."

For the first time since she'd taken her mask off, Langwidere looked startled. And then she started to laugh. This time, there was nothing cruel about it. It was the laughter of a much younger and more innocent girl. Maybe the person she'd once been, before the Nome King got to her.

I was starting to feel almost sorry for her. Almost.

"You can rest here," she said. "For now, at least." She glanced at Nox, her eyes hardening again. "Until I decide what to do with you."

"So you're keeping us prisoner?" Nox asked.

"I'm entertaining you as very honored guests." She smiled mirthlessly. She'd said "honored" like it was a curse. "These are strange times," she added, looking out the window again. "You're the second visitors we've had from Oz in a matter of days. The Nome King's up to something, and I want to know what it is."

"The *second* visitors from Oz?" I asked.

She turned back to us and raised an eyebrow. "You mean you didn't know?"

"Know what?" Nox asked.

"Dorothy's here," she said.

Nox and I looked at each other and then back at her. "Dorothy's *alive*?"

"Very much so, I'm afraid." She shrugged. "Until I kill her, that is."

SEVEN

DOROTHY

I wasn't sure I'd heard the Munchkin right.

"*My* wedding, Bupu? Whatever do you mean?"

She looked around anxiously. "It's why he brought you here," she whispered, as if the Nome King was standing behind us.

"He wants to *marry* me?" I didn't blame him, of course, but I had to say I was surprised. In all the time I'd been in Oz, the Nome King hadn't even tried to kiss me yet.

"I wasn't supposed to tell you," she said, hanging her head. "But you have been very nice to me. I wouldn't like for the Nome King to hurt you, mistress."

My gaze sharpened. "What do you mean, hurt me?"

She jumped back, alarmed, as if she had said too much. "Just that he hurts people! Mostly," she added fearfully. "Maybe for you it will be different. Just ignore me."

"Hmmm," I said, pacing my chambers to try to get some of the soreness out of my muscles. "He's up to something. But

I can't imagine what it is yet. It's more than just marriage he's after, I'll bet all of Oz on it."

Bupu nodded. "You are very wise, mistress."

I sighed. "I know that, Bupu. But I need more information before I can figure out what to do next. Help me get ready, will you?"

I wanted to look my absolute best for my big rendezvous with the Nome King—I've always felt better when my ensemble is on point. But without magic, I was having trouble achieving the results I wanted. I brushed furiously at my hair, which was absolutely *full* of split ends. Disgusting. And I was willing to bet the miracle of conditioner had yet to reach Ev.

Bupu, bless her little heart, was more or less useless. She didn't know a stiletto heel from a strainer, she couldn't name a single type of fabric to save her life, and she'd clearly never dressed a member of the royal family, let alone done hair and makeup. I was going to have to do a lot on my own, and I was going to do it fast.

But surprising as it might sound, I was rather enjoying the challenge. I'd gotten soft in the Emerald City, I realized. Everyone was just so adoring all the time. My every whim was satisfied before I even whimmed it. I'd had rooms full of gorgeous dresses, plus all the magic in Oz at my disposal to alter them as I saw fit.

Here, I was outside of civilization—all I had was a wardrobe full of ball gowns the Nome King had selected himself, a grubby little servant with no experience, and, at least for now, no magic.

Ensuring my style was up to my rigorous standards in these survival-only conditions was just the thing I needed to give me an extra dose of pep. Plus, as I realized when I examined myself in the mirror, I was a hot mess: battered, bruised, and haggard-looking. This was going to be a challenge for the ages.

It was already late in the afternoon, Bupu told me; I'd slept in, and our little chat after the Nome King's visit had swallowed up the hours. If I wanted to look as beautiful as I was, I didn't have much time to get myself in order.

As I pinched color into my cheeks and brushed my hair to a glossy shine, I thought about my new friend. Enemy. Whatever. I almost—almost—admired him. He was fearless and ruthless, he knew exactly what he wanted, and he refused to let other people's motives and desires stand in his way.

When you got right down to it, our styles had a lot in common. Committing to a big-picture vision takes serious guts, especially when everyone around you is telling you ridiculous things like your approach is too dictatorial, or you should factor in human—or Munchkin—rights. Where were the human rights defenders when I was growing up in filthy poverty in the middle of nowhere, I'd like to know? I had to feed the chickens at five in the morning—every single day! And on top of my endless chores, I had to put up with the doubts and snickers of all the other people in Kansas who refused to believe the magical things I'd seen in Oz. That kind of oppression would have had a lasting effect on someone who wasn't as strong and determined as I was.

Luckily for me, I had an incredible wealth of inner resources.

"Draw my bath, Bupu," I said, briskly flipping through the gowns he'd left for me. None of them were suitable, of course. The Nome King's style seemed to veer directly toward crypt-keeper. Maybe he should have kidnapped a vampire princess and not an ex–farm girl turned royalty like me.

"I don't suppose it's possible for you to find me something that's a color?" I added crabbily, fingering layer after layer of black. I limped around the room, trying doors—most of them locked tight—until I opened one that led to a bathroom. Bupu was right on my heels, eager to help.

But from what I could see, I wasn't going to need Bupu to fill my bath after all. A marble pool was already filling with steaming water as if it could read my mind. I happily discarded the Nome King's creepy lingerie and slid into the water, hissing sharply as my battered flesh came into contact with the hot liquid.

"Oh no!" Bupu cried at the sight of my cuts and scrapes. She bustled about clumsily, returning with some kind of ointment that smelled like mold and looked like rotten flesh. "This will help," she said. "Made from the finest healing funguses." Mush-rooms were apparently the cornerstone of everything around here.

"Oh, that's all right," I began, but the little Munchkin was already smearing the horrible-smelling stuff on my bruised shoulders. And while it was going to take another bath altogether to get rid of the stench, to my surprise the ointment actually worked. A soothing warmth spread through my muscles, and I sank back into the water with a sigh, allowing her to rub the salve gently into the rest of my bruises.

Bupu was inept, certainly; stupid, without a doubt; but she was the first person I'd met since—well, since Aunt Em and Uncle Henry, may they rest in peace—who seemed to have only my own best interests at heart. There had been Scare and the Lion, of course, but it had often seemed to me like they had secret agendas of their own. And poor, devoted Tin—but he was so blinded by his (understandable) love for me that he often failed to respect my wishes. And of course, once upon a time, I'd had Toto. Toto had been everything I wanted in a friend: sweet, cuddly, endlessly loyal.

Toto, however, was a dog.

And even Aunt Em and Uncle Henry, my own flesh and blood, had never believed me about Oz until they'd actually come here. And they'd quickly proved how unwilling they were to support me once I'd actually arrived. But here was this gentle, humble creature, seemingly with no agenda of her own.

Bupu watched nervously as I sank in stages into the water. Slowly, thanks to a combination of her ointment and the hot water, the pain subsided to a low, dull throb, and I leaned back against the tub's stone rim and thought about what I was going to do next.

Why had the Nome King rescued me? What was I doing in his palace? Why on earth did he want to *marry* me? It couldn't only be for love. There was something he wanted. Something I had. Something more than my amazing beauty and legendary charm.

And then it hit me. Of course. The shoes.

They might be his, but he couldn't use them.

No one could use them but me.

In that moment I sent a silent thank-you to that treacherous, awful witch Glinda. She'd pretended to be my best friend and then she'd betrayed me. She was basically dead to me for all intents and purposes.

But she'd given me the shoes. And maybe her reasons hadn't been entirely—or remotely—aboveboard, but possession is nine-tenths of the law. I knew the shoes couldn't come off my feet—which meant that if the Nome King wanted them, he had to have me, too. Inadvertently, Glinda had given me my first bargaining chip. I wasn't sure exactly what he wanted them for, but I knew exactly how powerful they were.

If I could figure out how to get my magic back before he could get the shoes, I'd be in an even better position to bargain with him. And maybe, just maybe, I could turn this situation to both our advantages—assuming the Nome King behaved like enough of a gentleman to convince me of the value of generosity. Otherwise, the only advantage I'd be taking into consideration would be my own. Fair is fair, after all.

It might take some figuring out, but if Glinda's shoes were powerful enough to take me from Kansas back to Oz, they had to be adequate when it came to zipping me across the Deadly Desert and back where I belonged.

I'd been ruminating in the bathwater for long enough. Aunt Em always used to say that action is the best course of action.

Okay, she never actually said that, but she would've definitely agreed with me that keeping myself alive was first priority. I was officially in survival-of-the-fittest mode. Whatever it took, I was going to get out of the Nome King's clutches.

But a tiny voice nagged at the back of my mind. I'd never met anyone like him. Not in Oz. Not in Kansas. I'd never met anyone who made me feel so . . .

Challenged. Alive. On my toes.

And it was a feeling I liked.

Maybe even a feeling I could love.

"Bring me a towel, Bupu!" I declared. "Mistress is putting her dress on now." I sloshed out of the tub and dried myself off.

Time to pick out the least awful of the Nome King's dresses. Looking good was the best armor a girl could put on.

EIGHT

I wasn't sure I'd heard her right. "Dorothy's alive? But we dropped a whole palace on her. There's no way she could have survived that. We barely got out ourselves."

Lang shrugged. "She didn't have to survive it. The Nome King was waiting all along for the right opportunity. He tunneled under the Deadly Desert into the Emerald Palace years ago. He knew exactly when the palace began to fall, and he got her out of there before you'd even cleared the castle walls. She's been in Ev for days."

I didn't believe it. It wasn't possible. I hadn't meant to let Dorothy live. I just hadn't been able to kill her myself. I thought of Lulu's face after the Emerald Palace fell, when I'd told her I hadn't been able to bring myself to kill Dorothy. The way Lulu looked at me as though I'd personally betrayed her.

And, in a way, I had. Killing Dorothy was why I'd been brought to Oz in the first place. It was the first, most important—and, ultimately, the only—task I'd been given. It was why I'd trained so hard, learned magic, learned how to fight.

I'd thought it was compassion that had made me leave Dorothy when the palace fell.

But if Dorothy was still alive, it was more like failure.

Except that some part of me had known there was a chance Dorothy might survive. Which mean that some part of me believed I didn't have to kill her to save Oz. What if that was what Lurline had meant when she'd told me to find another way?

Was I a failure—or was I still Oz's only hope?

"Wait a minute," I said. "I thought I was the only one who could kill Dorothy. Isn't that why you brought me to Oz in the first place?" I asked Nox.

Lang snorted. "You're not *that* special," she said. "Dorothy might be from the Other Place, but she's still human. And you don't seem to have gotten the job done, so maybe it's time for someone else to take over."

I bristled. Just because *I* knew I'd failed didn't mean I was up for this crazy witch telling me where to go. But before I could snap back at her, Nox interrupted hastily.

"What's the Nome King up to?" Nox asked.

Lang shot him a murderous look, as if she was offended he'd even opened his mouth. There was some *seriously* bad blood there.

And then it hit me. It was so obvious, I don't know why it took me so long. Langwidere had been in the Order—or, at least, she knew Nox and Mombi. Had the Road of Yellow Brick dumped us in Ev for the world's most awkward reunion with Nox's *ex?*

"I don't know yet," she said coolly. "But it's not your problem. I don't know why the road brought you here either, but I have no use for you. You can rest here for a day or two, but after that, go on your way."

"We don't know what our way *is*, Lanadel," Nox said in frustration.

"That's not my name anymore," she snapped.

"Uh, it seems kind of obvious?" Madison interrupted. "Everybody wants to kill this Dorothy chick, right? So . . ."

"So let us help you," I finished, seeing exactly where she was headed. "Like I said, that's why the Order came to me in the first place. There's no reason for you to fight Dorothy alone."

This time both Nox *and* Lang looked at me in surprise.

"Dorothy is everybody's problem," I pointed out. "And we've been fighting her for a long time without, frankly, a whole lot of success. What makes you think you can take her on your own?"

Lang frowned. "Exactly," she said. "You weren't strong enough. So why would I want your help?"

Now was definitely not the time to mention that I could have killed Dorothy but hadn't been able to bring myself to do it. That being Wicked was one thing, but it wasn't the same as being good. That no matter what Dorothy had done in the past, I hadn't been able to bring myself to murder her when she was defenseless.

I remembered what it had felt like to stand over Dorothy in the cave underneath the Emerald Palace. She'd been vulnerable and weak; I'd been strong and powerful. I'd had the perfect opportunity to end it then and there. She'd murdered hundreds of people, including plenty of people I cared about. She'd almost destroyed Oz with her insane quest for power. And I still couldn't bring myself to do it.

And the truth was, I wasn't sure I could do it now. Because if I did, that would make me just like her. And if I killed her, would it really end there? And what if Oz's magic warped me so much that I became just as evil in her place?

Nox had told me once that he wouldn't hesitate to kill me if I turned into a monster. But a lot had happened between us since then. If I did start to become a monster like Dorothy, corrupted by the magic of Oz, what if he couldn't bring himself to do it? What if, deep down, the only difference between me and Dorothy was that Oz's magic had twisted her into something unrecognizable?

But I knew Dorothy had to be stopped, whether that meant killing her or finding another way to defeat her. And I also knew there was no way Lang, whoever she was, could do it on her own. She needed us, whether she liked it or not. And I was going to find a way to convince her.

Whatever it took.

I looked up. Lang was staring at me as if she could read my mind. Suddenly I *really* hoped she didn't have Gert's power to listen in on people's thoughts.

"Guys?" Madison piped up. "I'm pretty hungry over here? Can we lay off the conference and eat something?"

"Of course. Forgive me, I've been a terrible hostess," Lang said, not sounding very sorry at all.

As soon as the words left her mouth, a massive, shiny black beetle the size of a cow scuttled into the room from a doorway I hadn't noticed, bearing an assortment of chairs, trays, and dishes improbably balanced on its immense back. But that wasn't the weird part. The weird part was that its neck and body sprouted dozens of heads of different sizes and shapes. Some of them were almost human, others distinctly insectoid. The humanlike heads wore various expressions; some were smiling, revealing more than one row of teeth, and others were weeping or snarling with rage. Hundreds of beady black beetle eyes glittered at us from its insect heads. Its humanlike mouths moved as though they were speaking, but no sound came out as their jaws worked noiselessly. It was definitely up there with the Wheelers in the category of super-gross, super-creepy creatures that I never, ever wanted to see again, let alone stand next to while it set up the table and laid out the dishes with its long, segmented black legs and spikily jointed talons.

Madison looked slightly faint.

"I don't think it will hurt us," I said softly, although I wasn't sure if I was trying to reassure Madison or myself.

"I'm terrified of bugs," she whispered. "Like, irrational paranoia, get-the-sweats terrified."

"All this time and I never knew," I said with a grin I couldn't help. "A well-placed cockroach at school could have changed everything."

"Greta is not a *cockroach*," Lang snapped, silencing us both immediately. "And she can hear you. Several of her bites are quite poisonous, so I'd watch my mouth around her if I were you."

"Sorry," Madison said hastily, but she still flinched as the beetle set a chair down in front of her.

If a many-headed beetle is capable of bowing sarcastically, Greta was definitely doing it. She set down chairs for the rest of us and delivered the dishes to the table in front of the princess, who uncovered them and shoved them toward us.

"Eat," she said unceremoniously. "And sit."

We sat. I wasn't too excited about the eating part. Whatever Lang was serving us looked a lot like mushrooms. Lots and lots of mushrooms. At least there was water.

"It's more than most people get here in a week," Lang said shortly, watching me stare at the unappetizing brown mess.

"Of course," I said quickly, helping myself to a spoonful. "I'm sure they're delicious."

They weren't, not even a little bit, but at least they were filling. The three of us chewed in polite silence.

"Now that we're all tight and stuff, can I ask about the heads?" Madison asked, swallowing a glutinous mouthful of mushrooms. Lang raised an eyebrow. "You know, the whole heads-on-sticks thing outside? And your decor? It's a little unsettling, to be honest. Like way more Vlad the Impaler than Martha Stewart Living."

"I don't know your Vlad or Martha," Lang said, her tone

polite. "These are witches of the Other Place, presumably? But the heads are decorative, yes."

"That stuff out there—those people—are *decorative?*"

"Those heads aren't real," Nox said. "They're a glamour. An illusion. All of this"—he gestured at the palace, the mirrors, her nondescript clothes—"is an illusion. A mask. Right?"

"That's the point," Lang said with a shrug. "I know what people say about me. That I wear my murdered subjects' faces stitched together over my own. That I swap identities the way other women change clothes. I don't mind the rumors; I'm the one who started most of them. It pays to be unrecognizable. To have no one know for sure what I look like. I could be anywhere, or anyone."

"So that stuff Nox was saying about you skinning people alive or whatever—that's not actually true?" Madison asked.

Lang smiled. "I learned plenty about torture in the Order," she said in a pleasant voice that belied her words. "Nox can tell you all about that. But actually hurting innocent people isn't my style. The rumors let me move around Ev as I please. They keep the palace safe from trespassers, along with the Wheelers. Even the Nome King doesn't know how much of it's true and how much is just embellishment. Skinning people alive is certainly *his* style."

That shut Madison up pretty quickly.

"And you and the Nome King . . ." Nox trailed off. I could guess at what he was about to say. How could she work for that monster? Especially if she'd been in the Order?

Lang glanced involuntarily at her silver bracelet. And now that I looked more closely, I could see that the pale skin of her wrist was circled with a web of silvery scars.

"It's unbreakable," she said, following my look. "The Nome King takes service contracts very seriously. I've tried to get it off with magic. Metal hammer, enchanted knives, half a dozen spells. He just laughed at me." She pulled the fabric of her robe away from her neck briefly and I saw more scars knotted across her back, thick and painful-looking. "Or sent me to the Diggers to be whipped," she added matter-of-factly. "After a while, it got easier to make him happy. I've had a lot of practice lying."

"But the Order sent you here to spy. How did you become his prisoner?" Nox said. "What happened?"

Anger flashed through her green eyes.

"The *Order?*" she spat. "What did the *Order* ever do for me, Nox? The Order couldn't even take out Dorothy. I don't work for anyone. I do what the Nome King asks in order to stay alive long enough to find a way to take him down. Him and Dorothy both."

"It seems to be working out for you," Nox said, indicating the lavish palace with a nod of his head. I wanted to kick him. It was obvious that whatever work she was doing for the Nome King, she hated him. If he'd captured her when the Order sent her here and turned her into his slave, no wonder she hated the Order so much. Nox seemed dead set on antagonizing this girl and I didn't understand why. That, or he was just oblivious to the fact that everything he said to her was exactly the wrong thing.

Which, knowing Nox, was just as likely. Fighting, he was good at. Tact, not so much.

"The Nome King didn't buy me this place. I earned it. The few wealthy people in Ev pay a lot of money to gamble in my clubs."

I thought I'd misheard her. "Your clubs? Like . . . night-clubs?"

She shrugged. "No matter how poor people get, they have to drink. And gambling makes them feel like they have a chance to make their lives better. It's a public service of sorts, but it also puts me close to the action. There's not a lot to do in Ev. Every-one who's anyone comes through my clubs, and I pay attention to what comes out of their mouths. That's the work I do for the Nome King. The work I do for myself . . ." She let that trail off, leaving us to digest her words.

"You cheat people and steal information from them for a really evil guy who's magically keeping you a permanent pris-oner?" I countered.

"It's an exchange. I give them a place to forget their troubles for a while. Ev is a dangerous, violent place, but inside the walls of my clubs, my patrons are safe. I guarantee it. That's a huge piece of why they do so well. And no one's dumb enough to talk real politics within my walls—they know who I work for. I get just enough information to feed the Nome King useful tidbits to keep him satisfied. The rest of my intel I keep for myself."

"So you're a mobster," Madison said. She sounded impressed.

Lang shrugged. "I prefer the word *entrepreneur*. I saw an

opening and filled it. And in a way, my clubs bring people together. Rich and poor alike mingle at the roulette wheels and card tables. I have a dress code, but I don't turn anyone away— unless they misbehave. That used to happen at first. Now that my reputation has spread, people don't misbehave so much anymore."

Most prisoners did not run Vegas-like empires. "So the Nome King just lets you . . . have all this?"

"The Nome King likes to think of himself as generous. And gambling provides a healthy distraction for the masses, which benefits him."

"Distraction from what? Do you know why the Nome King rescued Dorothy and brought her to Ev?" Nox asked.

Lang shook her head, her clean, glossy hair rippling around her shoulders in a way that made my fingers itch for magic. I could've at least touched up my filthy and ragged dress, smoothed my hair to something resembling cleanliness. A little lip gloss— wait, who was I? Madison? Nox had seen me covered in blood, dirt, and worse. He'd seen me turn into a literal monster, and he was still around. I was tough, awesome, competent, and good at fighting. It wasn't like she was flirting with my semi-maybe-non-boyfriend. If anything, her attitude toward him suggested she despised him.

But then I thought of that line from *Romeo and Juliet* that our sophomore year English teacher had drummed into our heads: *My only love sprung from my only hate.* You had to feel strongly enough about someone in the first place to hate them. Was this what jealousy felt like? Sort of being sick to your stomach all the time? I'd never had a reason to be jealous before.

I'd never been in love with anyone before Nox. My dopey kindergartener's crush on Dustin was nothing compared to what I felt for Nox. And realizing that I had absolutely no idea what was going on in his head, that he might have an entire history with someone that ended before I'd even met him—a history that I wasn't part of, and knew nothing about—was enough to make me insane.

If being in love felt like this all the time, then being in love kind of sucked.

I sighed out loud. Jealousy was exhausting; I was giving myself a headache.

"Did you have something you wanted to share with the class, Amy?" Madison said drily. They were all staring at me.

"I'm fine, thanks," I said hastily.

"You said something about resting?" Madison asked hopefully.

"You can't stay here for long," Lang said. "If the Nome King realizes you're here it could jeopardize everything I've worked for, and I'm not his only spy. The magic outside hides much of what goes on here, even from him, but it's still only a matter of time before he realizes you're in my palace."

"If you don't want our help, we'll be on our way," Nox said haughtily. "Clearly, the road brought us here for something else."

I wanted to shake him. What the hell was he thinking? Nox

was always strategic but it felt like he was acting on pure emotion here. We were in a completely different country where Lang was the only potential ally we'd encountered. Our magic wasn't working and we had no idea why. We had no food, no water, no shelter, and no way to hide from the Nome King. Prickly and unstable as she was, Lang was the only chance we had to figure out why the road had brought us to Ev and what we needed to do next. Nox might have some bad history with her, but her magic was obviously powerful. We needed her more than she needed us, especially if we couldn't fully access our own power. Pissing her off was completely the wrong strategy.

"What he means is, we don't want to put you in any danger," I said quickly. "But if we could rest for a while before we travel on, we'd be grateful."

Nox opened his mouth again to speak and this time I did kick him. He shut it with a snap.

Lang looked at me warily. "One night only," she said.

"That's really generous," I said. "Thank you." One night wasn't much time. But hopefully it would be enough for me to figure out how to convince her to help us. Or to let us help her. Which, I was guessing, she was smart enough to figure out was basically the same thing.

Lang beckoned Greta, and the beetle clicked forward, looming over us. Madison swallowed hard.

"Greta, show them to the guest chambers," Lang said. She smiled thinly. "You'll forgive me if I leave you now." The air around her face shimmered and seemed to solidify. As I watched, the silver mask re-formed over her face. But her magic disappearing act didn't stop there. The shimmer spread outward, enveloping her entire body. The kimono swirled around her.

And then she was gone.

Madison's mouth was hanging open. "Whoa," she said softly. "That was . . ."

"Magic, yeah," I said.

"Can *you* do that?"

"I've never tried the mask part. But disappearing, sure."

She stared at me. "Prove it."

"Right now it's complicated," I began, but Greta was already clicking toward us. One of its—her—heads nodded toward a mirror-framed doorway, and she pointed with one long, segmented leg.

"Ugh," Madison muttered under her breath, staying as far away from Greta as possible as the beetle led us out of the room and down a hall. I hoped Langwidere's sinister servant wasn't easily offended. If anything, Greta seemed almost to be smirking. If a multiheaded giant beetle whose faces all had completely different expressions could be said to smirk, anyway.

Greta stopped in another long hallway studded with doors. The decor was just as sinister here as it had been in the other parts of Lang's palace. Bodiless heads grinned at us crazily from the walls, and where the hallway ended, a huge wooden guillo-tine with a polished silver blade sat where a normal person might have put an end table.

"Home, sweet home," Nox said. Greta indicated three of

the closed doors with another wave of her leg, and then clicked back the way we'd come. Madison shrank against the wall as the beetle passed her. I could've sworn Greta brushed up against her deliberately. I also could've sworn the giant beetle was laughing.

But despite the horrible murals in the hallway, the doors Greta had shown us opened up on small, plain bedrooms with blank walls and simple furnishings. I sank onto a bed with a sigh of relief, grateful to have escaped the eerie stares of Lang's creepy wallpaper.

"Now we rest?" Madison asked hopefully, sitting down next to me. But Nox was pacing the floor, deep in thought, and I shook my head.

"You can if you want," I said. "But we have to figure out what to do next—before Lang throws us back out there. Once the Nome King realizes we're here we're in danger. And I don't know how long we have. The Wheelers seem to report to Lang, but if they give him information, too, or if he can sense when someone crosses the Deadly Desert . . ." I trailed off. As usual, there was so much we didn't know. If Lang had found us, odds were, the Nome King wouldn't be far behind.

But first, I wanted to know where we stood with Langwidere, and why she was so eager to kick us out. Which, I was pretty sure, had at least something to do with Nox. Possibly a lot. Possibly some stuff I would regret finding out. But if there was one thing I'd learned the hard way in Oz, knowing the truth was always better than being in the dark.

Even if the truth totally sucked. Which, in Oz, it usually did. So at least I had practice.

This time, though, I had feelings. And if Nox's history with Lang was what I thought it was—if he had been in love with her once—I knew there was no way it wouldn't hurt.

And I also knew that even if it did, I was strong enough to deal with it. Old, Kansas Amy might've blamed her problems on her druggie mom or Madison's bullying or her significant lack of friends. But I was a different person now. And I'd learned that everyone has a story—even Madison.

Whatever Nox told me, I could handle it.

I looked at him. "So, now that we're alone—it's time you tell us how you know Langwidere."

He looked stricken and stopped pacing. I watched his face as grief and worry moved across his features, and I steeled myself for what was coming.

What if he's still in love with her? I thought suddenly.

Okay, new Amy or no new Amy, if he was—that was one truth I might *not* be able to face.

I was so wrapped up in my new worry that I barely realized he'd already started talking.

"She was Lanadel when I knew her," he was saying.

"I got that part. Who is she to *you*?"

"She trained with the Order before Mombi sent her here. It's a long story." I raised an eyebrow. "I'll tell you," he said. "I promise. But I really don't think it's important right now. I'm sure she's not happy that we're here, but I don't think she'll hurt us."

"You don't *think*?" Madison asked.

He shrugged. "I haven't seen her in years and we didn't . . . well, we didn't exactly part on the best of terms." I stared at him intently. There was no sign he was about to say anything about having been in a relationship with her. But if Nox was anything, it was totally unreadable. If he did still have feelings for her, I'd never know unless he actually told me.

Which was not his strong suit.

"But I know she hates Dorothy—maybe even more than we do," he continued. "And it sounds like she's no fan of the Nome King either. We're more or less on the same side."

"Is that Wicked? Or Good?" Madison asked.

"Same thing," Nox said.

"Sometimes," I muttered. He smiled at me. My heart did this gross flip-flopping thing. *Knock it off,* I told it.

"Okay, sometimes," he agreed. "The side that's fighting Dorothy, anyway. And if Dorothy is somehow allied with the Nome King now . . ."

"Enemy of my enemy is my friend?" Madison asked.

"Welcome to the wonderful world of Oz," I agreed.

Nox leaned against the wall opposite us, sliding down until he was sitting on the floor with his long legs stretched out in front of him. "If Dorothy and the Nome King are working together it makes sense that the road brought us here to stop them," he said.

"Unless the road brought us here completely at random," I said. "Which it's been known to do."

Nox grimaced. "Let's try for the best-case scenario."

"I like how 'we have no idea why but we think maybe there's some reason we're probably supposed to be here to do something we can't figure out' is the best-case scenario," Madison said.

I laughed. "Yeah, that's Oz for you. The road has seemed to act randomly in the past. But I think it's always just had a mind of its own. It's always acted for the good of Oz before. Nox is right; it's the only answer that makes sense. But if we were barely strong enough to fight Dorothy on our own, there's no way we can take on both of them. The Nome King is incredibly powerful."

"And so is Lang," Nox said, meeting my eyes. I could tell he was thinking the same thing I was.

"The road brought us *here*," I said. "To her doorstep, basically. Which means: if we work with her, we have a chance. I think."

"It means there's *something* here we need," Nox agreed. He looked pensive. "I wish we had some way to contact Ozma. If anyone could tell us something about what the road wants, it's her. But she . . ."

He trailed off. I thought about what he wasn't saying: that we had no way of knowing if Ozma was even alive. That with Mombi dead and Glinda in control of Glamora, things in Oz were very likely . . . bad. Really, really bad. Maybe even worse than they'd been when Dorothy ruled.

No, I thought. *Nothing could be that bad.* When Dorothy was in charge, Ozma had been enchanted so that she was basically three sheets to the wind. She wouldn't let Glinda trick her again. And she was incredibly powerful—surely as powerful as Glinda, especially now that she knew the only side Glinda was on was Glinda's. I couldn't start thinking straight-up doom and gloom. The road wouldn't have bothered to rescue us from the Nome King and carry us all the way across the Deadly Desert if we'd already lost Oz, I told myself. There was still time to find out what we needed to do in Ev, get back to Oz, and restore Ozma to her rightful place.

And once all that was done, maybe, just maybe, Nox and I could settle in for a solid makeout session.

"Why can't you talk to Ozma? You can't just, like, enchant a telephone?" Madison asked.

Nox knitted his brows together. "A telephone?"

"You know? E.T. phone home?" He looked even more confused.

"Madison, they don't have telephones in Oz," I said. "Telepathy, yes. Telephones, no. But trying to contact Ozma all the way across the Deadly Desert with no magic . . ." I stopped. There was something I wasn't thinking of. Something important. Something Lurline had said.

I tried to remember what she'd told me during my brief visit to her world. I'd drunk the water from her spring. I'd walked through her garden with her. And then . . .

The words materialized in my mind as clearly as if she was standing next to me repeating them. And as I heard her voice, my boots began to flash with a faint but unmistakable silver light.

I will help you as much as I can. I will hear you when you call me.

Be strong. There is more power aiding you than you know.

"Amy? What are you doing?" Nox had jumped up and was staring at my shoes with an expression of awe. "*How* are you doing that without your magic?"

"It's Lurline," I said. "We have to call her."

At that, Nox gave me a questioning look.

"She told me she'd be able to hear me when I really needed her," I said excitedly. "And the shoes are hers, right? They're fairy magic, not just Oz magic. They're like . . . *original* Oz magic. I might not be strong enough to use them to get all of us back to Oz, but I bet I can contact her with them somehow."

Nox was nodding, although he looked uncertain still. "'Somehow' leaves a lot of room,'" he said. "Are you thinking a specific spell? I don't know how you can use the shoes if you can't use your magic."

"I don't either, but it's the only thing I can think of," I said.

"It's worth a try," he agreed. "What do you need?"

"I'm not sure," I said. I closed my eyes, reaching within myself the way I'd always done in Oz, searching for that indescribable feeling of power. Of feeling *something* wake up inside me—something that only existed in me in Oz. Something I'd worked incredibly hard to learn how to harness.

And like before, it was as if I could see my magic through a thick, dense wall of Jell-O. I couldn't reach it. I couldn't feel it. But I knew it was there.

But I didn't have what I needed to reach it. *Come on, Lurline,* I thought. *Show me what to do. Please.*

And then Nox reached forward and took my hand. I felt something stir to life within me at his touch. Not magic, exactly—something else. Trust. Love. Safety.

Home, I thought. *Nox is home.* And with that one word, the wall between me and my power began to dissolve. *Lurline,* I said. *Help me.*

I didn't know whether I spoke the words out loud or in my heart. But as I said them, they took shape in front of me. A door began to form in my mind—and somehow, I knew that asking Lurline for help had made it appear. I squeezed my eyes shut more tightly. Still holding Nox's hand, I stepped through the portal I'd created.

And then, without warning, I began to fall.

NINE

DOROTHY

I did my best to get Bupu to dress herself for dinner, but at the very suggestion she recoiled in horror. At first I thought she was offended because the dress was so ill-fitting—I'd have beheaded any of my chambermaids in Oz who suggested such a thing— but then I realized she was absolutely terrified at the prospect of attending the dinner herself. When I pressed her further, she cowered on the floor of my bedroom.

"They'll kill me! They'll roast me and eat me alive!"

"They certainly won't," I said, although I wasn't at all sure. I would probably be tempted to do the same on a relentless diet of the awful stuff I'd had for breakfast. "Bupu, it wouldn't be proper for me to attend the banquet without a handmaiden. Besides," I added, hit with a flash of inspiration, "I have a job for you."

She looked up at me, her eyes brimming over with tears. "A job? For me? Other than the one I already have?"

"Yes, dear," I said, waving a hand regally. "You spend a lot of time out and about in the palace, correct?"

"I had many tasks before I came into your service, mistress," she said uncertainly.

"And so no one would notice if you were to, say, wander around a little when we are released from this chamber for the banquet?"

"No, I don't think so," she said, still confused.

I sighed, reminding myself to be patient. It's just not reasonable to expect everyone to be as quick on the uptake as I am, other than Scare. And you can't expect anything from him anymore, because he's dead, thanks to that bitch Amy Gumm. I mean, I suppose technically *I* killed him, but *she* ruined him so that I had no choice. Oh, how I missed Scare! He was a little creepy, sure, and I have to admit some of his experiments were a bit—well, I wouldn't say out of *hand*, exactly, but maybe a touch over the top. But he'd always been there for me. Mostly. He'd certainly had the same goals I did. And he'd been so clever. He knew practically everything about the history of Oz. He'd been with me from the very beginning—from before he'd even had a brain. He'd made me laugh back then, and once the Wizard had given him his gift, he'd helped me make myself into the woman I am now.

But Scare was dead, I reminded myself firmly. In the end, even he had failed me.

The truth was, at this point, Bupu was all I had.

"So if you were to overhear certain . . . conversations," I continued. "Related to your mistress's future in the palace? Just like you found out about the Nome King's plans to marry me?"

At last comprehension dawned in her foggy little eyes, and she drew herself up with an expression of pride that was quite comical but also carried enough dignity that I restrained my snicker.

"I go many places," she said, nodding vigorously. "I stay away from the Diggers and the other servants. No one thinks I hear anything. They think I'm just an idiot slave. I know *lots* about what's going on." She beamed with pride. "The palace servants say many things around me," she added, waggling her eyebrows at me for emphasis.

"Then you must attend the banquet with me," I said. "I want you to listen to everything everyone is saying. Everyone I can't hear. And I want you to remember all of it. Is that clear?"

"No one has ever trusted me with an important mission before, mistress," she whispered, her eyes wide with awe at the enormity of the responsibility before her.

"Very good, Bupu," I said. She looked like she was about to literally jump with joy. I cleared my throat and she froze, halfway between a leap and a lurch.

Privately, I had my doubts as to whether Bupu would come up with anything resembling valuable information—assuming she didn't get herself killed trying to spy at the Nome King's banquet, which, I had to admit, was a distinct possibility. But she was better than nothing. Plus, having an important secret mission put a real snap in her step. She bustled around my chamber, fluffing pillows, straightening dresses, and hmmm-hmmming

imperiously. "Out, dust, out!" she muttered, flicking at an invisible speck on the bedcovers. And finally, at my direction, she
consented to swap out her dumpy, shabby sack dress for a—
well, a velvet dress several sizes too big for her that still looked
rather sack-like. At least it was a formal sack. I told her she
looked every bit of an Oz Munchkin. She twirled around at my
compliment and I felt something like pride. It was probably the
first thing I'd done for someone else since I landed in Oz. Aside
from spreading Happiness, of course.

And when more of the Nome King's servants came to fetch
us, she was ready and waiting. These servants were Munchkins,
like Bupu, but they were seriously bitchy Munchkins. They
wouldn't even look at the poor creature. She did her best to pretend their obvious derision had no effect on her. But I wondered
privately if I should point out to the Nome King that he'd clearly
bestowed his second-best Munchkin on me—and I wasn't used
to inferior quality, let alone being insulted.

Bupu was sweet, though. Maybe he'd thought I'd be won
over by her personality.

The Nome King's liveried Munchkins—who were even paler
than Bupu—led us down a maze of stone tunnels lit with sconces
filled with dimly glowing lumps of some kind of crystal. As we
turned down corridor after corridor, I tried to keep track of the
direction, but I soon lost count of all the turns we made. I wondered if they were trying to get me lost on purpose, as if to keep
me completely dependent on the Nome King. Even Bupu looked
a little confused after a while.

Plus, I couldn't help but notice how *many* of his servants the Nome King had sent to fetch me. There were eight of them. And some of them had lumpy shapes under their uniforms that looked distinctly like weapons. Their paste-white skin was crisscrossed with ugly scars and several of them were missing fingers or pieces of their ears, as if they were seasoned fighters who'd seen more than a few battles.

They weren't household servants at all. They were soldiers.

I wasn't being escorted, I realized. I was being *guarded*.

That, combined with my locked bedroom door, added up to an answer I didn't like at all.

It was becoming increasingly clear that whether I cooperated with him or not, the Nome King was determined I obey his will.

You probably don't need me to tell you there's only one will for *my* way.

And it's mine.

Privately, I was seething. Who did the Nome King think he was? He might be the ruler of Ev. But I was Dorothy the Witchslayer. And I was *not* going to be treated like a prisoner. But I smiled like the queen I was. I might be at a disadvantage now, but I certainly wasn't going to give in. I could still find a way to get what I wanted out of this situation. I knew I was up to manipulating the Nome King.

And like I said, I was thrilled by the challenge. I'd gotten a lot done in Oz. But I'd never won over a centuries-old despot who thought I was his prisoner. I was starting to feel positively alive again.

Finally, the Munchkins pushed open a heavy, ornately carved wooden door, revealing a cavern whose ceiling was easily twice the height of my chambers. The banquet hall was beautifully lit with elaborate candelabra that sprouted from the stone walls like branches.

Much to my surprise, dinner at the Nome King's wasn't half bad. It wasn't what I was used to in Oz, of course—not at the Emerald Palace, anyway, where the parties I'd thrown had been absolutely legendary. Whoever had set the table didn't know the difference between a salad fork and a dessert spoon. But at least everyone had dressed up. Velvet seemed to be the fabric du jour in Ev, closely followed by satin, brocade, and a few outfits that looked as though their wearers had basically dressed themselves in tapestries.

The company was exceptionally dreary. In addition to more Munchkin servants, there were a few other pale, lean creatures who resembled the Nome King—his kindred, perhaps?—and about thirty non-Munchkin soldiers. These must have been the Diggers that had so terrified Bupu, and looking at them more closely over the mushroom terrine, I could see why. *They* weren't dressed nicely at all. But that had nothing to do with why they were terrifying.

They were lean and muscular and pale as bread mold, dressed in armor pieced together from plates of metal and hardened leather. Most of them had sinister black tattoos crawling up their arms, or were missing fingers or eyes—or, in one case, a chunk of an ear, so that what was left was just a misshapen lump of scar tissue clinging to the side of his head.

Most of them were hairless, but one or two had thin strands scraped together into braids interwoven with bits of leather and bone. I was awfully miffed that they hadn't even bothered to dress up. If Bupu's information was accurate, the Nome King was planning on proposing marriage over the dessert course. Surely that deserved a little more ceremony?

After all, I'd done my absolute best with very little. I still looked every bit the desirable future queen of two kingdoms. Bupu turned out to be as hopeless at hairstyling as she was at everything else, but I'd at least insisted she give my hair the hundred strokes—not a stroke more or less—it deserved. (I'd had to teach her to count, too, bless her heart.) I'd found the best-fitting of the dresses the Nome King had left me and, while there was nothing I could do about the ridiculously outdated style or dreadful color, I'd repurposed a part of one of the wall hangings as an impromptu sash, cinching it tightly to show off my tiny waist and extremely admirable figure. I was, without a doubt, the prettiest girl who'd graced the Nome King's tables in their history, although from the look of things that wasn't an especially high bar.

More Munchkins carried in silver platters of food. Some things looked familiar, but others were totally foreign.

A self-important-looking Munchkin, visibly healthier than the others, was ordering the rest about in a curt manner. She had a green velvet bow perched at a drunken angle on her bald head and she wore a ring of keys around her neck. I perked up. That must be Esmerelda, I thought. And maybe, just maybe, one of those keys unlocked the door to my room.

Maybe I didn't need to win the Nome King's favor to escape after all. Maybe I just needed a plan and a little help from Bupu.

One of the little Munchkins offered me a bowl of what looked like strange, glowing roots, but as I reached for the serving fork they began to slither about like worms.

"No thank you," I said quickly, putting the fork back. I caught the Nome King smiling with amusement at my distress, but he dropped the smirk as soon as he saw me looking at him. I picked daintily at a crust of bread—which, although a bit on the dry side, was at least recognizable as food—and helped myself to the wine.

At least they got *that* right in Ev.

I glanced down during the final course—some kind of spiky thing that looked distressingly like a pile of beetles in a brown sauce, which I only pretended to eat—at where Bupu had been huddled at the foot of my chair. She was gone. Much to my surprise, I hadn't even noticed her leave. Next to me one of the Diggers roared in delight and stabbed its—his?—taloned fingers into the bowl of beetle-like things in front of him. They emitted a squeaking noise and began to run across the table in terror. I swallowed hard and smiled hugely, trying to hide my revulsion. Casually, I glanced around the room, but Bupu was nowhere to be seen.

Maybe Bupu was going to make a better spy than I thought.

Had the little creature tried to *escape?* Surely not. She'd only been with me for a few hours but she seemed loyal enough.

Abruptly, the Nome King set down his fork with a thunk and stood. Everyone immediately stopped eating.

"My dear guests," he began, "thank you for attending this banquet honoring the rightful ruler of Oz, the beautiful and powerful Dorothy Gale." I smiled demurely at my plate, where several sets of legs waved at me. "She has graciously agreed to honor our realm with her most esteemed presence." I smiled even more brightly at the assembled guests. The Diggers looked at me blankly. *When I'm running the show again you'll show me the respect I deserve,* I thought, gritting my teeth and grinning like a beauty pageant contestant facing the worst panel of judges in the world.

"In fact," the Nome King continued, "I have been so struck by her beauty and nobility, that for the first time in several hundred years or so, my heart has been moved by her queenliness."

Well. I knew he was lying, of course. He had some sinister plan to take over Oz and he needed me to do it. But what girl couldn't help but be swayed, just a bit, by the most powerful person in two kingdoms proclaiming her superiority? Of course, the fact that he had taken away my magic somehow undercut the compliment. I snuck a glance up at him.

And to my surprise, he was looking at me. And the expression on his face was—

If I didn't know any better, I'd say he was almost telling the *truth*. My heart skipped unexpectedly.

Was it possible that the Nome King had feelings for me in

spite of myself? And if so, could I use that to my advantage?

I ignored the nagging little voice at the back of my head. The one that suggested that maybe, just maybe, I was feeling an answering spark. He wasn't what I would call traditionally handsome. He wasn't young. He wasn't particularly nice.

But he was powerful. Incredibly powerful. And power is something I've never been able to resist.

I fluttered my eyelashes at him and he blinked. I'd startled him, I saw with a flash of pleasure. For just a moment, I had the advantage.

And I loved it.

"It has occurred to me," he continued hurriedly, trying not to let me see I'd caught him off guard, "that there is one truly perfect way to join our two kingdoms."

I widened my eyes as if I had no idea what he was talking about, even though I knew what was coming.

"Dorothy," the Nome King said, "will you rule at my side . . . forever? As my queen?"

Forever. That was a word I didn't like the sound of. Especially not coming from him. Forever was an awfully long time.

But *queen.* Now *that* was a word I liked quite a lot. None of this "interim ruler until Ozma cleans the bats out of her belfry" nonsense. No frumpy little coven of wicked witches breathing down my neck. No backstabbing Glamora. Glinda. Whoever she was now. And, best of all, no Amy Gumm. I'd have as long as I needed to restore my magic, thwart the Nome King, find a way back to Oz, and take back my throne. The Nome King was offering me the best possible solution to my dilemma, and I hadn't even had to ask for his help. Plus, while I figured out how to get Oz back, I'd be in charge of Ev. My first order of business would be doing something about the food. And then I'd get some new clothes.

The only thing I'd have to worry about if I was Queen of Ev would be its king. And I was sure I could handle him.

Pretty sure, anyway.

I realized everyone in the banquet hall was staring at me, even the Munchkins.

"I won't take no for an answer," he purred. He even managed to make it sound not menacing. How sweet.

"My lord," I gasped prettily, fluttering one hand over my (lovely, if I do say so myself) bosom. "What a marvelous shock you have given me!"

I rose to my feet, gazing proudly out over the silent hall. I'd show them what a queen looked like. My chin was high, my hair glossy, my waist tiny. I had more power in my two red shoes than the rest of these creepshow carnies had in the entire room. I was going to show them just what Dorothy Gale was made of.

And they weren't going to forget it.

I took the Nome King's hand and held it high over our heads. "I am honored to accept your proposal," I said regally.

The room was absolutely silent. The Munchkins stood motionless, gaping up at me. I saw a gray blur out of the corner of one eye that might, just might, have been Bupu.

"Well, my darling, you could hardly refuse," the Nome King

said in a low voice at my side. He reached out with his bony fingers and traced the outline of my cheek, a smile ghosting across his death-white face. I shot him a radiant look.

"I wouldn't dream of turning down such a marvelous offer from such a wonderful man," I said, my voice husky. Once again, I saw the faintest flicker of uncertainty cross his face.

He'd expected me to put up a fuss. To make demands. And the fact that I was going along with him without a peep of protest was making him nervous. My smile got even brighter.

Two could play at this game.

"In fact, my lord—" I began, but then something happened that I hadn't expected at all.

My shoes flared to life with a stabbing red light that split the still air with a sudden resounding crack like a clap of thunder. The shoes were blazing like a bonfire, scattering dazzling, bloodred sparks.

I was so surprised I didn't even realize the light was coming from *me* for several seconds. I took a startled step backward. Diggers leapt to their feet; Munchkins scattered. The Nome King grabbed my hand again, this time squeezing so tightly I thought he'd snap the bones of my fingers.

"What are you doing?" he hissed in my ear.

"I don't know! It isn't me!" I protested, but I could tell he didn't believe me. He yanked me fiercely from the banquet hall, practically dragging me down the hallway back to my chambers. Behind me, I could hear frantic panting—poor Bupu, desperate to catch up.

"I don't know what you think you're doing," he snarled, flinging me into my room, "but you're not going to get away with it in my palace, *darling*." Just in time, Bupu darted in behind me. The Nome King stared at me, his silver eyes burning with rage. "Stay here until I figure out what you've done," he growled.

"My lord—" I protested.

But he had slammed the door in my face. I sank down on the edge of the bed while Bupu tried to comfort me.

But I wasn't distraught. I was in shock at what I'd seen in the Nome King's banquet hall.

In that first flash of red light, it had been unmistakable. Amy. I'd seen a vision of Amy. In a cavern somewhere, with that tedious little warrior boy behind her. She had my shoes. But that wasn't the most important part. I knew, as surely as I'd ever known anything, that my vision was real. And that Amy was in Ev.

Amy was *here*.

And from the slow-sparking tingle in my toes, I knew I could use my magic again.

"Mistress?" Bupu asked in a quavering voice.

"I need to think," I snapped.

The little Munchkin tugged at my sleeve. "Mistress, please forgive me, but it's very important."

"Be *silent*, curse you!" I screeched. She cowered but continued to pluck at my dress.

"I learned something very important at the banquet!"

Finally I opened my eyes and looked at her. "You did? How?"

"I hid under the table," she said proudly. But then an expression of terrible anxiety flitted across her homely face. "But I heard the king's guards whispering about you," she said. "It's very bad news."

"Oh? How bad?"

She looked around, her eyes huge, and then lowered her voice even further.

"Mistress, the Nome King isn't going to marry you. He's going to murder you."

TEN

Nox, Madison, and Langwidere's palace vanished in a flash as I tumbled forward into darkness. I cried out in surprise and fear but my scream was swallowed by the thick dark that surrounded me.

But I wasn't falling, I realized.

I was *flying*.

At my feet, the shoes glowed faintly with a comforting silver light. And suddenly I wasn't afraid. I felt the same rush of emotion that had gone through me as I reached out to Lurline.

Home. I felt home.

All around me, the darkness began to glow. Golden rays of light streaked past me as I flew, and overhead, the sky lightened as if the sun was rising somewhere. I was flying over a lush, beautiful jungle. Towering trees carpeted the earth below me with green. At their tops, huge red flowers bloomed, unfolding to greet the warm golden light. I gasped. I'd seen a lot of beautiful things in Oz, but this was something else. Something totally alien and strange—and impossibly familiar at the same time.

I'd never been here. But I knew where I was.

"Welcome back, Amy," Lurline's voice said. She was everywhere and nowhere at the same time. Her voice surrounded me. It was part of the air I breathed and the breeze that carried me endlessly forward over the blooming forest.

"Where am I?" I asked. But before she answered, I already knew.

"You are back in my country," she replied. "The world between worlds. In this moment, you are safe. But I am afraid it won't be for long, my dear. As I told you the first time we met, your task is not yet finished."

"I know," I said. "But it seems . . . impossible. Not that we can't tackle it," I added hastily, in case she thought I hadn't learned anything since the last time I'd seen her. "I'm just not sure what to do next. Mombi's dead, we can't reach anyone back in Oz, Dorothy's allied with the Nome King, Lang doesn't want our help—I'm not sure why the road brought us to her."

"The road is wise in its own way," Lurline said. "As I told you, there is much still that is not clear to me. I'm a fairy, not a clairvoyant." I could hear the smile in her voice. "But I do know that Langwidere is crucially important to your quest. You must gain her trust."

"She hates us," I said.

"She is hurt," Lurline said simply. "More than you can

imagine. So are you. In fact, so is Dorothy. But as you are learning, my dear, we must come to terms with the wounds of our past if we are to survive the future. And I have some hopeful news that will cheer you."

The air in front of me shivered and almost solidified. It was as if I was flying toward a giant window that stayed just out of reach. And behind the solid barrier, I could see—

"Is that Oz?" I gasped, recognizing the ruins of the Emerald City where Ozma had held her coronation. Hundreds of tiny figures surged back and forth. I realized I was watching a battle.

"It is indeed, and right now there is a great battle," Lurline's voice said gravely, reading my thoughts. "Look more closely, child. All is not yet lost."

The vision on the other side of the window sharpened and zoomed in. I saw battalions of Glinda's soldiers in their identical armor, wielding weapons and fighting like demons.

But they were battling my *friends*. There was Lulu, whirling through the fray, her pistol firing shot after shot and her mouth open. Although I couldn't hear anything, I knew from the look on her face that her howl was one of glee. Winkies, Munchkins, and monkeys—Winged and Wingless Ones—battled side by side, matching Glinda's soldiers blow for blow. Gert was standing in the middle of them all, leveling a dozen of Glinda's soldiers with an appropriate pink wave of smoke.

Despite the chaos, I could see it: Glinda's army was losing. It was a beautiful sight. For the first time in a long time, something that felt like hope flared up in my chest.

And then the vision shifted to a different part of the battle-field, and this time I gasped in surprise: Ozma hovered over the melee, her beautiful wings unfurled, hurling bolts of magic at Glinda's army. And beside her was Mombi.

"Mombi's—Mombi's *alive?*" I said in shock. I couldn't wait to tell Nox. I had been terrified by her the first moment I met her—purple webs and all. But I was glad she was here—and I knew Nox would be, too.

The figure next to Mombi turned and I recognized the gorgeous profile that once upon a time I had crushed on before I fell for Nox. *Pete.*

"Pete is fighting for *us?*"

"Ozma and Pete are still connected, you know," Lurline said. "He betrayed you to save himself. But the guilt haunts him still."

"It should," I muttered.

"And Mombi survived the Nome King's attack. He was distracted trying to rescue Dorothy from the Emerald Palace. Ozma's army is fighting the last battle of Oz. She is a credit to us all." Lurline's voice was filled with pride.

And then I almost shouted out a warning: Glamora was zooming toward Ozma on a wave of crackling pink magic. There was no mistaking the truth now: all of Glamora's kind benevolence was gone. Her face was twisted and evil, and the terrible scar that Glinda had given her looked ugly and raw, as if her sister's controlling her body had opened the wound all over again.

But Ozma saw her coming and was ready. She moved her hands, and a web of golden threads spun itself around her as

Glamora hurtled forward. Glamora crashed into Ozma's net in a burst of sparks, but Ozma's defenses held. And when Glamora pulled away I could see a network of fine, smoking lines all over her body where Ozma's web had burned her.

The witch and the fairy clashed again and again. And while Ozma looked fresh and strong, Glamora was clearly flagging.

"The magic holding her to her sister is exhausting her," Lurline said. "Glinda has warped too much power for too long, and now it is costing her. Stealing magic from Oz, enslaving Munchkins, refusing death when it was her time . . ." I could feel disapproval in Lurline's voice, but there was something more than that, too.

Regret.

"Is there another way to stop her?" I asked. I was watching Ozma battle Glamora toward the ground but I was also thinking of someone else who needed to be stopped.

Lurline sighed. I could almost feel her shrug.

"Power will always corrupt those who have not learned to serve it properly," Lurline said. "What is happening now has happened before, and what has happened before will happen again."

"The same thing?" I asked in astonishment.

"Some cycle of it," Lurline said.

I reflected on that as, in front of me, Ozma struck the final blow. A powerful bolt of golden lightning hit Glamora in the chest and knocked her out of the sky. As the witch lay power-less on the ground, Ozma extended her hands. I turned my head away, not wanting to watch the killing blow.

I had no love for Glinda. But Glamora had once been my friend. And whatever she was now, I didn't want to see her suffer. Although I believed that the Order was wrong in trying to use our love to move Nox and me around like chess pieces, I loved the witches—all of them. They had taught me about magic. They had helped me shed Salvation Amy and become *me*.

"Isn't there something you can do?" I asked desperately.

Lurline shook her head. "It's up to her now. Glinda and Glamora have been battling for so very long. Imagine that much Good and that much Wicked occupying the same body. But you should look now." Reluctantly, I raised my head.

Ozma's face was peaceful and calm. Almost gentle. Rays of golden light flowed from her fingers, wrapping Glamora in ropy cords that solidified in front of my eyes. Within her bonds, Glamora's form grew blurry and indistinct.

And then Ozma lowered her arms with a fierce motion, shouting an incantation I couldn't hear, and Glamora and her bonds disappeared.

"She didn't kill her," I breathed. "But what if she escapes?"

"What if she does?" Lurline said. "She will remember Ozma's mercy. And, while it might not shift the course of what she chooses next, the balance of compassion will be preserved."

Compassion, I thought. Not Good. Not Wicked.

Forgiveness. And empathy. And love. But who had she saved? Was it Glinda or Glamora?

Ozma looked up from the battlefield and for the briefest

second her eyes met mine. She squinted—and then smiled.

"Good luck, Amy," she mouthed.

"She can see me?"

"She can see me," Lurline corrected. "But she knows you are with me now. Don't lose heart, Amy. Your path lies through Ev. You must complete the task you were brought here to do. You must defeat Dorothy."

The vision of Oz disappeared as if someone had flicked off a television.

"I couldn't do it, Lurline," I said. "I couldn't kill her."

And then I realized what she'd said.

Not kill Dorothy.

Defeat her.

I was right. There was another way. That was what Lurline was trying to tell me. That was why she'd shown me the battle Ozma had just fought. The Wicked had been wrong. Killing Dorothy wasn't the only way to defeat her. But if that was true, it was up to me to find another way.

I felt her smile again. "Dorothy was just like you once, you know. Headstrong and intelligent and brave. Looking for adventure wherever it found her. None of us are entirely Wicked or entirely Good. Or entirely evil, for that matter. We are made of what shapes us."

That was pretty cryptic advice, but I had a feeling it was all I was going to get.

"Be brave, my dear," Lurline said. I felt a brush of lips across my forehead.

A fairy's kiss. Just like Gert had kissed me once, after my first battle in Oz. The battle where I'd thought I'd watched her die. Warmth spread through my body. Her kiss washed away my exhaustion and fear. I felt completely safe.

"Good-bye for now, dear Amy," she said. But her voice sounded farther away. Below me, the verdant jungle was crumbling into dust. Darkness swallowed me again, but this time I wasn't afraid.

"Amy!" Someone was shouting my name in the distance. "Amy, what happened? *Amy!*" The voice was full of panic— and familiar.

"Nox," I said.

"Amy!" His voice was tinged with relief. I opened my eyes. I hadn't even known I'd closed them. I was in Lang's guest chambers. Nox and Madison were staring at me, their eyes huge with fear.

"Holy shit," Madison breathed. "What just happened? Are you okay? You just had, like, a seizure, and your shoes were glowing, and your eyes were like rolling back in your head—"

I interrupted her babble. "It's okay," I said. "I'm fine, I really am. Nox, you're not going to believe this, but Mombi's alive."

"What?"

"I saw it," I said eagerly. "Just now. I was with Lurline."

"You were having a seizure," Madison said, her face suddenly concerned. "You didn't go anywhere, Ames."

I shook my head impatiently. "No, listen. I *saw* them—I saw her. She's alive, Nox."

Nox turned his back, his shoulders hunched. I had never seen him cry, but when I wrapped my arms around him I realized he wasn't crying—he was laughing.

"It's hard to kill a witch," he said. I smiled sadly but before I could respond I heard footsteps pounding down the hall. Seconds later, Langwidere flung the door open, her eyes wild with fury—and fear. Her mask was gone, her kimono clutched tight around her chest, and she was breathing hard.

"What the hell is wrong with you?" she snarled. "What are you *doing?*"

We all looked at her in surprise.

"What were you *thinking*, using magic like that here? You couldn't have told Dorothy you were here any more clearly than if you'd marched up to the Nome King's palace and banged on the door. Whatever you just did sent up a signal flare of power so huge they probably felt it in *Oz*."

Nox and I exchanged glances. "I didn't think—" I began.

"No," she said. "That much is clear. You have to get out of here before they come looking for you. I'm not going down with you just because you're a bunch of idiots."

"I'm sorry," I said hastily. "I know it was a huge risk. But I saw Lurline, Lang. She told me we have to work together. The road brought us to you for a reason. You know it as well as I do."

"Lurline is a myth," Lang snapped. But for the first time, she seemed almost uncertain. She was wavering. Somewhere, some part of her knew I was right.

Nox could feel it, too. "We don't have anywhere to go," he

said. "Lang, we want to kill Dorothy just as much as you do—and bring down the Nome King while we're at it. They were going to find out we were here sooner or later. We just have to move faster. You have to let us help you."

"I don't think you're in a position to be issuing ultimatums," Lang said. "And I fight alone."

"That's not what you learned in the Order," he countered.

"I learned a lot of things in the Order," she said. "Thanks to you, I learned how to abandon the people you trust and send your allies into danger."

Nox looked at her for a long beat, then said, "I'm sorry, Lanadel!" At the sound of her old name, she started. "I know you think I made a mistake. But I didn't have a choice. I had to do what was best for the Order. You *know* that. I would never have put any of you at risk if I didn't have another option."

"You killed her!"

And then he really looked at her. "Lang, Melindra isn't dead."

Melindra? What did she have to do with any of this? I knew Melindra and Nox had . . . history. And I knew Melindra wasn't my biggest fan. But we'd trained together, fought together. I might not like her, but I'd trust the half-metal, half-human girl with my life.

"You're lying," Lang said. "No one survives the Scarecrow's workshop. No one."

"She did," I said. "He's not lying. I've met her." I had no idea what was happening, but if Nox needed to convince Lang that Melindra was alive, I could at least help him do that. "She was alive when we left Oz, anyway."

I felt a small well of pity for Lang rise up in me. She had built her life around an elaborate vengeance plot—only to learn that Melindra was alive after all.

"What did he do to her? How did she escape?"

"Melindra's the best fighter the Order's ever seen," Nox said. "You know that as well as I do. She survived. She's . . . different. But she survived."

Of course, I thought. Lang had been part of the Order before Melindra was tortured, transformed into one of the Scarecrow's twisted creations. But if Nox was leaving that part out, it was on purpose, so I kept my mouth shut.

To my utter surprise, Lang's eyes filled with tears. She turned away from us, staring sightlessly at the wall. Nox reached out to touch her shoulder, but thought better of it and pulled his hand back. All her disguises had fallen away; her face was filled with raw emotion and so much pain I wanted to grab her up in a bear hug, even though I knew prickly, easily angered Lang would be more likely to take it as an assault than a gesture of comfort. Finally, she reached some kind of inner decision. She sighed and straightened her shoulders, pushing her long hair out of her face.

"I'm not going to work with you. I don't like you, and I don't like anything about this. But I'll take you to one of my smuggling hideouts," she said. "It's warded—it will hide you for now. And then I can decide what to do next—and how to get rid of you without risking my own skin."

I let out my breath slowly. We were that much closer to Lang helping us. But I had no idea what had just happened between her and Nox. I shot him a look, but he shrugged helplessly. And Nox was a lot of things, but he was never helpless. I bit my lip, keeping my own questions to myself. Right now, we had to stay alive long enough to defeat Dorothy and get the hell out of Ev.

"Let's go," Lang said. Without waiting to see what we'd do, she stalked out of the room.

We didn't have much choice but to follow.

ELEVEN

Much to my relief, this time we weren't traveling by Wheeler. I had seen so many creepy things in Oz that it was surprising anything could still make my skin crawl, but I would be happy if I never saw those awful creatures again as long as I lived. Instead, Lang led us underground, down a twisting series of steps and tunnels that led to a huge, torch-lit cavern.

At one end of the cave a black stream flowed into a high-ceilinged tunnel; nearer to us, it spread into a broad, shallow pool. A long dock stretched out into the water, and tied to it was a black boat carved into the shape of a dragon. Jet-black scales glimmered along its sides, and leathery black sails shaped like wings waved gently in the breeze drifting off the river.

Another many-headed beetle dressed in a captain's uniform—complete with tiny sailor hats perched atop each of his heads—jumped to attention as we approached. Lang led us out onto the dock, and the captain helped each of us climb aboard.

Madison refused his outstretched, segmented leg with a shudder, muttering a curse under her breath as she whacked her shins on the edge of the boat. The beetle untied us from the dock—and the boat stretched its wings. Madison squeaked in surprise and even Nox looked alarmed.

"It's alive!" I exclaimed.

"Of course she's alive," Lang said, looking at me in puzzlement. "How do you travel by water in the Other Place?"

I thought about explaining that Kansas was landlocked, and that we used cars, not dragons, but decided against it. Instead, I sank back into the bench carved into the boat's hollow body.

Except it wasn't carved, I realized—it was a smooth ridge of bone covered in leathery skin that was warm from the heat of the dragon boat's body. Peeking over the side, I saw huge, scaly legs paddling strongly underneath us. The captain controlled the dragon boat with a set of long leather reins. I tried not to think about our boat's long, sharp, and very deadly-looking teeth.

The river carried us through a seemingly endless series of dimly lit tunnels and underground canals. In places, we saw other traffic—mostly emaciated-looking peasants dressed in tattered rags, poling along in skiffs pieced together from bits and scraps, but also a few boats like ours ferrying people who were obviously much richer.

As we traveled, I told Nox and Lang about what Lurline had showed me. And I couldn't be sure, but I almost sensed Lang softening as I talked. As if she was finally, finally starting to believe that we might be on her side, too.

Each time we passed another boat, Lang gestured for us to duck down. The boat spread its wings even wider as we sailed past, hiding us under its huge wings.

I was well aware of how important it was to stay hidden. Still, I couldn't help looking around every chance I got. The scenery was eerily beautiful and totally unlike anything I'd ever seen in Oz.

Nox caught my eye and I leaned over to him.

"Are you *sure* it was real?" he asked.

"She's alive. And they're winning."

Nox leaned into my shoulder. "I hate her sometimes. Most of the time. But I want her to be in the world so I can keep hating her until I can't anymore. Does that make sense?"

I nodded. "I could have said the same thing about my mother for most of my life."

"But not now?"

"She's better. She's trying. It doesn't erase the years when she was so messed up. And it doesn't mean it won't happen again. But I don't hate her today."

The boat shifted suddenly, knocking me into him. Before I could right myself, Nox pulled me closer and kissed me. It wasn't like our other kisses. It was deeper and needier. I left myself fall into it, blocking out our surroundings if just for a moment.

Lang cleared her throat and we broke apart.

"We're getting close now. It's time for me to change." She turned away from us and I saw the silver choker glow brightly for an instant. Lang faced us again, and I gasped. She now wore the face—or was it the head?—of a homely old woman. Her clothes had been replaced by a nondescript coverall made of unremarkable gray-green fabric. She looked like a workman borrowing her boss's fancy boat to run an errand.

Which was exactly the point, I realized. Lang was turning out to be a master of disguise.

"So some of the rumor is true," I said grimly.

She shrugged. "I don't actually kill people and take off their heads. With magic I'm able to 'borrow' other people." Madison looked green, as though she might hurl over the side of the boat at any minute.

"Does everyone in Ev live underground?" I asked, trying to change the subject.

"Some of the farmers keep surface settlements," Lang said. I thought of the sad, shabby villages we'd passed on the way to her palace. "Most people work as slave labor in the Nome King's jewel mines and forges."

"Slaves?" Nox asked. Lang gave him a sharp look.

"We're not as enlightened here as you are in Oz," she said sarcastically. I thought of seeing the Munchkins mining for magic when I first landed in Oz.

"Dorothy's Oz isn't exactly what I'd call enlightened," I said. "What about the Wheelers?" I asked, grimacing at the memory of the awful creatures who'd so cavalierly borne us across the desert.

"They serve a purpose," she said. "They keep people afraid of me."

"By terrorizing the farms around your palace?" Nox asked drily.

She bristled. "The Wheelers are the only creatures of Ev that are surface-bound. They're easy enough to escape in the underground tunnels; they never go belowground. And they make good guardians, if unpredictable ones."

"But they were ready to burn people's villages on the way," Madison said. "And they wanted to hurt us."

"They know their place," Lang said curtly. "They would never dare contradict my orders. And as for the villages . . ." She shrugged. "A few casualties are unavoidable in service to the larger cause. I learned that from the best, after all."

She shot Nox a bitter look. Something like pain flashed across his face and was gone so fast I wondered if I'd seen it at all. I had to know their history or it was going to drive me out of my mind, but I'd have to wait until I could talk to Nox alone. It was anyone's guess when that might be.

Lang was matter-of-fact about the extreme poverty, which was obvious all around us, despite the beautifully carved tunnels decorated with jeweled murals and elaborate dragon boats. I thought about Dusty Acres as we floated by the tiny structures that passed for homes along the river's banks. Injustice seemed like a way of life here. I wondered if Lang had always been so hardened to it, or if something had happened to her when she was part of the Order that had made her into this ruthless, pragmatic double agent. Perhaps that was the point of all the different faces she wore—she didn't want to remain as one person.

Everything I'd seen and done, all the suffering I'd witnessed, starting with my very first hour in Oz—I'd thought I'd hardened myself to it, just the way she had. That had become clear when I'd been explaining things to Madison earlier. I'd had to, or else I'd have lost my mind. I'd had to fight to kill without regretting the death I left behind me. So did Nox.

And ultimately, so did Dorothy.

But Dorothy had taken it a step further from the very beginning. She wasn't fighting injustice—she was creating it, ever since she'd returned to Oz. The first time she'd come to Oz, she'd been like me. She'd just tried to help her friends and keep them safe. But when she came back, she'd killed and tortured people for fun. She'd made war into a hobby. She'd enslaved her subjects and warped them into her soldiers. Something had happened to make her that way. Something had turned her from a girl like me into the monster she'd become. Whatever that thing was, it was the key. I knew it. That was what I had to find out if I wanted to end her power forever without killing her. If I wanted to use compassion—but still win. I'd stopped short of killing her directly, so I knew I was different.

I felt like I had a dozen different strands of varying textures and lengths, and I was almost ready to braid them together—but threads were still slipping through my fingers. There was something important I was missing. Something about how all of this tied together. Something that Lurline had hinted at.

The thing that bound me to Dorothy and turned orphaned kids like Nox—and, presumably, Lang—into battle-scarred warriors. If I could just undo the tangle and weave the threads together . . . but for now, the knot was too dense for me to unravel.

And, I realized, I didn't just want to defeat Dorothy because it was my mission. I wanted to defeat her because I wanted to stay alive. I wanted to see my mom again. I wanted to have a chance at a real life with Nox—a relationship that wasn't constantly thrown into turmoil by war and intrigue. I wanted to make sure that Madison got home safely to her family and her kid. I had responsibilities that were bigger than me. Bigger than the Order and what they wanted for me. I had family. I had friends.

The dragon boat slowed down and I stopped thinking. For now, we just had to stay alive. I could figure out the next step when we were safe.

As safe as you could get in Ev, anyway. Which didn't seem very safe at all.

"My lady, we're here," the captain said, several of his mouths speaking at once. His eerie, rustling voices broke the silence.

"Good," Lang said, her voice flat and distant. "You know the way in. Take us home."

The dragon boat stilled in the fast-moving water, its legs moving powerfully against the current to hold us in place. The captain held up long, segmented limbs and began to chant in a low, haunting singsong. Each of his mouths shaped different words and different melodies, the individual songs weaving together into a tapestry of sound that sent a chill down my spine. The music was full of pain and longing and somehow, even though I didn't understand any of the words, I knew all of them were sad.

Was there anything in Ev that wasn't about heartbreak and loss?

As the boatman continued his song, a fissure appeared in the rock face in front of us. Slowly the boat moved toward it as the chant increased in intensity. The fissure widened just enough for us to slip through, and then the rock slammed closed behind us and the boatman's song trailed off into the sudden silence.

The darkness was so intense it seemed almost alive. Suddenly I could feel the tons of rock above us, the distance between us and the open sky. I swallowed hard, trying to ease the suffocating feeling that was taking over me. *Breathe,* I told myself firmly. *Just breathe. The ceiling isn't collapsing. The stone isn't moving. You're fine.*

"It takes some getting used to," Lang said in the darkness beside me. I jumped. She sounded almost sympathetic.

There was a crack and a hiss, and then the boatman was lighting a lantern with a match. The light barely made a dent in the smothering darkness around us, but at least I could see something now. We were in a low, narrow tunnel, the rock just inches over our heads. The boat's wings were furled tightly to its sides now, and its head was lowered close to the water to avoid brushing the tunnel roof.

"I think I liked it better when it was dark," Madison said. Even in this dim light I could see that she was pale.

"I hated it at first, too," Lang said as the boat moved forward again. "It's funny how much a person can change. Now, when I go aboveground I feel naked. It'd take years up there to get used to it again."

Nox was looking a little pale, too. I reached over and squeezed his hand, and he gave me a brief, grateful glance. Lang saw the touch and frowned, looking away again.

"We're almost there," she said. "Just a few more minutes."

"What was that song?" I asked the boatman, but he didn't respond.

"He only speaks to me," Lang said. "It's a spell that all my servants know; it can only be sung by a single person with many voices. It's the only way to get to the place I'm taking you."

"Why'd you set the magic up that way?" Madison asked. Lang was silent and Nox answered her.

"So no one can torture it out of her," he said. "I'm guessing her servants don't feel pain."

After that, none of us felt like talking for a while.

Finally, the tunnel opened up into a larger cavern where the water formed a broad, flat lake that was big enough that the lantern light didn't reach to its shore. I felt my spirits lift as the ceiling did, as if the rock itself had been oppressing us. The dragon boat sped up, probably sensing it was nearly at the end of its journey, and soon the lamplight fell on a narrow, pebbled beach. Lang kicked off her shoes. In one smooth motion, she swung herself over the boat's side and into the water, wading toward shore.

"I guess we follow," Nox said under his breath.

I climbed out of the boat as Nox offered Madison a hand. She waved it away. The pitch-black water was almost hip-deep, and freezing cold. I splashed my way toward the beach and something very large and very scaly slithered past my calves. Panic flooded through me and I half ran, half sloshed toward the shore. Madison made an awful noise behind me and I knew that she'd just encountered whatever it was that had passed me.

"They're harmless!" Lang called from the beach. I didn't stay in the water long enough to find out whether or not she was telling the truth, and Nox and Madison were right behind me.

"You can change," Lang said, indicating our soaked clothes with a jerk of her head. She'd unearthed a waterproofed leather bag of supplies from somewhere and was pulling on tight black leather leggings, a loose shirt, and boots. With her dark hair pulled back from her face in a high ponytail, she looked like a cross between a rocker and an aerobics instructor.

I rummaged through the bag, choosing a similar outfit. My shoes had stayed miraculously dry despite the slog to shore; apparently magic boots were water-resistant. Who knew. Nox changed with his back to us, his lean muscles rippling as he pulled on a clean shirt.

"You're staring," Madison said, elbowing me in the ribs.

"I am not," I said, blushing.

"Mmm-hmm," she said, and rolled her eyes.

Behind us, the dragon boat was paddling away, steered by its strange captain. Lang lit another lantern, its flickering amber light playing over the rocky beach and sending looming, sinister shadows ahead of us.

"Come on," she said. "You can rest for a few hours before we figure out what to do next. I have enough alarm spells set up to wake the dead, but we shouldn't need them for a while. No one but me knows this place exists."

Rest. Just the word sent a flood of longing through me. When was the last time I'd really been able to rest?

I thought of the little bedroom my mom had set up for me in Kansas while she waited for me to come home, even though everything pointed to the fact that I was dead. How she'd refused to give up on me, gotten sober in case I came back, finally started dating someone who wasn't a greaseball or a loser. I plodded after Lang's wobbly beacon, across the stone beach and into yet another tunnel. This one was more rough-hewn than anything in her palace. Thankfully, it also didn't sport the Headless Horseman–themed decor. There were fewer branches and turnings; it was as if Lang was leading us deep into the heart of the earth itself. We were silent, our breath echoing in the dimly lit, narrow tunnel.

For the millionth time I wondered what my mom was doing now.

It wasn't just me who'd vanished this time—the Nome King's magic had destroyed the high school and pulled Madison into Oz, too. We were both missing persons—me for a second time. I wanted to believe my mom would be okay, but I knew better. She'd barely been sober for a month when I disappeared a second time. She'd lost our home, me, everything. Even her pet rat, Star. Her new boyfriend, Jake, seemed like a nice enough guy but I wondered how good he'd be at helping her stay sober, or if she'd fall back into her old bad habits.

She'd been right to hope that I was alive the first time I'd disappeared. But I couldn't imagine that she'd be able to keep up hope a second time.

And even if we finally defeated Dorothy and I found a way to get back to Kansas, I wasn't sure I wanted to go.

"You look really sad," Madison said quietly.

I jumped. "Yeah, sorry," I said. "I was just thinking about..."

"Kansas?" she supplied.

"Yeah. Are you—"

"Trying not to think about it? Yeah," she said. "I just keep going over that moment in my head, you know? When Assistant Principal Strachan turned into that freaky-ass dude and dragged me through—well, through whatever that was. And I dropped Dustin Jr. I *dropped* him! My kid!" She shook her head. "I can't stop wondering if there's something I could've done different. What mistake I made to end up here without him. I don't belong here, Ames. I don't want to be here. And now everything is . . . This all seems like some awful, fucked-up dream."

"I know," I said.

I did know, was the thing. I knew what she was going through in a way that no one else in Oz possibly could. Lang and Nox might've lost their parents, but they were still living in the place where they were from. They hadn't literally been pulled out of their own world and into one that they'd grown up believing was just a story—a funny movie with cheesy old actors in bad face paint and a pretty girl in a checked dress.

There was no way to describe what that felt like to someone who'd grown up in a world where magic was normal, witches were real, and the Cowardly Lion ate people in front of you.

But what I wasn't telling Madison was that when I first landed in Oz, I was happy to not be in Kansas anymore. Happy to have escaped the trailer, and my mom—and Madison. Happy to be needed by the Order, and to be chosen for something for the first time in my life. Oz had made me stronger, had given me magic and friends and love. Oz had given me something to fight for.

But I didn't say any of that to Madison, who was missing her baby. Who was one crazy, creepy thing away from having a meltdown.

"There's nothing you could've done," I said. "I mean, I know that doesn't help, but you didn't do anything wrong."

"I dropped him," she said again, and then she looked away. "I don't want to talk about it anymore."

"Did you ever visit Sky Island, Amy?" Lang cut into our conversation as if she hadn't been paying attention, but I knew she'd been listening. She was giving Madison something else to think about. For the first time, I felt almost grateful to her.

"No," I said.

"Amy learned magic in the caves," Nox said. "After you—left, it got too dangerous to take people there. Maybe when all of this is over, Amy, you can see it."

"What's Sky Island?" Madison asked.

So, as we walked, Lang told us. About the place where she'd

learned magic from Mombi, the old, abandoned tourist resort: a floating island, clear as glass, that drifted through rainbow-colored clouds that changed colors to the beat of your heart. The river made of lemonade, the clear blue sky, the way it was always sunny and never too hot. After all the time we'd spent underground, even just the thought of blue sky seemed so impossibly, unreachably beautiful, but the way Lang talked about the swirling, colorful mists that moved across the island was so vivid I could picture myself there. Next to me, Madison sighed softly.

"I wouldn't mind seeing that," she said.

"It's hard here, I know," Nox said. "But there are beautiful things, too. That's what we're fighting for."

I could see Lang's back stiffen and I knew Nox had said something wrong. "Is it?" she said, her voice low and hard. "Is that what the Order does, Nox? You'd think you would have at least changed the speech after all these years."

"Langwidere . . . Lanadel," he said, and then sighed and shrugged. "Believe what you want," he said. "For now, we all want the same thing. To take care of Dorothy once and for all."

"For now," Lang agreed in that same rough tone.

All visions of Sky Island were pushed aside by the harsh intrusion of reality. Because I knew that Lang was only protecting us to protect herself. And as soon as she found a way to leave us behind, she would. I had to find a way to convince her to fight with us, or we were screwed.

Luckily, we didn't have to walk much farther before the tunnel ended in a solid iron door. Lang placed one palm on the metal and murmured something that sounded similar to the chant her boatman had sung. At first, nothing happened. Then the door swung open with a creaking groan.

"Need to oil the hinges," Lang remarked. "Haven't had to use this place in a while."

On the other side of the door, the tunnel broadened into a room off of which branched out several hallways. One led to a little kitchen, another to a bathroom where, I saw happily, there was a tub. Others led to small sleeping chambers. The main room had a rough wooden table and few comfortable-looking chairs scattered here and there. The whole place was lit by glowing veins of crystals in the walls. It was small and modest, but extremely cozy.

Lang showed us the pantry, where shelves practically groaned under the weight of jars and barrels of preserved food.

"You could last a long time in here," Nox said.

"That's the point," she said coldly.

"Well, I'm passing out now," Madison announced, and Lang softened.

"You can take any of those rooms," she said. "Mine's farther down the hallway. Help yourself to anything you want to eat or drink. I need to figure out what to do with you. It's almost morning. It won't take long for the Nome King to realize he doesn't know where I am—and put two and two together." She glanced involuntarily at the silver bracelet around her wrist. She saw me follow her look.

"It tells him where I am," she said quietly. "But the wards

around this place are too strong for it. He'll figure out soon enough that I've gone somewhere he can't find me."

I still didn't completely trust her, but I realized how much Lang was risking to help us even this much. She could just as easily have thrown us out of her palace—or turned us over to the Nome King. She didn't care about helping us, she cared about hurting Dorothy. But for whatever reason, she was keeping us safe, no matter how she talked to us.

Somewhere, some part of her was on our side. Enough to keep us alive, anyway, even though it put her in terrible danger. For the first time in a while, I started to actually feel hopeful. Maybe there was a way out of Ev for us. Maybe we could defeat Dorothy after all. And when we did, I was getting out of this underground hell as quickly as I could.

Lang might be used to the unending, unrelenting darkness, but I ached for open air and sunlight, the smell of flowers and growing things. Anything but cold stone and blackness and dark, cold water full of unseen, terrifying creatures.

Lang brushed past us and was gone, her footsteps swallowed up by the stone as she walked down the hall.

"Okay then, good night, I guess," Madison said.

Her voice sounded small and sad. But I knew there was nothing I could say or do to make it better. I'd check in with her in the morning, but it wasn't like I could reunite her with her kid or send her back to Kansas with a snap of my fingers. She disappeared into one of the bedrooms, closing the door behind her with an unmistakably firm snick. She didn't want to talk, and I wasn't going to push her.

"I'm going to look for some tea or something," I said. I was exhausted, but too jittery to sleep. I had suddenly realized that I was alone with Nox for the first time in a very long while and I was nervous. Despite all the drama with witches trying to separate us and pit us against each other, and then dying and not-dying, Nox and I were getting closer.

The truth was, I didn't have much—okay, any—experience with guys, aside from fending off my mom's creepy ex-boyfriends and their super-inappropriate interest in her teenage daughter. When it came to someone like Nox, I still had no idea what I was doing.

"Tea sounds good," he said.

I poked through Lang's pantry until I found something that looked vaguely tealike—a jar of small, dried gray-brown twigs that smelled like the green tea my mom drank by the bucketful when she got clean—and hoped I wasn't accidentally brewing up a potion that would turn us into frogs, or beetles, or something even worse.

While I heated water on the stove, Nox threw together some odd-looking green batter and poured it into a pan.

"Who are you and what did you do with Nox?" I joked.

He smiled. "Mombi never stopped being a witch, even when I was a little kid. She kept odd hours and was sometimes gone all night—but whenever she came home, she would make these." He plated two green pancakes and handed one to me.

"Her Mombi way of taking care of you?" I quipped as I took

the tea to the table. Nox sat next to me on the wooden bench, so close our thighs touched, and my heart skipped a beat.

"I should tell you about Melindra," he said quietly, and my thoughts screeched to a halt.

"Okay," I said neutrally.

He licked his lips and pressed them together, staring off into space as though he couldn't figure out how to start. I took a deep breath.

"You're in love with her?" I offered.

He looked startled. "What? No! Is that what you—no, Amy, that's not it at all. *Lang* was in love with her."

I stared at him. "Wait, what?"

"When Lang came to train with the Order, she had no one. Her family had been killed in one of Dorothy's early raids. This was a long time before you came, before we understood just how bad Dorothy was going to be. All we had were rumors at that point—we just knew we had to be prepared to fight if it came to that." He laughed softly, bitterly. "Which, as you know, it did. Anyway, Lanadel journeyed through the mountains alone, on foot, starving. For weeks after her family was murdered. Trying to find the Order based on stories she'd heard that we existed. She almost died, but Gert found her. She started training with us. She was good. Very good, actually. One of the better fighters I'd ever worked with, even though she had no training, no experience. She was driven. All she had left to keep her going was the idea of avenging her family. And then she got close to Melindra."

He took a deep, ragged breath. I didn't say anything. The

pain in his face was awful. Without thinking, I put one hand on his knee and he took it, lacing his cool, dry fingers through my own. "You never met Melindra before she went through . . ." He cleared his throat and continued more strongly. "Before she went through the Scarecrow's . . . workshop. She was the most gifted fighter I'd ever seen. But it was something more than that. She had this warmth, this kindness, this generosity. Other people with her strength could've turned into a bully, but not her."

Melindra? Warm and kind? That didn't sound anything like the bitter, scarred warrior I knew, the half-tin, half-human girl the Scarecrow had turned into the Order's resident mean girl. But I might not have much kindness left in me either, if I'd been through his torture.

"Lang—Lanadel—hadn't had much friendship in her life, I don't think, even before her family was killed. And Melindra took her under her wing. For Melindra, it was just the way she was. But for Lanadel—I couldn't see it then, but I think it was much, much more. And then Melindra—" He stopped. His fingers were squeezing mine so tightly that my hand was losing sensation. I held my breath, not wanting him to stop. "This is the hard part," he said. "The part where I—where I made a mistake."

I'd never heard him admit anything like this. That he could be wrong. That something he'd done for the Order was a bad decision. My heart ached for him. But at the same time, I couldn't help feeling an admittedly selfish sense of relief. He wasn't in love with Melindra—or Lang. I knew that should have been the least of my concerns, but my feelings about Nox didn't obey rational rules.

"Melindra didn't feel the same way about Lang, but she did feel that way about me," he said uncomfortably. "I . . . I cared about her, of course. I think if I hadn't been so wrapped up in the Order, in trying to take care of all the trainees while keeping the witches happy, I might have been able to love her, too. But it wasn't the right time. She wasn't the right person. I didn't have anything to give someone else then. I could have handled it better. She—we—had an awful fight about it, and Lanadel overheard. The next day, I sent Melindra to spy on the Scarecrow. She went because I'd told her I could never return her feelings. Lanadel thought I'd sent her away because I couldn't stand what she'd said to me, that I didn't know how to think for myself, that I was just Gert and Mombi's puppet."

"But you didn't," I said.

"I don't know, Amy," he said, looking me in the eyes. "That's what I'm telling you. I sent one of our best fighters into a situation she couldn't possibly survive. She knew it. I knew it. Lanadel certainly knew it. And I didn't know *why*. I told myself it was because we needed the information. But for all I know, Lang was right. And she's right to hate me for what I did. Gert and Mombi sent Lanadel to Ev to spy on the Nome King right after Melindra left for the Emerald City. They worked up some kind of spell to get her across the Deadly Desert. She was supposed to send back reports but we never heard from her again. I thought—we all thought—she was dead. When we started hearing rumors about Princess Langwidere, some crazy tyrant who worked for the Nome King and who cut off her subjects' heads and wore them as her own . . . well, none of us even thought of connecting her to Lanadel."

"Can we trust her?"

"Lanadel?" He sighed, running his hands through his blue-black hair. "I don't know. Probably not. Although now that she knows Melindra is alive, she doesn't have the same reasons for revenge. But the road brought us here for a reason, and the road always does what it does for the good of Oz. It comes from Lurline; its magic is older than anything else in Oz except for the Great Clock. I think there's something much, much bigger going on here than just Dorothy and the Nome King. And maybe that's ultimately what we have to find out if we want to end all of this."

"I wonder why the Nome King rescued Dorothy," I said thoughtfully. "He didn't seem like the kind of guy who needed much help in the magic department."

"The Nome King has always wanted to rule Oz," Nox said.

I groaned and rubbed my eyes with the heels of my palms. "Three worlds, two pairs of shoes, sixteen villains . . . It's too much. But I don't know if there's anything we can do about that right now. We're stuck here with that crazy mobster, or whatever she is. In all these years, she's never taken him down and she seems awfully comfortable here."

"She's not crazy," Nox said gently. "She's in pain. More pain than you can imagine." I nodded. Lurline had said the same thing. "She has nothing," he continued. "She's lost everyone she loves, everything she cares about. For better or for worse, our paths are tied to hers now. And I think she's right, about taking care of Dorothy for good. I know how hard it was for you back in the Emerald City to be faced with that choice. And I don't want you to be the one to have to do it. But as long as Dorothy's alive, we're in danger. There's no other way."

"But I still don't understand why Lang—Lanadel—hates you so much. You were just following orders."

"No," he said. "I wasn't. I was the one who decided to send Melindra to the Scarecrow. That's the thing Lanadel will never forgive me for. Gert and Mombi sent her to Ev, and she came here thinking that Melindra was dead, and that I'd good as killed her. And if Melindra had died, it *would've* been my fault. What happened to her *was* my fault. She would still—"

"You can't blame yourself for what the Scarecrow did, Nox," I said urgently. "You can't carry this thing around for the rest of your life, letting it eat you up inside. You told me every time I had to do something awful that we were at *war*. We're fighting so that other people don't have to make the kinds of decisions we do. I understand that you think everything the Order does is your responsibility—but you can't blame yourself forever. You just can't. Melindra wouldn't have gone if she didn't think she could survive."

"Melindra wouldn't have gone if she thought I loved her," he said.

My heart hurt so badly, thinking of what Nox was putting himself through, all for something that was so much larger than anything he could control.

For so long, we'd all been Gert and Mombi and Glamora's pawns. He might've made a decision he regretted, but they were just as responsible. They had been calling the shots all along until now. They'd literally controlled him until the road had taken us out of Oz. They'd told him he and I could never be together. They'd controlled his entire life.

And now he had to carry this burden, feeling like he deserved Lang's hatred, all because of what he'd done trying to save the world.

"Nox, do you believe that I make my own choices?"

"Of course."

"I chose to join the Order. I chose to take the mission. I choose you. Melindra and Lang, they chose, too. It's not on you."

He opened his mouth to protest but he closed it again.

"And I choose to do this now." I kissed him with all the love and compassion I had in me, with everything inside me that told him I understood that there was nothing to forgive.

I didn't need magic to tell him everything I wanted to know with that kiss: that I was hopelessly, helplessly, unconditionally in love with him, that I'd stick it out with him until the end, whatever that end looked like.

And he kissed me back—hesitantly at first, and then with a hunger I could feel through his mouth, his hands buried in my hair. It was a long time before we came up for air.

"Amy—" he said hoarsely, but I put a finger across his lips.

"No talking," I said. I took his hand and pulled him up from the table and practically dragged him into one of Lang's open bedrooms. He kicked the door shut behind us and I shoved him backward onto the bed. Finally, he smiled, grabbing my hands and pulling me down on top of him.

We had made out before. But this felt different. When Nox's lips brushed my neck, I felt the kiss wash over me.

I sat up, and my hands hesitated at the hem of my dress. And then I pulled it upward. I had taken off my dress a hundred times without falling over, but this time I began to. Nox caught me and helped me off with the dress. When I emerged from underneath it, he threw it on the floor. We were both laughing until I placed my hand on his chest.

He paused for a moment, running one callused palm down the bare skin of my back. "Are you okay?"

I rolled over to face him, covering my chest with one arm. "I'm, um, really nervous," I said. I felt myself blushing. And then I blushed some more because I knew he could see me blushing.

"It's okay," he said, his voice gentle. "We don't have to do . . . this. We don't have to do anything at all. I can go. Do you want me to go?"

"No!" My voice came out as an urgent squeak. "It's just that I, um, I've never . . . I've never done this before. The thing that, um, it seems like we're maybe about to do."

"*Oh*," he said. He blushed too. "I, well." He sat up, and I thought I'd ruined everything. My heart sank. "I've never done this—um, that—before either."

"But . . . Melindra?"

"No!" he exclaimed, and then backpedaled. "I mean not that, no. We were just . . . we just, um . . ."

"Got it," I said quickly. I definitely did not need the gory details. Or the comparison.

"When I first met you and I saw you fight, I told you you had to change. That you had to learn to be the knife. But I was the one who needed to learn. I never thought about myself. I thought of the Order. But I was the knife. I was the fight. You taught me how to love. You taught me how to choose. And I choose you. Always."

My heart clenched in my chest. "Nox . . ."

Nox and I had fought back to back on the battlefield. We had kissed and touched before, but there was always a stopping point. A holding back. This was letting go. I felt almost more a part of my own skin and at the same time more in the moment than I had ever been. Every touch and kiss was a call and response of skin and feeling. But it wasn't like the movies. We still giggled a lot and it was awkward and funny and a little weird but also completely, totally perfect. It was nothing like I thought it would be and everything that I ever thought it would be all at once. Afterward I pillowed my head on his lean, muscular chest and his sandalwood smell enveloped me like a cloud as the pounding of his heart slowed to a regular beat. He put an arm around me and I burrowed into his side.

"I love you," he said softly into my hair.

"I know," I said, yawning, and then I fell into the deepest, most contented sleep of my life.

TWELVE

A repeated thumping on the bedroom door pulled me out of the depths of sleep and out of Nox's arms. I sat bolt upright. For a long second, I had no idea where I was. The crystal veins in the cavern had dimmed while we slept, and I could barely make out the stone walls in the dim light.

I wasn't wearing any clothes, someone was pounding on the door, and I wasn't alone in the bed—and then I remembered. Nox was the person next to me. Nox. I'd slept with Nox. For another second I sat there, with a grin that did not need the aid of PermaSmile. If I was honest with myself, the Amy I was before my trailer landed in Oz hadn't even allowed herself to really imagine having a boyfriend. Being close to Nox was a whole new kind of magic.

Next to me, Nox stirred and groaned, flinging an arm over his eyes in protest before he sat up.

"Hi," I said. I was blushing again, but at least this time it was dark.

"Hi," he said. His smile looked the way I felt. "Come here." He pulled me to him into a long, passionate kiss. And then there was an even more forceful thump at the door.

"All I want," Nox said in low voice, tracing my collarbone with one finger in a way that *definitely* should not have made me feel the way it did—it was just a collarbone!—"is to spend the rest of my life in bed with you. But I guess we have to save the world, or something."

"Or something," I agreed reluctantly. I stretched and stood up with a sigh, locating my clothes at various points around the room, and flushing yet again as I remembered how they'd ended up there.

"Don't put those on," Nox protested.

"Shut up," I said. I couldn't stop the idiotic grin that refused to leave my face. Then again, I didn't want to.

"I mean it."

I threw his shirt at him. "We have to go kill Dorothy. You said so. Also the Nome King is coming to kill *us*."

He flopped backward dramatically. "Who cares anymore? I can think of way better things to do." I joined him on the bed, our shoulders touching. I always wanted some part of him touching some part of me.

"What happens now?" I asked.

"We get married, obviously. Oz custom," Nox said.

"Shut up!" I cried, elbowing him. "What happens for real, after we finally beat Dorothy and the Nome King?"

"Amy Gumm, always thinking about the future," Nox said, rolling over and toying with my hair. "I wish I knew."

Madison kicked the door again. "Hurry up!" she bellowed.

"We're coming!" I yelled.

Madison muttered something and stomped away.

"You can't hate her forever," I said as her steps died down.

"You can't not still hate her a little. Or a lot." He searched my eyes. "She hurt you."

"When I came back, she . . . it didn't seem important any-more, hating her. It was so small compared to all the things we faced here. We need to be on the same page, Nox. All of us. There's no room for hate. We're fighting Dorothy and her super-scary fiancé.

"If it were up to me no one would hurt you." While he said this his finger was tracing tiny circles on my arm. The action was unconscious on his part, and it affected me all the same.

"I love you for that. I mean . . ." I had said the words without thinking about it, but I meant the words. We had said it last night. But it was different in the light of day.

Nox pushed back my hair and looked into my eyes. "I love you, Amy."

"I love you, Nox."

"When you asked before about our after . . . I don't care where we end up. As long as we're together."

"Together isn't a place, Nox."

"It is to me."

Nox kissed me long and deep, and I knew then that we were going to be very late for breakfast.

A half hour later, I headed down first.

Lang and Madison were hunched over the table, talking in low voices. They looked up when I came into the room, but they didn't move apart. They looked like they'd been there for a long time.

"Where's Nox?" Lang asked.

"He's, uh, he's . . . I don't know," I said. I could feel how hot my cheeks were. Madison started to laugh.

"Sure you don't, Ames."

"I do not! I have no idea where he slept last ni—"

Nox chose that exact moment to emerge from the same bedroom I'd just come out of, and Madison rolled her eyes.

"Sleep well, Nox?" she asked sweetly. He looked confused.

"I slept fine?" he said, and she collapsed into giggles.

"I *bet* you did," Madison snorted.

"Knock it off," Lang said sharply.

She wasn't joking—and she wasn't talking to Madison either. My temper flared. At Madison for bringing up where Nox had slept. And at Lang for thinking she had any reason to weigh in. But mostly, I was angry at the situation. No matter how much I wanted the opposite to be true, we were here for a reason that had nothing to do with what was happening between Nox and me. And at the same time, what was happening between Nox and me was what we were fighting for.

"I'm ready for business," I told her, sitting down at the table. Nox sat next to me, his thigh touching mine. I let myself lean into him a little. Madison's eyes flicked over me, but she didn't say anything this time.

"I don't know if you're ready for this," Lang said.

"The Nome King's on his way?" Nox was suddenly very, very serious.

Lang shook her head, and for the first time, I realized that she was almost at a loss for words.

"I've been invited to a wedding," she said.

"A *wedding*?" I wasn't sure I'd heard her right.

"A wedding," she repeated. "The Nome King and Dorothy are getting married."

THIRTEEN

DOROTHY

I have to admit, Bupu's news that my new fiancé was planning on killing me didn't come as a total shock. But still, I was
miffed. I knew I'd sensed a spark between us. And the idea
of ruling our twin kingdoms together wasn't entirely unap-
pealing. I don't like to share, it's true, but I've also never met
anyone who came as close to being my equal.

"Okay, Bupu," I said. "What exactly did you hear? *Why* did
the Nome King go to all this trouble to rescue me if he's only
going to kill me? That doesn't make any sense at all."

Bupu snuffled a little and dabbed at the corner of her eyes
with her sleeve.

"The shoes," she said miserably. "He wants mistress's shoes."

"I *know* that," I said, rolling my eyes. "He thinks they're his,
the ninny. But he can't have them. They're bound to me. If he
kills me, they'll be useless."

It occurred to me as I said this that I had no idea if it was true. Except in a way, I did. If he could get the shoes back just by offing me, I'd have been dead the minute he found me. So it was something else.

He needed to marry me to get the shoes. But why?

Something occurred to me.

"Bupu, what's a wedding like in Ev?"

"Your wedding will be the most splendid ever seen in all of Ev," Bupu assured me.

"Bupu, I don't want to have a wedding if I die at it, do you understand that part?" She nodded vigorously. "So," I said patiently. "Before the Nome King kills me, what happens exactly at a traditional Ev wedding."

Bupu looked thoughtful. "Vows?" she offered.

I reminded myself to be patient.

"Yes, dear, I understand that. But what do the vows *say*? What about the ceremony? *What else happens?*"

Realization dawned in her eyes. "Oh! You want to know about the *magic*."

"Yes, Bupu," I said, excitement flooding through my veins. I knew it. There was something about the wedding itself. Something important that the Nome King wanted. Some part of the ceremony. "Is it something to do with my shoes?"

Bupu nodded eagerly. "Yes, the shoes! They are bound to you, mistress."

"I know that, Bupu," I said through gritted teeth. "But the Nome King doesn't want me to use them. Do you know why?"

"He wants their magic back?"

"I need to know why he wants to kill me!" I shrieked, unable to control myself any longer.

"Oh," Bupu said. "You should have said that to begin with, mistress. The shoes are bound to you, but Ev's wedding vows are magical. All magic is shared between the spouses."

"So I can siphon off the Nome King's magic?" I asked. That didn't make sense at all. Why would he risk making himself vulnerable? Bupu was already shaking her head.

"That's not his plan, mistress. He doesn't like to share anything. Magic can be stolen once it is bound. With blood."

It took a second for her words to sink in. "With *blood*?"

She nodded, her lower lip quivering. "The king will bind his magic to yours. And then use your blood to steal it. All of it. That's why he will try to kill you."

A wedding followed by the traditional bloodletting reception. And I'd had my heart set on a multitiered wedding cake.

She puffed out her little chest. "But I will protect you!"

In spite of myself, I smiled. "I'm sure that will be very helpful," I said. She beamed. "Hmmm," I said, thinking out loud. "That's awfully *nasty* magic, really. But that's not a huge surprise either. Ev seems to be a fairly nasty place. All this slavery and cave dwelling and bad fashion."

Bupu nodded. "Very nasty. You will take me back to Oz when you defeat the Nome King, won't you? I could help you there, too."

And there it was. My little seed of friendship had grown into a full bloom. The little creature wasn't quite as stupid as she looked—and her motives weren't entirely altruistic. Her eyes were wide and pleading, but I caught a spark of cunning, too. I wasn't angry; I was pleased. At last there was something to this sad, shabby Munchkin.

"Is that why you're helping me, Bupu?" I asked sweetly.

"No!" she said hastily. I raised an eyebrow. "Maybe a little," she admitted.

"You have nothing to be ashamed of," I told her. "Helping yourself is the most important thing of all—unless you work for me, in which case it's helping me. But I think I can make this work out for both of us. And yes, Bupu, I'll bring you back to Oz."

"So I can help you there?" She brightened.

"I'll tell you what," I said. "If—when—we both make it back to Oz in one piece, I'll set you free."

She stared at me with her mouth hanging open.

"Free?" she whispered. *"Free?"* Her eyes filled with tears. It was a word that she clearly hadn't let herself even dream of in a long time.

I put out my hand. A moment later, she took it, gazing up at me in bewilderment. "We're shaking on it," I explained, gravely shaking her wrinkly hand. "It's a deal."

"A deal," she echoed. And then she squared her shoulders and stood proud and tall. "If you help me escape I will lay down my life for you, Dorothy Gale," she said.

And do you know what? I was almost *moved.*

Ev was making me soft. But I couldn't help it. I knew what

it was like to be stuck in an awful place with no hope of ever getting free again—and I knew how much worse it was when you knew how beautiful the alternative could be. When I'd been stuck in Kansas a second time, with no way back to Oz . . . Well, it didn't bear thinking about. But I knew exactly what Bupu was going through. I'd been tortured in Kansas, too. I'd suffered terrible privation. I'd wept into my pillow every night, desperate to regain what I'd lost.

Okay, so maybe it wasn't *literal* torture. But the mind is the most sensitive organ. What I'd gone through in Kansas was just as bad as whipping and imprisonment.

I clapped my hands, and Bupu jumped. "Let's get down to business," I said. "If I'm going to thwart my own murder and get us out of here, I need to come up with a plan."

I thought for a while.

I couldn't deny that I was intrigued by the Nome King— even now that I knew he wanted to kill me. He just wanted his power back—and that much I could understand. It wasn't his fault I stood in his way, although I was a little miffed he hadn't even asked me to share. I was clever, rich, and beautiful; what ruler wouldn't want me at his side? But the Nome King was ancient; it was no wonder his power had run down dark and ugly paths in the centuries he'd been holed up underground, hating the outside world. And from the look of things, he and I had very different approaches to the way we cared for our kingdoms. Queendoms. Whatever.

I know a few malcontents have had complaints about the way

I did things in Oz, but I've only ever wanted for my subjects to be happy. I'd never have enslaved any of them if they would only do what they were told. Plus, when they were miserable, I'd ordered them to follow the Happiness Decree. And when that failed to cheer them up, I'd insisted on PermaSmile. Aunt Em always used to say that no one could stay under the weather as long as they had a smile on their face.

I would *never* let my subjects suffer the way the Nome King did. Why, he didn't even insist they look happy when he was *around* them.

I mulled over what to do next as Bupu brushed out my hair.

I didn't want to die, obviously. Who would? But I couldn't let go of the idea that the Nome King was missing out. On me. We were two of the most powerful people in the world, whichever world you picked. We balanced each other out perfectly: he was grumpy, mean, and lived in a cave, and I was beautiful and all my subjects loved me. Or else.

Together, the two of us would make a formidable team.

To be honest, I'd never been one of those little girls who'd fantasized about my wedding. But now that the possibility was in front of me, I was starting to have ideas. A whole entire day that was basically a holiday for me? A party where I was the star? An event that involved hundreds of people coming from all over the world to bring me presents and tell me how beautiful I looked? Who could possibly resist? And realistically, the Nome King was the most eligible bachelor I was likely to run across in Oz *or* Ev. There were about a million single, powerful witches running around, but the last gentleman caller I'd had was Tin.

Ugh.

No, I was simply going to have to convince the Nome King that I was more use to him alive than dead. I'd have to use every ounce of power I had to charm his pants off. (Figuratively speaking! I would *never* sacrifice my precious chastity before marriage, of course.)

In short, I had to make him fall in love with me.

And if that didn't work, I had to kill him first.

I certainly had my work cut out for me, considering I was a girl locked in her room. I was going to have to take care of *that* right away.

I wiggled my toes experimentally and felt the shoes stir to life. I had one small advantage: the Nome King might have realized I could use magic again, but I was pretty sure he hadn't seen that awful idiot Amy the way that I had. I was never going to forgive her for stealing my *other* shoes. Those were mine, and the little bitch had no right to them. But whatever she'd used them for, it was through her channeling their power that mine had been awakened. So in a way, I owed her a favor. Technically. Not that I'd ever tell her.

And if she was in Ev, it was for one of two reasons: she wanted to kill the Nome King, or she wanted to kill me.

"I just need a plan." I frowned and chewed on one knuckle thoughtfully. "Bupu, where will the Nome King hold our nuptials, do you think?"

"Mmmm." Bupu tocked her head back and forth, considering.

"There is the Major Hall. It has not been used in many years. But it is a powerful place. Also big." She gestured toward the ceiling with the hairbrush. "Very big."

"Powerful?"

"Old Magic. Very dangerous." She shivered. "Diggers," she said. "Diggers used to sacrifice people there."

"That'll be the place, then," I said cheerfully. "Good work, Bupu. How many entrances does it have?"

"Only one, mistress."

Well, I'd just better be sure I killed him, then, if I couldn't make him fall in love with me. A single exit from what was, I was sure, going to be a very well-guarded event? Even at the height of my powers that would have made for a tricky escape. And while my shoes seemed to be waking up again—or whatever it was they were doing—I could tell my magic was still hard to access this far from Oz. It made sense that the shoes would work here, if they'd really come from the Nome King somehow. And it made sense, too, that my own magic would work best in Oz. But if I could practice with the shoes maybe I could find a way to amplify my power.

Except that based on what had happened at that sad excuse for a banquet, the Nome King could tell if I used them.

But there was another weapon I could use against him if I had to.

Amy Gumm.

I sighed heavily.

And, right on cue, the door opened.

"Oh, hello, darling," I cooed, jumping to my feet. Thanks

to Bupu's efforts, my hair spilled around my shoulders in glossy waves, and I was still wearing the dress I'd put on for the Nome King's banquet. It wasn't my best look by a long shot, but I'm an enterprising girl.

The Nome King did *not* look thrilled at the sight of me.

"Don't think you can fool me, Dorothy," he growled. All pretense of the dashing suitor was gone. His tone was threatening.

I widened my eyes and looked up at him prettily through my lashes. I'd be wasting my time playing dumb at this point. But I could still take him by surprise.

"You need me," I purred. "So be a little nicer."

To my satisfaction, he actually looked taken aback. And then he laughed.

"You are a prisoner in my kingdom who couldn't use magic until an hour ago," he said. "And I'm guessing you're not up to full strength quite yet. I hardly think I need you."

"I'm your *guest*, not your prisoner. Be respectful when you address me," I snapped. "I'm not some dimwit glitterball like Glinda. You don't have any idea who it is you're trifling with. I can make you regret the day you were born, you doddering old coot."

His face contorted into a frown. Well. That got his attention.

"I'm not trying to *trick* you," I added with dignity. "Believe me, I have no idea what happened back there." That was the truth and I made sure to look him in the eye when I said it. "And I have no idea how—or if—I could make anything like that happen again."

So that was maybe the teensiest fib. I knew my magic was

back. I just didn't know to what extent. Or if I could even harness it fully. So it lent my little white lie the gloss of truth. He
looked closely at my face and then seemed satisfied.

"When we are married, my darling, there will never be any
secrets between us," I promised, batting my eyelashes again.
Other than the fact that you want to kill me, I thought. But really,
over my dead body. I'd find a way to stop him come hell or high
water.

"Of course not," he said smoothly. His smile was bland and
pleasant now.

He knows I'm lying, I thought. *He just doesn't know what about.*

I moved quickly to distract him. "Darling, perhaps you'll
allow me to make a few . . . suggestions about the wedding,"
I purred again, looping my arm through his. "Might I see the
venue? And the rest of your palace? I've barely set foot outside
these lovely rooms since you brought me here." I refrained from
adding that this was because he'd locked me in them.

He cocked his head at me. I knew he was trying to figure out
what I was up to. But apparently he decided there was no harm
in showing me around a little.

"As you wish," he said gravely, bowing like a perfect gentleman and opening the door for me. I gave Bupu a wink over his
shoulder. She nodded fiercely. "First, I will show you the palace.
And then the cavern where our wedding will take place."

Well, the grand tour was a grand disappointment. Just a
bunch of miserable old caverns and dusty tapestries and creepy
staircases that went nowhere.

Sure, some of the caves were sort of cool, if you were into that kind of thing—glowing crystals, and weird underground springs that ran into underground rivers, and tunnels that led you around in circles. Caverns that were obviously storerooms that hadn't been touched in decades: dust-covered wooden barrels full of who knows what. Ancient weapons: spike-balled maces so heavy I couldn't lift them, huge crossbows that seemed designed for giants, cannons rusted into immobility.

The Nome King droned on about the history of his various ancestors, and, although I tuned out his sonorous voice, I was acutely conscious of the weight of his arm in mine. He hadn't changed either. He was still dressed in his velvet suit. The material was soft and cool against my skin.

"How fascinating," I murmured, every time he paused. At least he seemed to have relaxed.

It was as though he'd never had anyone to listen to him before. Some men were like that; let them get going, and they'd never stop. It never occurred to them to ask if anybody *else* wanted to talk about herself. As if I had nothing interesting to say.

Then again, maybe he was just lonely.

As he talked, I surreptitiously looked around me, trying to memorize the layout of the palace. But it was an absolute maze. Every corridor branched off into a thousand others. Every room looked like a room I'd passed already.

And everywhere, I realized, the hallways were empty.

The Nome King had his forces. His Munchkins and his Diggers and the other Nomes I'd briefly seen at the banquet. But the palace dwellers were engulfed by this enormous place, rattling around like peas in a glass jar. No wonder he needed my magic. As powerful as he was, his forces were nowhere near enough to take Oz. It all came down to him.

And that, I understood. Because at the end of the day, while I'd had armies at my disposal, Oz was all about me. It was exhilarating, having that kind of power. But it was also isolating. A huge responsibility.

The more time I spent with him, the more I realized how much alike we were. But the Nome King could have learned a thing or two from me—I had kept Tin, Scare, and the Lion around for a reason. Not just because they were useful. They were also company.

"But you must be bored with all of this," he said suddenly, as if he'd read my mind. "Tell me about the history of Dorothy Gale."

"You mean, how I came to rule Oz?" I asked, blinking up at him.

"No," he said. "Your history before."

"I prefer not to talk about that."

I never talked about the Other Place. I had had people's fingers cut off at the mere mention.

"But, darling, how are we ever going to know each other if we don't . . . share?" he asked.

I hesitated. I needed him to trust me. Was this the price of admission?

"Dorothy . . . ?"

I took a deep breath and told him about Kansas. At first, I

told him everything I'd hated about growing up there. The miserable winters that lasted for months. The miserable summers the rest of the time. Working like a serf on Aunt Em and Uncle Henry's farm. My so-called friends who'd turned on me after my first visit to Oz.

But then I started thinking about the good things. About the parts I hadn't even realized I missed: the first big snowfall of the year, when the prairie turned into a sea of white that stretched all the way to the horizon. The happy *cluck-cluck* of the chickens every morning when I brought them their feed. The warmth of the egg-laying shed in winter. Aunt Em's apple pies. The way the prairie grass smelled in summer before the heat settled in to make us all miserable.

I'd never told anyone as much as I told the Nome King. Not Ozma, back when I thought we were friends. Not even Scare and Tin and the Lion the first time I traveled with them in Oz.

Back then, I'd spent the whole trip to the Emerald City chanting "home" like a mantra.

I stopped talking. Something unfamiliar was happening.

A lump. In my throat. It hurt terribly. Was I dying?

"Dorothy, you're crying," the Nome King said quietly. He brushed a tear from the corner of my eye with a long, silvery finger.

"Certainly not," I said quickly, clearing my throat around the unfamiliar sensation. "I don't know why I went on so. I don't miss the Other Place for a minute. It was barren and boring."

"Coming to Oz must have been very strange for you," the

Nome King said, drawing me forward again. I hadn't realized we'd stopped walking.

"It was wonderful," I said decidedly.

"I'm sure it was," he agreed. "But to be separated from your family so young, orphaned like that, forced to make decisions as a ruler of a nation . . ."

I'd loved my family. That is why I'd brought them with me to Oz. But they were gone. I was here, and that was all that mattered. "I'm perfectly capable of handling pressure, if that's what you mean," I said coolly. This was going all wrong. I was supposed to be *pretending* to be vulnerable, not *actually* vulnerable. What on earth was wrong with me?

"I don't doubt that," he said with a smile.

He had led me to another hallway, this one much wider than the rest. The ceiling towered above us. The hall ended in a huge set of iron-bound wooden doors.

"Welcome to Major Hall, my ballroom," he said, flinging the doors open.

I couldn't help it. I gasped. Ballrooms were the cure for almost anything.

The Nome King's ballroom was more than beautiful. It was magnificent. The ceiling was so far overhead it was lost in darkness. Massive ruby chandeliers, dark now, floated overhead, glittering redly in the scant light from the hallway. The floor was made of polished red stone.

I took a few steps into the enormous room. The click of my heels echoed eerily through the darkness. I was reminded of a

Halloween haunted house Aunt Em had taken me to once long ago in the Other Place. There had been a room that felt like this. Vast. Empty.

But not entirely empty.

Haunted.

I was suddenly very aware of the fact that the Nome King and I were deep within the bowels of his palace.

And we were entirely alone.

A shiver ran through me.

Not fear.

Something else entirely.

I turned to him. "It's perfect," I said, and I meant it. I had no intention of dying here, of course, but he didn't need to know that.

"I thought you might like it," he said.

And, I realized, he meant it, too. For once we weren't playing a game. We were standing in this enormous room, surrounded by darkness, two of the most powerful people in the world. Alone. Together. I stepped forward and let my hand slide down his arm. My fingers twined with his. He didn't resist.

And so I kissed him.

His cool lips parted in surprise—and then he leaned into me and returned the kiss. His arms wrapped around me, his fingers tangled in my hair.

And I knew in that moment, whatever else was to come, whatever we might do to each other in the end, this moment was real. Neither one of us was pretending to be anything other than what we were.

But I couldn't lose control. Because no matter what, I had to remember that this man intended to kill me. There was nothing about him I could trust.

Reluctantly, I broke away from him. I lowered my eyelashes, giving me time to recover my racing thoughts. I couldn't let him see he'd caught me off guard.

"You are full of surprises, Dorothy Gale," he murmured.

There was a shift in his tone. I could see in his eyes that he, too, had forgotten the game for a moment. So it was my turn to take advantage.

"I'd like our wedding to be very grand," I said in the same hushed tone he'd just used. "Hundreds of guests."

"Of course," he said, his eyes a little glazed. But then his gaze sharpened. "Hundreds? I was thinking a more intimate affair."

I'll bet you were, I thought. Perhaps even his subjects drew the line at human sacrifice. If he was still planning on killing me, he wouldn't want an audience.

But I needed Amy in the palace when I made my move. If I knew she was coming, I could defend myself against her. But with any luck, the Nome King wouldn't. She was my backup plan: if Amy didn't kill him, she could distract him long enough to give *me* a chance to escape. It was a risky plan, but I didn't have a lot of options.

"I insist," I said, my tone flirtatious. "I want a celebration that shows off your riches, my treasured love. I want your subjects to be able to appreciate your magnanimity and your largesse. My love, your kingdom is ever so much older and finer than Oz. Surely you have nobility . . . princes and princesses—dukes and duchesses—all sorts of important persons whom you wish to witness our union?"

"Why?" he asked.

I concealed my irritation with considerable effort. "Because that's how it's done, my darling," I said. "In royal circles, anyway. The citizens of Ev don't even know their future queen is among them."

"You want a party?" I was getting used to his hairless eyebrow-arching, and recognized it as what he intended it to be.

"Not a party," I clarified. "A *wedding*. With musicians, and canapés, and pretty dresses, and a battalion of servants, and a mandatory dress code, and a feast. Wine and spirits."

Dress code. Inspiration hit me. Amy would have an even better chance of getting into the palace if the guests wore disguises. "In fact," I said, "let's make our wedding a costume ball. Wouldn't that be fun?"

He looked at me for a long time. I could tell he was running through what I'd just said, trying to figure out what I was up to. The game was back on. I hid an exhilarated smile.

"That does sound fun," he said thoughtfully. "I believe we once did that sort of thing here, ages ago. I even went to these balls you speak of. Though it's been a century or two, and I do think fashions might have changed."

"Balls never go out of fashion," I said at once, pressing my advantage. "And how often will you be married, my darling?"

"Only once, I hope," he said drily, looking at me. I kept my smile even and serene. "Would you like . . . help in planning our ball?"

"Just your guest list," I said brightly. "And perhaps a few connections to the kitchen staff."

He smiled, showing all his teeth. "Certainly, darling. Let me know if you need any help. But our wedding will take place tomorrow regardless."

"*Tomorrow?*" I said, trying not to show my shock.

"I simply cannot wait a moment longer to be united with you forever," he said.

"But that's nowhere near enough time to plan a ball, let alone a wedding," I protested. "These things take weeks. Months! I must insist on more time!"

"There is nothing you cannot do, my love," he said with a smile that looked almost genuine. "I have utter faith in your abilities. Tomorrow morning we shall be wed."

"Next week," I said. "Give me a week, my treasure."

He frowned, impatience stealing across his cadaverous features. "Tomorrow afternoon, if you insist."

This was ridiculous. I had less than twenty-four hours to plan the most important day of my life? I wanted to throw something at him.

"Darling, it's not possible," I purred.

His frown deepened. "Are you reluctant to join our two kingdoms, Dorothy?"

There was no mistaking the veiled threat in his voice. Any

stalling for time I did now, he would use against me. I knew, of course, the real reason he wanted to rush our nuptials, but I couldn't show my hand. I had to play along.

"At least give me a day to prepare, my beloved," I murmured, fluttering my eyelashes. "Can we agree on the stroke of midnight tomorrow night? After all, our guests will need time to travel to the palace."

Impatience and doubt were replaced by amusement on his face. "My subjects do not live so far from the palace, dear Dorothy. I do not allow them to stray. Not the important ones, anyway. I find it convenient to keep them close if I need them— or if I need to punish them." Involuntarily, he touched the knife at his side. I swallowed hard. "But I am aware that Oz's customs are not Ev's. Let us wed at midnight, as you wish. Shall I show you to your rooms now?"

I nodded, my mind racing, and let him guide me back to my chamber. His hand rested on the small of my back as we walked and I couldn't shake the pleasure of his touch. At the door he leaned down and moved to kiss my cheek, but I turned my mouth to his instead.

This kiss was even more passionate than the first. And I saw with no small amount of satisfaction that he was breathing hard when he finally ended it.

"Good night, Dorothy," he said quietly.

This time, he didn't bother to lock my door.

"Mistress!" Bupu cried, leaping to her feet.

I clapped my hands. "All right, Bupu, no slacking about. We

have work to do. Mistress is getting married tomorrow."

"But—"

"No buts," I said. "Trust me. I know what I'm doing."

"You are very clever," Bupu breathed, her eyes huge.

"Yes," I said. "I know."

My first mission: better clothes and better food. And a source of cocktails. Finally, Bupu turned out to be useful; the Nome King seemed totally indifferent to the day-to-day mechanisms of his palace, but Bupu knew everyone from the humblest kitchen slave to the best seamstress. There was no time to sleep; I sent Bupu to her with a message to begin my costume immediately. As it turned out, Bupu also knew where the spirits were kept. I should've asked her ages ago.

The Nome King sent a secretary to my chamber to draft up a list of important and wealthy personages that ought to be invited to the nuptial ball, and I set him to work hand lettering invitations worded as thinly veiled commands. The absolute worst thing is throwing a party and having no one come; I figured threats would fill the room, even on such short notice. I had already figured out that the Nome King's subjects took his commands very seriously. That was one more thing the Nome King and I had in common; we valued loyalty and obedience, and we weren't afraid to enforce the things that were important to us.

I decided to costume myself as a serpent. Powerful, dramatic, deadly. But the scales of the dress would also bear my signature gingham print. I wanted the citizens of Ev to see their future queen looking her absolute finest. Who knew, maybe they'd even rally behind me. I entertained myself briefly with a fantasy of overthrowing the Nome King in a citizens' rebellion and ruling Ev and Oz by myself, but soon dismissed those thoughts and turned back to my work. I had a lot to do, and very little time in which to do it. I had a seamstress to oversee, menus to revise, a bloodthirsty tyrant to either seduce or escape from, and the pungent but highly effective liquor in the Nome King's stores wasn't going to drink itself.

FOURTEEN

"What do you mean, Dorothy and the Nome King are getting *married?*" Nox was as close to speechless as I'd ever seen him.

Langwidere handed him the piece of heavy, engraved parchment she'd been examining. Greta had realized the invitation was important and had delivered it to her since we were in hiding. I read it over his shoulder.

> HER HIGHNESS, DOROTHY GALE, QUEEN OF
> OZ, AND HIS MAJESTY THE NOME KING INSIST
> YOU TAKE PLEASURE IN THEIR COMPANY AT
> THE CELEBRATION OF THEIR MARRIAGE AT
> THE STROKE OF MIDNIGHT TOMORROW. DIN-
> NER AND DANCING TO FOLLOW.
>
> MASQUERADE REQUIRED. REGRETS WILL
> NOT BE ACCEPTED.

"What the *hell* is she up to?" I asked.

Lang was looking thoughtful. "More like what he's up to, I think. He's looking for a way to control her magic."

"By marrying her?" I asked.

"I'm sure things are much more enlightened where you come from," she said drily, "but in Ev a marriage contract is one way of controlling someone's power. Magic becomes the common property of both partners. It's magically binding."

"Creepy," Madison said with a shudder.

"In our world women used to be property," I pointed out. "It's not so different."

Lang shrugged.

"We don't do that in Oz," Nox said hastily.

"No," Lang said, her voice cool, "you just send the people you don't love to die, which is so much more civilized."

"We do that with real estate in Kansas," I said, hoping to divert what looked like it could shape up into something very nasty very quickly. "Like if you buy a house and then you, um, get married, then you both own . . . the house," I finished weakly, as Nox and Lang ignored me, shooting daggers at each other.

"Anyway," Madison said, "we get it. He puts a ring on it, he ends the world. Or whatever. So we have to stop the wedding?"

"We have to kill Dorothy," Lang said.

"That would definitely stop the wedding," Madison agreed.

"Not necessarily," I said with a shiver, thinking of Jellia's awful, animated corpse. If Dorothy could turn a once-living person into a jerking puppet, I was pretty sure the Nome King could pull off a convincing wedding to a dead girl if it suited his purposes.

"I'm sure he wants Dorothy's magic," Lang said. "But he really wants her shoes. Wants them back, technically."

"Wait, back up. He wants them back? The shoes were his?"

"Rubies are to Ev what emeralds are to Oz," Lang explained. "They're not the source of Ev's magic, but they can be used to store it, and the older they are, the stronger their magic becomes. The Nome King created a ruby necklace centuries ago that he infused with an incredible amount of power. Glinda stole it from him right before Ozma imprisoned her, but managed to transform the necklace into Dorothy's new red shoes. He still has a certain amount of power over the stones, but he can't use their magic; they belong to Dorothy now, and they're useless without her."

"I am so lost," Madison muttered.

"All you need to know is that killing Dorothy before they can be married will stop him from being able to use the shoes ever again."

"That's why he wanted *my* shoes," I said, looking down at my glittery boots. "But he couldn't control me, so he tried for Dorothy."

"But what possible motivation would *she* have for marrying *him*? If he's going to be able to control her magic, why would she agree to it?" Nox asked.

"Maybe she doesn't know. I mean, Dorothy has the biggest ego in the world. Maybe she thinks he actually wants to marry her. Or, maybe she doesn't have a choice," I said. I looked at Lang. "He's powerful enough to kill her, right? He must be threatening her somehow. Or maybe he's keeping her prisoner."

Lang nodded. "He could definitely kill her if he wanted."

"And solve half our problems," Nox said.

"But the two of them united . . ." I shivered. "If she *is* working with him voluntarily, I can't imagine how awful that would be."

We all stared at the table in silence.

"But if Ev is affecting her magic the way it is ours . . . ," Nox said slowly. "She'll be weak right now. Even if the Nome King's protecting her."

Lang nodded. "You're right. The wedding will be the perfect opportunity to take her out. It's the chance I've been waiting for for years. Defeating him in his own palace will be next to impossible, but she at least will be vulnerable, even if she's with him."

"What if she isn't?" Nox countered.

"Then she and the Nome King will realize I've been hiding you," Lang said. "It'll be the end of me either way. I can't keep going like this, anyway." She waved at the room around her, but I could tell she meant the gesture to encompass her entire life in Ev. I couldn't imagine what it had been like for her here, completely isolated, working for a tyrant she hated but who wouldn't hesitate to kill her if she defied him.

I felt a pang in my chest for Lang that surprised me. Like me, she'd been thrown into a situation she hadn't asked for, and she'd learned a whole new way of surviving, a whole new set of skills.

I also didn't blame her for wanting out, even if it killed her.

"When do we leave?" I asked.

She looked at me, startled. "*You're* not going anywhere. You'll only be in my way. She'll recognize you and you'll get us all killed."

"You can't possibly go into the Nome King's palace to kill Dorothy alone," Nox said in disbelief. "Plus, as far as we know, the only person who can kill Dorothy is Amy."

"I couldn't *possibly*?" she asked, her tone dangerous. No matter what he said to her, it seemed to be exactly the wrong thing.

But he was right. And there was no way I was going to sit around here waiting for the worst.

"Dorothy's hurt us, too," I argued. "And as strong as you are, it's always good to have backup. Besides, it'll be even more dangerous for us here without you. And it's a masquerade. We'll be in disguise."

Which, now that I thought about it, was a weird choice for a wedding. Especially for Dorothy. I wondered if it was significant or just another one of her insane whims.

"I don't care if it's dangerous for *you*," Lang said. But I could tell she didn't entirely mean it. Under that hard shell was a person who was almost . . . caring. She wasn't going to leave us to be discovered by the Nome King's forces like rats in a hole.

"I can fight," Madison piped up. "I mean, I can't do magic. But I have a pretty mean right hook."

I knew firsthand about Madison's right hook.

"This was my fight. If I had killed Dorothy before the palace fell on her, she wouldn't even be your problem. Let me help you finish her," I said.

Lang looked at each of us, her expression torn. And then she sighed.

"Fine," she said. "You can have Dorothy. But the Nome King is all mine."

She was still putting up a tough act. But I could tell she was grateful for the help. As strong as she was, she needed other people, too.

So did Nox. So did I. So many times in Oz it had felt like I was completely on my own. As if the Wicked had cut me off completely from being able to ask other people for help.

But now I had Nox and Madison and, for the time being, Lang. In a strange way it felt like my own makeshift family. Not Wicked. Not Good. Just . . . together. We wanted Oz to be free because it was home. Because we cared. Not because someone else was telling us what to do.

Home. That word again. Without warning, a memory of my mom flashed through my mind. One of the few times she'd been sober before I came to Oz. There had been a snowstorm and she didn't want me to have to wait for the bus in the cold, so she'd driven me to school. On the way she'd started crying.

"Mom?" I had asked.

"I just wish you knew how much I love you," she had said. "I know I'm hard to live with. But underneath it all, there's just love."

I'd just looked out the window. She had hurt me too many

times by then. Forgotten about me when she was drunk or high. Left me stranded somewhere for hours while she was out partying with her friends.

And while I was gone, she'd gotten sober. For me.

I hadn't even had time to tell her I loved her before I came back to Oz.

"Amy?" Nox said. "Where'd you go?"

I blinked. They were all looking at me.

"Sorry," I said quickly. "Just thinking. About strategy."

"Once the ceremony is complete, her magic will be bound to his," Lang said. "We'll have to make our move before then. The Nome King's ballroom is enormous, but there's only one entrance."

Before the guards killed us all, was what she meant. I was grateful she didn't say it.

"What about me?" Madison asked.

Lang smiled. "You can stick with me," she said. "As a bodyguard."

Lang needed Madison as a bodyguard about as badly as I needed a winged monkey for a pet. But she was the strongest of the three of us and the most likely to be able to protect Madison if anything went wrong.

When something went wrong, I amended silently.

"So we're sailing into the palace in disguise, hoping nobody recognizes us," Madison said.

"Pretty much," Nox confirmed.

"Cool, just wanted to check our odds of survival." She sat

back. I knew she was thinking about Dustin and her baby. Whether she'd ever see them again.

I'm going to get her home safe, I thought. *Whatever it takes. If I have to die doing it.* Madison hadn't asked for any of this. I owed it to her to protect her.

"We need a better plan than that," I said. "I'd like at least *some* chance of coming out of this alive."

Lang nodded, toying thoughtfully with the silver bracelet on her wrist. "The Nome King always wears a silver knife at his belt," she said. "It's made out of the same metal as this thing." She held up her wrist. "It's magical, obviously, and it's incredibly old—older even than he is. It's probably strong enough to kill Dorothy, even though she has the shoes."

"Probably?" Madison echoed dubiously.

"Can we use it?" I asked.

"I've never tried," Lang said. "He never lets it out of his sight."

"But he'll be distracted at the wedding," Nox pointed out. "And he'll be so preoccupied with stealing Dorothy's magic that the odds are good he won't notice us until we're close enough to take him out."

"I think we should split up when we get to the wedding," I said. "If the Nome King kills one of us, there will still be two more of us to try for the knife."

"We'd be stronger as a team," Nox argued.

"You're letting your feelings get in the way," Lang said. Her tone was matter-of-fact, not her usual bitchy snark. "Amy's right. More of us, more chances to defeat him."

Nox shot me a complicated look.

"Believe me, I don't like it either," I said frankly. "I'd way rather stick with you both. But this might be our final chance to defeat Dorothy and get the hell out of this crappy kingdom. We can't blow it."

Nox nodded reluctantly. "Okay," he said. "We split up."

"We don't have much time," Lang said. "We'll have to get dressed and leave as soon as we're ready if we want to make the ceremony."

Something was still nagging at me. "It's just so weird," I said. "Why invite people, if the whole point of the ceremony is for the Nome King to get control of her magic? Why go to all the trouble? And why costumes?"

"It could be a trap," Lang said slowly. "But for who? Neither one of them knows you're here."

"For you?" I asked her. She shook her head.

"If the Nome King wanted me dead, he has plenty of ways to kill me without going to all this trouble." She sighed. "You said it yourself, Amy. This could be our only chance. Trap or no trap, we have to take it."

Nox nodded. "She's right," he said. "We'll be cautious, but we have to do this."

Lang looked at him, obviously surprised that, for once, they agreed.

I smiled at them both. "I never said we shouldn't do it. I just think we should be smart."

They grinned back, and after a second, so did Madison. It felt good. Like we were on a team for the first time since I'd joined the Order. Like maybe, just maybe, we all had each other's backs—even Lang.

The nagging feeling wasn't going away. But they had a point. Whether or not we were walking into a trap, this was our only chance. Once the Nome King had control of Dorothy, they'd both be unstoppable.

I had tried to finish this one way. I had chosen myself instead of putting the knife into Dorothy. But this time I did not have the luxury of walking away.

And this time, if I had to kill her, so be it.

FIFTEEN

DOROTHY

It was too bad, really, I reflected as I readied myself for my wedding with the Nome King, that I didn't have any girlfriends. I'd always had Tin and Scare and the Lion before, and of course I missed them and was mostly sorry they were dead, but I longed for the cozy rapport I'd once had with Glinda and Ozma—minus, of course, the backstabbing, betrayal, and secret motives. Even that blissed-out hippie Polychrome had had potential for friendship—after all, she did have an eye for fashion, even if it was outrageous—but of course, she was dead, too.

Ozma and I had once been close, before she'd refused to acknowledge that I'd obviously been brought back to Oz to rule it myself—a refusal that truly hurt me to the core, since I'd thought our friendship would prevent her jealousy. In fact, it was always other girls' jealousy that had gotten in the way of the kinds of relationships I craved: first, back in Kansas, when

none of my so-called friends believed me about Oz (the humiliation of my sixteenth birthday party was a moment I'd never,
ever forget—or forgive) and later when it turned out Glinda and
Ozma had meant to betray me all along after I'd given them so
much of myself. Jellia hadn't been my friend, exactly, but she'd
been very helpful, until it turned out she was actually a spy
working for the Order.

And that was it, really. I gazed thoughtfully at my reflection
as Bupu brushed my hair. Was Bupu a friend? Could servants
really *be* friends? I mean, they were barely people. But it was
true that around Bupu I felt something I hadn't felt in a long
time—human emotion, I guess. Which I'd found previously
to be a failing in all my doings in Oz, but Bupu didn't exactly
seem like the type to have some evil plan up her sleeve to undo
me. I was obviously the only person she'd ever encountered who
treated her well and talked to her as if she was intelligent (which,
in her own way, she actually was), and she was so grateful for
my attention and affection that she lavished all the love and ado-
ration pent up in her small, squat body on me.

And while she wasn't my equal, not by a long shot, I found
myself growing fonder of her by the day.

"I won't let the Nome King kill you," Bupu promised me
again. "No matter what."

"That's very sweet, Bupu," I said, but my mind was a million
miles away. My charm might be working on the Nome King,
but even a girl with my skills would have a hard time pushing
a cranky old despot to do a complete 180 in just a handful of
days. I didn't have time to convince him I was more use to him

alive than dead. I knew I'd managed to get through to him just the teensiest bit, but not enough for him to set aside his murderous plan. He was old, and let's face it—old people are lazy. I had given this a great deal of thought and I had realized that he would most likely stick with his boring plan of betrayal and carnage rather than open his mind to what I had to bring to the table. I sighed heavily. What a nuisance.

Now I had to kill him instead. At the very least, I had to escape him, but that wasn't going to be an acceptable long-term solution. He could travel back and forth between Oz and Ev, he wanted my shoes, and he'd stop at nothing to get them. Even if I managed to evade his clutches tomorrow night, he'd never stop until he hunted me down and got what he wanted.

And if Amy didn't do my dirty work for me the way I'd planned? I'd made sure the Nome King's secretary sent invitations to every corner of Ev, but with so little time before the wedding, it was possible word wouldn't reach her until it was too late. I couldn't depend on her being there to cause the distraction I needed, which meant I needed a backup plan—and fast.

Someone pounded frantically on my bedroom door, and Bupu dropped her hairbrush, rushing to see who wanted me now. It turned out to be the seamstress, her arms piled high with my outfit.

"It took you long enough," I said irritably. "I gave the orders *hours* ago. Now I'll barely have time for the custom fitting. Do you *want* me to look terrible?"

The seamstress, a pasty, sad-looking Munchkin like Bupu, shook her head. "N-N-No," she whispered fearfully. I liked her respectful attitude. The Nome King clearly had a lot of problems, but ensuring proper behavior in his servants wasn't one of them.

"Bring it here," I said, beckoning. "Ugh, are your *fingers* bleeding? Disgusting! Clean yourself at once!" Bupu marched the trembling seamstress to the bathroom to clean up and I sighed again. The buffoon couldn't complete a rush order without making a mess of herself? What was I supposed to do with that? I had a wedding to prepare for, an assassination attempt to thwart, a tyrant to escape, and a kingdom to return to—I did *not* have time to babysit the help.

When Bupu returned with the seamstress, trembling visibly, to my chamber, her fingertips were bandaged. "Let's get this thing fitted," I said. "If you stick me with a pin, I'll have the Nome King tear your fingers off one by one and make you eat them." I didn't think it was possible for her eyes to get any bigger, but at that, they did.

"Y-Y-Y-Yes, Your Majesty," she babbled, gathering up my costume and advancing toward me. "As you wish."

I rolled my eyes and stood still as the seamstress arranged drapes and folds of fabric around me, making minute adjustments here and there. Fine, so my costume was taken care of. On closer inspection, her work wasn't half bad. I'd look amazing, and that was half the battle fought already. Now what I needed was a plan.

"All right, Bupu," I said after the seamstress left, making a decision. "Come here." I beckoned her close, and the Munchkin put her ear next to my lips. "Are you ready? Here's what we're going to do. . . ."

SIXTEEN

Despite Lang's admonition that we needed to leave quickly, she didn't want Madison going into the Nome King's banquet hall completely unprepared. While Nox and I looked through her stash of weapons to see what we could hide under our clothes, Lang ran Mad through fight combinations in the main room until Madison's face was shiny with sweat.

"Your friend's a quick study," Lang said. Madison beamed with pride.

"Show me," Nox said. Unlike the two of them, he was serious. Deadly serious. It was like a cloud had descended on him, transforming him back into the battle-focused, emotionless warrior he pretended to be. I wondered what would have happened if I'd never learned there was a completely different person underneath the stony facade.

"Okay," Madison said.

She faced Nox confidently, squaring off into a fighter's stance.

She was still in good shape, I noticed; her pre-baby aerobics reg-
imen had given her toned arms and shoulders and muscular legs.
Madison and Nox circled each other in the open space beyond
the table. Madison already moved like someone who knew what
she was doing.

But when Nox launched a lightning-quick jab, she was too
slow to deflect it. To be fair, I probably couldn't have deflected
it either. I'd turned into an excellent fighter, but Nox had been
training since he was a child. I doubted even Lang could fend
him off for long.

Madison threw a punch and Nox dodged it easily, but I could
tell from where I stood that there had been serious power behind
the blow, and Nox nodded. "Good."

"Not that good," Madison said drily, "since I didn't actually
hit you."

"You're strong," Nox said, lashing out again. This time,
Madison was almost able to block the punch. "Very good."

"I told you," Lang said, the edge back in her voice. "Are
you trying to suggest I need your help to teach someone how to
fight?"

"Just making sure you did a good job," Nox said. I almost
groaned aloud. It was pretty much the worst thing he could have
said, and he realized it a second after I did. "I'm sorry, I didn't
mean—"

"Didn't mean to imply I wouldn't?" Lang said icily. Madison
swung a right hook at Nox's jaw, but even distracted he knocked
her fist aside. Madison gritted her teeth. I knew exactly how she
felt. Fighting Nox could be infuriating. He made the impossible

look effortless. Madison was no more a threat to his defenses than a mosquito.

He danced back and dropped his fists. Madison looked like she wanted to charge him and land a punch for good measure, but she put her hands on her hips and cocked her head instead. "Do I pass?" she asked.

"Your reflexes are good and you're strong," Nox said. "But you wouldn't last a minute against a trained fighter. With time, you've got a lot of potential. But I want you to stay as far away as you can from any fighting at the wedding. Got that?"

"Is this your plan now?" Lang asked sharply. Nox looked at her in exasperation.

"You know as well as I do that you can't turn an untrained novice into a fighter in an hour, and implying anything otherwise is setting her up for danger. She's not safe in a fight. She has no experience."

"She does, too," I said, and Madison shot me an apologetic grin.

"Ancient history, Ames," she said.

"Not *that* ancient."

"I apologized!"

"Enough," Nox said sharply. The rebuke stung. I'd thought we were past the part where he tried to boss me around. But I didn't want to give Lang the satisfaction of arguing with him in front of her.

"He's right. This is serious business," I said. "We're all risking our lives tonight. It's nothing to joke about."

Madison sighed. "I just wanted to feel a little more prepared," she said quietly.

"Why don't we try sparring for a few minutes," I suggested. The last thing we needed was Madison freaking out. "Nox and Lang can pick out weapons instead of me. I'll show you what I can."

Madison looked between Nox and Lang with one eyebrow raised, but shrugged. "Sure," she said. "If I'm going to die, at least I'll get in a workout first."

I ran Madison through a few new combinations, careful not to tire her out. Nox was right: her reflexes were great, and she knew how to use her strength and her weight. With a little time, she'd be an excellent fighter.

Too bad we didn't have any.

There was something satisfying about finally being stronger than she was, more capable and more lethal. She'd terrorized me for so long, and while I'd forgiven her for the past, I didn't mind showing off my new skills in the present.

"You're really good at this," she said when I feinted and jabbed, breaking through her defenses to land a light tap on her jaw that would've been a ferocious punch if I'd been in a real fight.

"Thanks," I said.

"You never were before. This place has really changed you."

"It does that."

She sank down to the floor with her back against one wall and her legs stretched out in front of her. "We're not getting home ever, are we?"

I sat down next to her and stared at my knees, not wanting to meet her eyes. I knew she'd see the truth all over my face. "We might get back."

"Do you even want to go home, Amy? Now that you have this hot magical boyfriend, or whatever?"

"He's not my boyfriend," I said automatically, and Madison laughed.

"Whatever you say, Ames. He's your something, though. You seem really happy."

"As happy as I can be considering the circumstances," I said.

"Yeah, well." She picked at a loose pebble on the cavern floor. "You have stuff here. People. A history already. I don't have anything. If we get through tonight, what happens next?"

There was no point in lying to her; she'd see right through me.

"I don't know," I said. "We find a way back to Oz, I guess."

"And when that happens?" Madison persisted. "Like, I get that all of this is going to be hard, and we're probably going to die, or whatever. I get that. But let's say for the sake of argument we don't. We make it through, Ozma wins, the Nome King goes away, Dorothy dies, everybody's happy, blah blah blah. What about you and me, Ames? We take up, like, corncob farming?"

"The Scarecrow's dead," I said.

"You know what I mean."

"Yeah, I know what you mean." I sighed and rubbed my eyes with the palms of my hands. "I don't know, Madison. We figure it out, I guess. I don't even know how you buy a house in Oz. Or get a job. Or, like . . . any of the stuff that goes into a normal life. Nothing's been normal since I got here."

"In the books Dorothy just wishes herself home," Madison said.

I looked down at Dorothy's shoes. Madison didn't know what they were. I'd never told her.

"She had her shoes," I said. "She needed those."

She followed my gaze and her eyes widened. "Your boots are *those* shoes? The ones that took her back to ? They're real? You've had them this whole time and you didn't even try and use them?"

"It's not that—" But she had jumped to her feet and was staring at me, her eyes filling with tears.

"This whole time all I've talked about is how badly I want to go home, and you've had the way back all along and didn't think to *mention* it? I get that you want to stay here forever with your hot little boyfriend, but did you think for a fucking second that maybe other people could use a free trip home? I have a *kid*, Amy. I have a *life*. And you hid this from me?"

"It doesn't work like that!" I said desperately.

"How do you know? Have you even *tried*? Why don't you give me the damn shoes if you want to stay here so badly?"

"Because I can't. I can't take them off, Madison. I can't use magic unless I'm wearing them, and apparently it's too dangerous for me to do magic here."

"So you're not going to help me?" She looked at me, her mouth twisting between fury and tears. "You've never really forgiven me, have you, Amy?"

"What are you talking about?" I cried. "High school? We

are so far beyond that, Madison." I thought that Madison and I had struck an understanding where we would not speak of all those years that she had tortured me. But she had dusted off Salvation Amy and brought her back out for us to deal with. And since she'd brought it up . . .

"Are we really doing this right now?"

She nodded. "I have apologized and apologized, but what Nox said about me ruining your life—"

"Madison, you were awful to me. My life at home was hell, and you made school, the one place that was my refuge from my mom and the trailer, hell, too. But when I got to Oz, there were bigger bitches in Oz than you ever were, and I have been fighting alongside them and against them for months now. I actually used my memories of you to make my magic work in the beginning. So I guess I should be thanking you."

Madison's face fell.

"I'm glad that you're sorry. I'm glad that it still bothers you. Because if it didn't, we couldn't be anything. I can't erase our past but I don't live in it. I am not ruined. I'm just done with it. What you did to me . . . it's a part of who we both are, and I carried it for a long time. But if you still carry it, that's for you to deal with."

I knew it wasn't exactly what she wanted to hear, but I couldn't lie to her, and I couldn't absolve her—the girl I was at nine who had her birthday party all by herself with her mom wouldn't let me.

"I get it, you're a great person and I am an awful one—" she bit back defensively.

"No, I don't get it. I never got it. I never understood why you hated me so much. Why me?" I could feel my face burning. And it was true. We were now friends, more or less. But since she'd brought it up, I had to ask.

She frowned. "I don't know. It was almost like a game. You know how when you shoplift it isn't about the junk you steal, it's about seeing if you can get away with it. And after you've done it once, you do it again. I could get a whole cafeteria to call you a name, Amy. Or pretend you weren't there. I kept waiting for someone to stop me, but no one ever did."

Madison had spent years seeking out my weakest places and striking at them with words, but hearing this description from her about why she did it almost stung worse than any name she'd ever called me. "Madison, I wasn't some pair of earrings you stole," I said firmly.

"I know. And I'm sorry. I'm so sorry, Amy. And I'm different now. I have a kid. I know I have to be a better person. The second I saw Dustin Jr. a switch went off. I looked at his little face and knew I had to be different. Better. Because I didn't want him to have a mom like me. I know that doesn't change what I did to you. But I do mean it."

I looked at Madison for a long beat. "I believe you," I said quietly.

"So will you help me, Amy? Will you help me get home?" she said, her tone pleading. There was a time I would have killed to have Madison Pendleton on her knees begging me for something. Today it was just another thing that hurt. "Please,

Amy . . . you could just click your heels together and drop me off and be back here for your war or whatever. From what I can see, everyone here can take care of themselves. My kid can't."

"I am sorry, Madison. I can't risk it. I can't risk doing magic when we don't know what will happen," I said, and I meant it.

Madison's lip quivered and her eyes flashed. "Fuck you, Amy. I thought we were something like friends. But you can go to hell for all I care. I'm stuck in this horrible weirdo universe, and it's *all your fault*."

It was no use. She was already stalking away from me and back into her room. She slammed the door behind her with a reverberating crash. I put my head on my knees, fighting back tears, and wondered if anything else could go wrong in the last few hours I had to live. And I still needed to find a costume.

SEVENTEEN

The lead-up to Dorothy's wedding was turning out to be a serious bummer.

Madison wouldn't speak to me, and Nox and Lang were barely talking either—they'd almost gotten in a fistfight over some stupid argument about who got to have which knife. We weren't a team—we were a circle of hate. If I didn't rescue the mood, our chances of saving Oz from Dorothy and the Nome King were about as good as my chances of winning a Nobel Prize in physics. (Do they even have those?)

"We'd better get ready," I said into the miserable silence. No one would even bother to look at me.

And then I lost my temper. Like, for real. Why was I trying to pretend everything was okay? If they didn't get it together we were all going to die. Like, for real.

"Are you all children?" I snapped. "We're about to take on the biggest bitch in Oz and you can't even talk to each other?" I grabbed one of Lang's knives off the table and threw it at the wall, where it hit with a resounding clang. "Get your shit together!" I yelled.

Madison jumped. Her scowl cracked. And she started to laugh.

"Dude, you should see your face right now," she said. "You're bright red."

"I'm fucking pissed!" I yelled. And then I began to laugh, too. A second later Nox and Lang joined in. Lang's beetle servants must have thought we were all nuts. But the laughter relieved the tension. And when we finally stopped, the air felt lighter.

"I have your disguises," Lang said, wiping tears from her eyes. She wasn't going to apologize, and neither was Nox, but they finally seemed willing to let the argument go at least. She snapped her fingers, and one of her beetles scuttled forward.

It showed us down a hallway I hadn't noticed before to a huge room lined with mirrors, and piles of clothing stacked on a long bench. Madison stripped out of her jeans and sparkly T-shirt and I stepped out of my borrowed clothes.

"Whoa," Madison said. "Where did she even get this stuff?" Her long blond hair hung down her back in loose bedhead waves, and her face—clear of the seventeen layers of lip gloss and foundation she typically applied—looked surprisingly young and almost vulnerable. Madison, I realized suddenly, was actually really pretty.

"They're not clothes," I said. "They're costumes. Look."

For Madison, there was a pair of tight leggings and a shirt covered with beautiful, shimmering silver scales and an elaborate, delicate headdress that suggested some kind of glorious tropical fish. I touched the leggings and realized they were made of some light but incredibly strong metal.

For me, Lang had provided a sleek fiery orange bodysuit painted with red and gold scales that gleamed softly in the light. They were made of the same material as Madison's costume—flexible and almost weightless, but incredibly strong. A ribbed cape of thin, soft gold leather hooked on to the bodysuit at my shoulders and wrists and spread out to look like wings. The coolest part was the mask—a gold head shaped like a dragon, with fierce-looking ivory teeth showing in a snarl. As I put the mask on, it molded seamlessly to my face, the way Lang's silver mask did. I couldn't feel it at all. But when I touched my face, I felt how strong the material was.

Our costumes weren't just costumes. They were armor. They fit perfectly. I had no idea if Lang had some kind of giant closet stuffed full of crazy outfits in all sizes or if she'd used magic to create them, but the costumes were beautiful and practical. I felt like I was wearing my old fighting gear back in Oz—the costume had the same familiar, protective feel.

We might not make it through Dorothy's wedding alive. But at least we looked good. And pretty badass, if I said so myself.

I took the mask off for now; although it had molded to my face, it came off easily. I'd put it back on when we were under way.

"Dude, you look amazing," Madison said, echoing my thoughts.

"So do you," I replied.

She fidgeted. "I'm sorry for yelling at you. About all that Kansas stuff."

"Forget it," I said, meaning it. "I know you want to go back. You have someone to fight for now. I get it. It's just that . . . Like I said, it's not simple."

"Dorothy just did the heel-clicking thing," Mad said, looking down at my boots.

"Yeah, I don't think they work like that anymore. Dorothy's shoes also weren't combat boots." I sighed. "I'm going to find a way to get you home, Mad. I promise. No matter what it takes."

"What about you?" she asked.

"Me?"

"If—when—you figure out how to get back. Are you going to come, too?"

"I don't know," I said.

She nodded. "I thought so." She paused, as though she was trying to decide whether or not to say whatever she was thinking. "We're going to die out there, aren't we." It wasn't really a question. I felt a fierce surge of protectiveness.

"I am not going to let that happen," I said firmly. "You're going home, Madison. Nobody's going to die except Dorothy." I said the words with such conviction that I almost convinced myself. And why not? I'd faced worse odds before and survived.

Okay, maybe not worse. But definitely almost as bad. Besides, I was tough as hell. So was Madison. So was Nox. And I was pretty sure, tough as we all were, Lang was tougher in spades. Despite the insane risk we were taking, we were stronger together. This was what I had trained for, sacrificed for. This was what Nox had worked his whole life for. This was all Lang wanted.

Maybe, just maybe, we were going to make it.

"I'm going to find a way," I said again. "As soon as this is over. You're going back to Kansas."

Madison looked at me for a long time. "Okay," she said. "I'm gonna hold you to that." I could tell the strength in my voice had reassured her.

Back in Lang's main room, Nox's expression confirmed how good Mad and I looked. The tension between Nox and Lang seemed to have finally dissipated, and I said a silent prayer of relief. The two of them had finished sorting through weapons, and had a whole stash of knives that could be easily hidden under our costumes. Nox was dressed as a panther, which seemed appropriate. His suit was velvety black, and a ferocious cat mask rested on the table, waiting for him to put it on.

"Good," Lang said approvingly, looking Mad and me up and down. "Very good. Give me a moment to change, and we can leave." She disappeared into her room. Nox put an arm around me, and I rested my head on his shoulder and closed my eyes briefly.

"I'll just, um, get my stuff together," Madison said, looking at us. She vanished into her own room and shut the door.

"Madison doesn't have any stuff," Nox said, confused.

"She's giving us some time alone together," I said, smiling at him.

Since it might be the last time alone together we ever get, I thought ruefully. But I didn't truly believe that. I hadn't come all this way to get killed underground at Dorothy's stupid wedding. We were all going to make it out alive. I refused to allow anything else.

"Oh," Nox said, understanding dawning on his face. "Right."

He took my hand absently, playing with my fingers. Even though our conversation was serious, a thrill ran through me. It was just my luck to find the person of my dreams in a war-torn world where I was in danger of losing him any minute, I thought.

But maybe that was what life was like for everyone. Okay, so people weren't literally on the verge of being killed all the time back in Kansas, but everyone around you was changing and growing all the time and turning into different people.

When my mom had turned into an addict, she'd completely wiped out the kind, generous, tough single mom who'd defended me against people like Madison. And when Madison had had a kid and lost everything, she'd become a person almost unrecognizable from the queen bitch she'd been before. No, that wasn't true. She still had her humor. Only now that was on my side instead of working against me.

Nox had changed, but he had only gotten better. He was a good guy with a moral compass that was fixed on North. And now he was my guy, with the same compass, but with a heart that was open to me.

I squeezed my eyes shut again, harder, as if by wishing fiercely enough I could airlift us out of this world and into a safe, secret space of our own, where we could spend all the time we wanted learning everything there was to know each other.

But I knew better. I'd known better all along. Falling in love with Nox hadn't changed why I'd been brought to Oz, and it didn't change how much I wanted Oz to be free. And anyway, I knew Nox would never be happy with me if I asked him to choose. Oz was his home. It meant more to him than anything— more to him than I did. I couldn't fault him for it, and I couldn't ask him to give up on it, even if I wanted to.

"What are you thinking?" he asked softly.

"Nothing worth talking about," I said honestly.

"You can tell me anything, Amy."

"No, really, it's okay. I just wish I knew everyone else was safe."

"You know what it's like over there." He sighed. "None of us have ever been safe. Not in years, anyway. They're tough. You saw them defeat Glinda. The Nome King's been in Ev. I'm sure they're fine. They'll still be there when we get home."

Home. That word again. The word that meant I had to choose—assuming I had the option. Was home here? Back with Lulu and Ozma and Gert and Mombi? Or was it in Kansas with my mom? I couldn't imagine going back to high school— again—after all of this. The idea was so ridiculous I almost laughed. But there was so much in my own world I hadn't experienced. I'd never even been outside Kansas.

Well, except to Oz. But Paris sounded pretty good, too. Maybe a nice beach on the Bahamas. Maybe college. I'd killed the Cowardly Lion; admissions essays would be a breeze after that.

There was so much I hadn't done.

But Nox felt more like home than either Oz or Kansas. And if he was here, would I ever be happy in my own world?

"What do you want?" I asked suddenly, lifting my head and looking at him. "When all of this is over, I mean. When we win, and Dorothy's gone, and the Nome King is—well, wherever we put him, I guess, and Ozma's back in charge. What do you want to do then?"

He was silent for a long time. "It's funny," he said finally. "I never thought about it until . . ."

"Until?" I prompted.

"Until I met you," he said simply.

"Oh," I said, blushing.

He smiled, squeezing my hand. "I lost my parents when I was just a kid. And Mombi—well, you know what she's like. I think in her own way she cared about me, but she wasn't much of a mother. She raised me to think about nothing other than fighting, than becoming the best, most powerful warrior I could. For a long time, that seemed like the end goal in itself. And then I got stronger and stronger, and soon I was fighting all the time, and Dorothy was getting worse and worse, and it was just—things kept going like that, so that I didn't have time to think about anything other than whether I was going to be alive the next morning to fight some more."

"Like dominoes," I said.

"Like what?" He looked puzzled.

"Oh, just a game we have in the Other Place," I said. "Little tiles? You can set them up so that if you knock one over all the other ones . . . you know what, never mind."

He laughed. "Okay, like that I guess. But that was it for me for a long time. I didn't think about the future because deep down I assumed there wasn't going to be one. And deep down I was fine with that. If I died fighting Dorothy, I would've made the ultimate sacrifice. I could finally just . . . rest. And I wouldn't have to feel like I'd failed Oz, or the Order, or Mombi, or all the trainees I sent into the Emerald City knowing they were probably going to die, too." The laughter was gone from his voice and his eyes were haunted. "It wasn't just Melindra, Amy. So many people I sent to their deaths. So many of them were just children."

"You can't think like that," I said urgently. "You *can't*, Nox. It's not your fault, it's Dorothy's. You didn't kill them. She did. Everyone who trains with the Order knows what they're getting into. I knew that from the moment I agreed to help Mombi. You're the one who keeps telling me we're at war. I don't understand why you can't tell yourself the same thing."

"Because they were my responsibility," he said roughly. "They were my charges, Amy. I trained them, every one of them. I knew their names, their stories, their hopes and dreams. I might not have believed in the future, but every last one of them did, or they never would've joined the Order."

His pain was so raw and so apparent. I wished more than anything I could take it away from him. But, I realized, that was something I was learning, too. I couldn't change his feelings. I could tell him what I thought, but he had his own path to work through. All I could do was support him through it and hope that someday he learned to forgive himself, that he realized he was caught in an impossible situation.

"What if you'd run away?" I said. "You'd hate yourself even more. You did the only thing you knew how to do, Nox. You did the only thing you knew *how* to do. Mombi brought you up to be a fighter, and you passed those skills on to a whole generation of trainees. Not all of us are dead, remember?"

He nodded, bringing my hand to his mouth. "You're tougher than you give yourself credit for, Amy."

"Thanks, but I still would've died without what you taught me about fighting and magic. 'Tough' doesn't do much against Dorothy, or her armies, or the Lion. Remember? I'm alive because of you, Nox. Not because you saved me, even though you have. We've saved each other. I'm alive because you're the one who taught me the skills I needed to survive. So is Lang. So is Melindra. So maybe you're doing better than you give yourself credit for, too. Okay?"

He snorted softly. "Amy—"

"Nox, I mean it. I'm not gonna hear any more of this shit about how everyone who died in Oz is your fault. It's the fault of the person who *killed* them, Nox. It's *Dorothy's* fault. Deal?"

He opened his mouth and shut it again, then shook his head. "I'm not there yet. I can't see it that way."

"I can."

"I know," he said. "And that's one of the things that I love about you. You make me feel like . . . like there's a reason for me not to give in to death."

That left me breathless. I didn't know what to say. What he was telling me now, I understood, was the most important thing another person had ever trusted me with. I felt like if I so much as breathed I'd shatter what was blossoming between us, like the night-blooming tirium he'd showed me what felt like a century ago.

"That's the thing I want you to know," he said in a low voice. "At first, when you came to the Order, I wanted to push you out. I wanted to make you leave. Because I could see it in you then, this goodness that you have, and I didn't want you anywhere near us. I was terrified I'd have to send you to your death before you were ready, too, and one more untrained warrior on my conscience would've been too much. But it was more than that. You were different. You saw the world differently. When you looked at Oz, you saw what Dorothy had done—but you saw the beauty in it, too. You knew what it was like to feel wonder. And I hadn't been around someone like that since I was just a child. Gert and Mombi knew it, too. They thought they could use what I felt for you to control me." He took a deep, ragged breath. "And now here we are."

I was so still I realized I'd forgotten to breathe. Silence spread over us like a blanket, sealing us into our own private world in the middle of Lang's hideout. For this moment, this instant, it was just the two of us and the way we felt about each other, this huge, beautiful thing that I could finally say out loud.

"I love you," I whispered. No matter how many times I said it, I knew I'd never get used to the feeling of the words in my mouth. The knowledge that it was true. That I'd never feel this way about anyone else again as long as I lived.

And neither would he.

EIGHTEEN

Lang swept back into the room, and she looked unbelievable. Her costume consisted of a closely fitted bodice of glossy black feathers studded with faceted obsidian that caught and held the lantern light. A long, spectacular train of more feathers left most of her black-stockinged legs bare. The final touch: a glorious black-plumed mask that fitted closely over her face and erupted into a headdress of towering feathers that arced behind her back like wings.

"*Wow,*" I said, and meant it.

"I do enjoy a particularly good disguise," Lang said modestly. "Are you ready?"

I grabbed Madison from her room and the four of us strapped knives to our thighs and ankles.

"Let's go," Lang said. I squared my shoulders, took Nox's hand, and followed her out of her hideaway and back to the eerie underground lake where the dragon boat was waiting for us.

"We want to be as unrecognizable as possible," Lang said when we had settled into the boat and it was paddling away from the shore. "The more time we have before the Nome King sees me, the better." She lifted her hands and closed her eyes. For a moment, nothing happened. And then Madison gasped.

The dragon boat's wings were unfurling, their surface glistening with an iridescent sheen like oil on water. White feathers sprouted from the dark, leathery skin, and its scaly, stubby neck elongated into an elegant, sinuous curve like a swan's. Lang's fingers were moving and I could smell something electric and spicy, like the sky before a thunderstorm.

Magic.

In front of our eyes, the dragon boat was turning into something unrecognizable: a swan.

In Ev, Lang used her magic to become a chameleon. Someone whose very face changed constantly. Her whole life was a disguise.

I wondered what would happen to her if we won. If she didn't need to hide anymore. Would she be able to ever go back to being normal? Someone who moved through the world as herself and not someone else.

I wondered if she even knew who she was anymore underneath all the masks. My journey down the Road of Yellow Brick had been a clarifying one—I knew myself better now. And I was stronger. Lang was strong, and crafty—and I just hoped she'd been rewarded with the same sense of self.

As the beetle captain navigated us along Ev's underground waterways, more and more boats packed with people decked out in spectacular finery began to crowd the river. Some boats were living creatures, like ours: huge swans in thread-thin gold bridles; car-size fish that swam half out of the water; even a giant, decidedly evil-looking crocodile. Others were made of wood and metal, some of them so delicate it looked like a single wave might swamp them, others as massive and solid as tanks.

Like us, the other guests were in disguise. I saw exotic birds and reptiles, wild animals I recognized—and plenty I didn't. One woman was costumed as an owl, in snow-white feathers scattered with diamonds. Another wore the inky-black pelt of some kind of jungle cat like a second skin, cut so low in the bodice that her overabundant assets threatened to spill out of her ensemble altogether. Their escorts were dressed as the Tin Woodman—*that* was in poor taste, I thought—and the Wizard of Oz, complete with a three-piece suit and a top hat. Unlike the actual Wizard, he was young, handsome, and possessed of a full head of thick, dark hair. Also unlike the actual Wizard, he was alive. My gaze flicked back to the center of the fake Tin Woodman's chest, and I thought back to when I held his glowing, throbbing heart in my hand. I shuddered.

I wonder how the people of Ev even knew about birds since they spent so much of their lives underground. Maybe they dreamed of faraway places just the way I had back in Kansas.

Even on the way to a party the huge difference between rich and poor in Ev was totally obvious. The wealthier people had elaborate, lavish costumes, studded with gemstones that sent rainbows of light shooting across the lamp-lit canals. The poor people had simpler boats and costumes; some of them wore only makeshift masks, carved roughly out of wood, and tied over their eyes with ratty bits of string.

"So many people," Nox said quietly, watching the throngs. Traffic in the canals had slowed to a crawl. Although our faces were hidden underneath our masks, we were careful not to make eye contact with any of the other guests.

"The invitation didn't offer an opportunity to decline," Lang said. "And everyone in Ev is afraid of the Nome King, even if they've never heard of Dorothy. He is not . . . kind to people who defy him."

I thought of the scars on Lang's back and shivered.

Finally I saw what had to be the entrance to the Nome King's palace: a huge, vaulted cavern that opened directly onto the water. The walls glittered with raw rubies the size of my head and burst out of the rock everywhere like flowers climbing through soil. Huge red lanterns floated in the air, casting a bloodred light over the hordes of boats that looked both eerie and ominous. Next to me, Madison's, Nox's, and Lang's costumes seemed almost to come alive in the unearthly light, as if the costumes themselves were living creatures.

A massive dock extended out into the canal, where a group of heavily armed, white-skinned creatures impassively watched the guests disembark. They were hideously ugly, heavily muscled and covered with scars and tattoos, and they looked mean as hell. Those had to be the Diggers. Liveried valets parked their boats along an obsidian marina.

I expected to hear excited chatter—the babble of voices, conversations, people gossiping the way people always did on the way to parties. But Dorothy's guests were eerily silent. Rich or poor, every one of Dorothy's guests had one thing in common: they looked terrified. Their eyes were wide with fear, their faces haunted. You could have heard the flap of a bird's wings in the huge cavern. I swallowed hard. I couldn't let my courage falter. Not now.

"This is it," Lang whispered. She looked at me, then Nox, and abruptly she threw her arms around us, squeezing us so tightly that she knocked the breath out of my lungs. "Thank you," she said softly. "I'm . . . glad to have your help."

The words came out rushed and stilted, as if she wasn't used to being honest.

"Obviously," Nox said, taking her hand. And then, "Lang. You have to know—"

But she shook her head, cutting him off. "Save it," she said. "There will be plenty of time to say everything after we kill Dorothy," she said. "Together." He nodded and pulled her close again in a tight embrace. When he released her, I saw tears pooling in her green eyes.

Our boat was drawing close to the dock now. The captain tossed a line to one of the valets, and she pulled us close enough to the black stone that we could get out. All around us, other people were doing the same.

We were here.

Whatever else happened at Dorothy's wedding, I had to give

her credit. It was the most impressive turnout of any party I'd ever seen, and that's including in my mom's collector's issue of *People* magazine from Princess Diana's royal wedding.

With all these people, staying hidden in the crowd wasn't going to be a problem. Again, that nagging worry went off in the back of my mind: something felt wrong here. Something like, this wasn't Dorothy's style. She was vain and shallow and careless, at least when it came to certain things, but she wasn't stupid. She always had a plan.

This many people, left to their own devices—it was too risky for someone as paranoid as she was. Even with the Nome King's forces, there were so many people filing down the gangway and into the Nome King's palace that it would be impossible to keep track of them all.

Why would Dorothy leave herself open to that kind of a threat?

I shook off my doubts and climbed out of the boat. There was nothing we could do now except stay alert. Even if I'd wanted to, the endless line of boats still streaming into the cavern would make it impossible to leave.

For better or for worse, we were in this mission all the way. Hopefully, we'd have a little luck—or magic—on our side this time.

We followed the crowds through a set of enormous metal doors studded with more rubies, and down a broad hallway. The walls were made of the same polished stone as the dock. The black surface was mirror smooth and I could see my costume's shadowy reflection. The air was hot and heavy. I could smell the other guests' perfume and sweat and fear. From somewhere ahead of us, a deep bass line thudded ominously.

It was like being at the world's worst rave. If this was really the end of everything I'd come to Oz to do, it was a strange backdrop.

The end. Could this really be it? If we didn't kill Dorothy, she would kill us. Kill us for real. And even if we did defeat her, we still had to face the Nome King. The odds were some of the worst we'd faced, but I had faith. We had come this far. I had come this far.

But what if we did what we'd come to do? If we won, it would mean I'd find a way to get us back to Oz. Which meant keeping my promise to Madison. But if I found a way back to Kansas, I'd have another choice to make.

Home, or Nox? Home, or Oz?

It dawned on me that, once upon a time, Dorothy'd had to make that choice, too.

We marched along until the hallway ended.

When I stepped into the Nome King's ballroom, right behind Nox, I gasped out loud. The ballroom was unbelievable. I'd never seen anything like it. And despite the situation, the tension— everything that we were about to do—I couldn't help one last feeling of reluctant astonishment. After all this, it was one of the most beautiful places I'd ever seen: a vast underground cavern, its high ceiling lit with ruby stalactites that burned with an eerie red light. The shiny floor reflected back up at me as we entered

the room. The walls sprouted candelabra like moss; years of use
had left twisted, molten sculptures of ancient candlewax col-
lected beneath them. Red moths with wingspans as wide as my
arm fluttered through the air, glowing with the same ruby light
as the stalactites, shedding shimmering dust with every beat of
their lacy wings until the air in the huge cave swirled and eddied
with red clouds that pulsed in time with the music.

Despite the cavern's size, the air was sweltering. Stern-faced
sentries ringed the cavern, pale as birds' eggs and lean as skele-
tons. Instead of costumes, they wore armor plated together from
tarnished steel and patches of leather. Their bare chests were
decorated with intricate designs made, Lang had told us, by
cutting into their own flesh and packing the wounds with coal
dust. They held spears and swords and other, even more sinister
weapons that made my skin crawl just to look at: spiky iron balls
that dangled from long chains, wooden staves bristling with iron
nails, leather whips with steel-barbed tails. I guessed the Nome
King liked to remind his guests that they were there thanks to
his generosity, and misbehavior was punishable—by death. The
Nome King himself was nowhere in sight.

Most of the guests had used the masquerade as an excuse to
bare as much skin as possible. They were dressed as old-fashioned
courtiers, in elaborate powdered white wigs, velvet suitcoats with
tails, and dresses cut dangerously low. Women dripped with jewels, their fingers blazing with golden, gem-studded rings, their
exposed skin dusted with glitter and sweat. Even the men wore
jewelry in the Nome King's ballroom: ruby-decorated cuffs and

rings, a nod to the Nome King's favorite stone. I thought of the people we'd seen starving aboveground and how many of them could be fed with what just one of those bracelets cost. Then I put the thought out of my mind. That wasn't why we were here.

The guests circulated in the immense cave, sipping bloodred liquor from red goblets. The room was as still and quiet as outer space. Half of the attendees were using the opportunity to eat as much as they could.

I snatched a goblet from a passing servant's tray and took a drink, the heady liquor burning the back of my throat and giving me courage. I noticed that Lang was talking with a man dressed as a fairy. Huge wings of wire and gossamer blossomed from his back, and he wore a crown of onyx and garnet gems. I had no love for the Nome King, but I had to admit, grudgingly, that he threw a good party.

I stayed where I was, directly in front of the raised dais where the ceremony was obviously to take place. It was currently empty. That was when I realized: I hadn't said good-bye to Nox. Which *really* meant that dying was not an option. He looked at me, and even behind his mask, his gaze said everything it needed to. He took my hand and squeezed it briefly, before he let me go for good and disappeared into the crowd.

I didn't see Madison. I could only hope that she was doing what she was supposed to—staying out of sight, and out of harm's way.

A noise like a clap of thunder suddenly shook the cathedral-like room. The music cut out and the guests immediately fell silent, apprehension spreading across their faces. A fissure in the wall on the far side of the room split open, revealing a yawning black doorway through which more guards carried an immense ruby and obsidian throne. The Nome King lounged in the throne, one black-clad leg thrown over the armrest and dangling lazily. He wore a spiky iron crown on his bald head and a black leather suit with no shirt, the jacket unbuttoned and revealing his pale, hairless torso. Around his neck, a single enormous ruby dangled from a thick iron chain. His long silver nails, filed to sharp tips, matched his pointy-toed black boots that were tipped with shining steel. I took special note of the huge, evil-looking knife strapped to his belt, and shuddered.

The guards set his throne down on the raised dais and immediately prostrated themselves, touching their foreheads to the floor. The guests followed suit, throwing themselves to the ground frantically so as not to be the last person left standing. I quickly did the same.

"Greetings, my loyal and devoted subjects," the Nome King said. Though he didn't raise his voice, it carried easily across the huge room. He put the slightest sneer into "loyal," like he knew most of his subjects were no such thing. They weren't loyal— they were just terrified of him. "Thank you all for attending my little party." *As if they'd had any other choice,* I thought. "Please, treasured peers of the realm, do not bow before your king," he added. No one moved. No one wanted to be the first to rise.

"Up, up," the Nome King said impatiently, and at that his guests scrambled to their feet. He looked even more pleased with himself than usual, and that was saying a lot. It wasn't until he looked over his shoulder that I realized there was a figure standing in the shadows behind him. A figure that, upon his glance, now stepped forward.

I sucked in a breath and took a step back, trying to stay out of sight behind the giant, feathered hat of a woman standing in front of me.

Dorothy. Her skin was pale and flushed from the heat under her elaborate, jeweled mask. She had chosen an appropriate costume: she was dressed as a serpent in a slinky, skintight red dress, encrusted with thousands of tiny red sequins that created the illusion of scales. It was cinched tightly at her tiny waist and then flared out in sinuous curves over her hips and long legs. Her red heels glittered on her feet.

"Dearly beloved," the Nome King began. "We are gathered here today to . . . oh, wait, I'm getting ahead of myself, aren't I?" The Nome King gave a sly, fey giggle and nervous laughter rippled outward among his confused subjects, none of whom understood what was funny but all of whom were eager to assure him they were in on his private joke. "That part comes later. I'm sure you're all wondering why you're here. Other than to drink my liquor and eat my food." He laughed again. "But I have wonderful news for you. As you all surely know, the kingdom of Oz has long been a thorn in our royal side. While Ev withers and its crops fail, Oz prospers. Instead of offering us their assistance, the citizens of Oz live in oblivious selfishness." Dorothy cleared her throat. The Nome King's bony hands tightened into fists.

"Today," he continued, "all of that will change. For today marks the day that Oz and Ev will be united as one. Two kingdoms, once sundered, brought together in peace and prosperity, governed by the most powerful and benevolent ruler either country has ever known." Next to him, Dorothy stiffened. If I'd caught his misstep, I knew she had, too. *One* ruler. Not two.

It wasn't hard to guess what that meant.

"All of you have the honor of witnessing the greatest moment in Ev's history," the Nome King continued, not realizing the mistake he'd just made.

He beckoned for Dorothy, who walked daintily up to the Nome King's throne, where he rose to his feet and clasped her hand in his and raised them both over his head for the crowd.

"My fellow citizens of Ev," the Nome King intoned, "prepare yourselves for—"

Dorothy cleared her throat again, more significantly this time, and the Nome King stopped, looking at her in puzzlement. If she suspected, like I did, that he was planning on sacrificing her right here, in front of the entire crowd, she didn't look too worried about it.

Instinctively I looked at her shoes again and felt an answering throb in my boots.

It dawned on me. *Of course,* I thought. *She can use them.* That bitch *always* had something up her sleeve, didn't she?

Now that I was looking for it, I could *see* the haze of magic pulsing around her, as if the shoes were even stronger now that they'd been returned to the land they came from. She surveyed the crowd with icy grandeur, one hand perched on the back of the Nome King's throne. A strange little creature huddled at her feet, costumed as a small shrub.

"My bride is correct to remind me of why we are here," the Nome King said finally. "Before the ceremony begins, we must celebrate this momentous occasion!" A rictus grin spread across his face. "Let us dance and be merry!" he crowed, clapping his hands.

The woman next to me shifted nervously on her feet. Other guests exchanged brief, uncertain glances.

"I said *dance*!" the Nome King screamed. "Be *merry*!"

He must have taken a page from Dorothy's book. The guests stood, stricken, and then one by one they began to shuffle their feet back and forth. They looked like animated corpses with their weird, sad, silent, shambling dance. Their hands and arms flapped aimlessly. Without music or rhythm to follow, they kicked randomly into the air, or spun around in place, their eyes filled with fear.

In a hidden corner I hadn't noticed, a ragtag orchestra of Munchkin musicians suddenly struck up a jerky, tuneless waltz. Now everyone was dancing their off-kilter, graceless dance, spasming back and forth like zombies at the world's saddest disco. The musicians looked just as awful. One of them, I saw, had his ankles chained together. Another was missing an ear; a third had a red-stained bandage wrapped around his chest.

I looked away. I couldn't help them. I could only do what

we'd come here for: finish Dorothy and defeat the Nome King, once and for all.

Dorothy threw her head back with a jubilant grin, keeping time to the beat as if she truly believed everyone was having the time of their lives. I lurched back and forth with everyone around me so as not to draw attention to myself, but unlike the others, whose movements were now growing increasingly frenzied, I was careful to conserve my energy.

Near me, they were already starting to flag. Half starved, exhausted, and terrified, they couldn't keep up the pace. While the Nome King clapped along to the horrible music and Dorothy cheerfully tapped her foot and shimmied her hips, more than one person around me collapsed to the ground. As soon as they fell, the Diggers descended on them, dragging their inert bodies out of the ballroom.

Once they were outside, I heard their screams over the music.

It took everything I had not to run out there. To rescue them. Whatever was happening to them was almost too horrible to contemplate—but I knew that helping them wouldn't do anyone in the room any good unless Nox, Madison, Lang, and I could first free them from the Nome King's sick little games forever. So I shut my ears against the terrible cries even as I felt bile building in the pit of my stomach.

At last, the Nome King held up a hand and the music screeched to a halt. The musicians were panting, wild-eyed and shaky from exertion. One of them had collapsed during it all, and his companions were deliberately avoiding looking at the place where he'd stood only moments earlier.

The guests stopped dancing immediately. Once more, silence fell upon the room. From outside, one more tormented scream pierced the quiet and then, abruptly, was cut off.

No one said a word. The Nome King got to his feet.

"Dearly beloved, we are gathered here today," he began again. Again, he giggled at a joke that only he could really understand. As he droned on about how much Oz owed Ev, and about how he and Dorothy were going to change everything, I could almost feel his voice slithering through my body like a bug that had crawled in through my ear and was now trying to eat my body from the inside out.

I wanted to retch, but I kept my eyes on the ground, terrified that he would somehow see me and recognize me. Dorothy hovered behind his throne, still smiling vacantly.

All I had to do was stay out of sight. Lang would wait until the actual ceremony to give the signal, I knew. I just had to endure this charade until then.

At last, the Nome King fell silent. He held out his hand to Dorothy, and she stepped forward. "My fellow citizens of Ev," the Nome King intoned, "I give you your future queen, the Witchslayer, the rightful ruler of Oz."

Dorothy pulled her shoulders back and lifted her chin with pride as she addressed her not-so-adoring audience. Never once had she failed to rise to an occasion. You had to hand it to her— the girl loved attention.

"Greetings, my dear subjects," she purred. "I'm *so* excited to

meet you all. But first, I have a *very* important announcement."
She raised her mask. "I want you to know we have *one* more
incredibly special guest with us here today," she said.

Her already huge smile widened even further than I thought
was possible as she continued. "I have to say, I normally loathe
party crashers, but I'm just tickled that someone as special as this
would show up for little old me. With or without an invitation."

Dorothy looked down at the crowd.

My pulse quickened. She was looking right at me.

"Hi, Amy," she said. Her grotesque grin had suddenly transformed into a joyful snarl. "Are you going to kill me now?"

NINETEEN

DOROTHY

Just before the festivities were about to begin, I looked in the mirror in my chambers and smoothed my hair out. I looked perfect, if I do so say myself. And I still couldn't help checking myself one last time, feeling a little tickle in my stomach as I did it: butterflies.

I know I exude a certain confidence, but I have a little secret: parties always make me just a little bit nervous! The anticipation. What dress I would wear. Who I would dance with. Would anyone die.

By now, you should know that I *always* have a plan—and my wedding surely wasn't going to be an exception to that. It was my special day, after all, and there was no way I'd let a few silly little assassination plots ruin it.

I was smart enough to have realized that despite all that I'd done, the Nome King was going to try to kill me.

I almost had to admire his nerve.

And even if he wasn't going to go quite that far, I was beyond certain that he wasn't going to let me get my way. The second most important thing you should know about me is that I always get my way. In the end, at least.

No matter what he was up to, I was two steps ahead of him. If there was one thing my beloved fiancé wasn't counting on, it was Amy Gumm and her little boy toy.

I have to admit, it was almost exciting! No matter what happened, this was going to be the party of the year.

Bupu entered and brought the last piece of my costume—a real-life snake that wound itself around me.

I looked at the Munchkin. "You are a good friend, Bupu." While I dressed, I told her about my friends, about Scare and Tin and the Lion, and the things that they had wanted when I first met them, and how I had helped them.

"I am not like them," she said. "I am not smart or courageous or full of heart."

"Bupu, you helped me when you didn't have to—that was heart. You helped me when you knew you could have been skinned alive. That's courage. And you were clever enough to find out that information I needed. If that isn't brains then I don't know what is."

Bupu smiled at me.

Friendship doesn't have to be selfless—but it works best when your interests line up. Bupu and I had an understanding now. And it was going to save us both.

I twirled around for Bupu to compliment me.

Everything was ready. My costume was ready, my hair was

ready, and my will to live was at an all-time, through-the-roof high.

So it was perfect timing when the knock came at my door and the Nome King stepped inside the room.

"Are you ready, my darling?" he asked. I have to say that he looked less than appropriately smitten. His gaze flicked to Bupu, who was perched at my side, looking serious, and nervous.

He gave a scowl. "What is she doing here?" he asked.

"She's my bridesmaid, beloved. It's traditional."

He let it go with a shrug. "As you wish," he said. He knew perfectly well that Bupu was hardly a threat. She wasn't meant to be. The real threat was on her way.

At least, I hoped she was.

I felt like a common prisoner as the Nome King escorted me to the ballroom, his guards flanking me on all sides. I ignored the indignity. After today, I'd never have to see these tiresome creatures again.

As we got closer I had to keep from beaming. Because my plan was working: Amy was out there somewhere. I could feel the power of her shoes burning in the distance, just as I could feel the power of my own coursing through my body.

That feeling only got stronger as I approached, and I knew that, wherever Amy was, she was close, and getting closer. We were both headed toward the same place.

It was almost ironic. She thought that she was going to kill me. She had no idea at all that she was playing right into my hands. *Someone* was going to die tonight, but it wasn't going to be me.

I was happy to let her and the Nome King have their little murder ball. While they were busy ripping each other to shreds, I was going to apply a fresh coat of lipstick and get myself back to Oz. Maybe I could even manage to snatch my other shoes back while I was at it. What a coup that would be! It wasn't outside the realm of possibility.

I wondered what Glinda's face would look like when I saw her again. When she realized I was still alive, and that with both pairs of shoes under my control, there was nothing in the world that she could do to stop me.

I'd killed a few witches in my day. I was *so* looking forward to doing it again. This time, I'd really be able to enjoy it.

I had come a long way, after all. That first Wicked witch— the Wicked Witch of the East—had been an accident. I couldn't help the fact that the tornado had dropped my house on her before I'd even officially set foot in Oz.

The second time, at least, I'd known exactly what I was doing, even if I hadn't been quite ready to bask in the glory of it all. It was the first time I'd ever killed anyone in my life. I'd been surprised then by how easy it was.

I wouldn't realize it until later, but it was that moment that had changed me forever. Killing the Wicked Witch of the West had unlocked the secret potential that had always lived inside me—the potential to be great. After that, it had just taken a little bit of living—not to mention a second trip to Oz—to realize exactly what that potential meant.

It meant that I was special. It meant that I was a *queen*.

I had the decisiveness and power it took to govern a country. To be truly great. Because what had all those hours in my history class back in Kansas taught me, if not that the most effective rulers are also the most ruthless ones? I was proud to be like them in that way, and grateful to the witches for sacrificing themselves (the poor things!) so that I could become the girl—no, the woman—who I was truly meant to be.

The Nome King and I were approaching the ballroom now. I wondered what my guests were doing. This was going to be the grandest event they'd ever witness in their miserable, mildewy little lives.

"You promised me an entrance, my darling," I said, turning to him.

"Indeed I did," he replied, with a smirk that was almost romantic.

My beau, I noticed just then, was wearing a wicked-looking silver blade strapped to his belt. Rubies studded its hilt. I felt the unmistakable throb of magic pulsing down the length of the knife and I understood immediately: this was how he was going to try to kill me. It was how he was planning to unleash the blood that would allow the shoes to return to him.

Let him try, I thought. Soon, at long last, I'd be going home—back to Oz, where I belonged. Back to the throne that was rightfully mine.

Home. For just a second, I faltered as that word echoed uncomfortably in the back of my head. It made me shiver, reminding me of something that I couldn't put my finger on. Something someone had said to me once.

A sliver of doubt festered in me where there had only been certainty before. I pushed it aside. The Nome King was just trying to get into my head.

Of course Oz was home.

Now the Nome King led me down a twisting hallway I hadn't noticed before, away from the main entrance to his ballroom.

"Nothing makes an entrance grander than a secret doorway," he said with a smile, pointing to a cleft in the rock wall. *Hmmm,* I thought, filing this away. For all I knew, it was too late for this information to be of any use, but I'd save it just in case. I shimmied through it. The cleft ended in a heavy red curtain. I peeked around it and saw a raised dais, and beyond it, the ballroom.

The place was packed. Absolutely packed. For a moment, I felt a wild glee. These people were all here for *me!* They'd dressed up in costumes, just as I'd told them to. The ruby light played over hundreds of faces.

But despite the massive crowd, the servants and Diggers and attendants and cooks and guests and hangers-on, the entire cavern was silent. Deathly silent. As if all of them were terrified to draw the Nome King's attention. They knew from experience that whenever he called for a crowd, something awful was bound to happen. They were all wondering which one of them it was going to be.

I felt Amy before I saw her. Her boots were calling to me, and I knew exactly where she was, pressed close to the stage, surrounded by bodies.

Silly girl. She thought her ridiculous getup was enough to disguise her. In those boots, I'd have known her even if she'd been wrapped in a fully body cast. They were calling to me so loudly that it almost made me wince.

Everything was working even better than I'd planned.

The Nome King gestured to the Diggers, and another group of them carried forward an enormous, glittering red throne. He settled himself into it with a yawn.

"Where's my throne?" I asked.

He smiled. "I thought we could share, my love. For now why don't you enter the room behind me?"

Bupu sniffled quietly at my feet. I reached down and patted her head comfortingly through the branches of her costume.

Well, like Aunt Em always used to say, make lemonade when the sun shines. I took a deep breath, squared my shoulders, and adjusted my mask.

It was showtime.

The Diggers carried the Nome King onto the dais. Bupu and I followed him like lackeys, but I just smiled, knowing that I'd have plenty of time later to make him regret the insult if I felt like it.

I sighed, and he glanced over at me, I suppose expecting to see the glum face of a prisoner. Instead, I threw him a radiant smile. He smiled back, but there was something uncertain about it this time.

What a waste killing him would be. But it's like they say— you can't teach an old dog new tricks. Even Toto refused to change his ways when he got older. The Nome King, I was sure, wouldn't be any better at it.

At any rate, he must have taken to heart what I'd said to him about weddings being a festive occasion. As the guests gaped up at him like sheep, he invited them to dance. And to my delight, they did. The musicians played a wonderful waltz. The guests danced in beautiful patterns, their faces glowing with joy and exertion.

I clapped my hands in delight, transported briefly from my more immediate problems. The dance was a little ungraceful, but perhaps that was just the local custom. I snatched a glass of something silver and sparkling off a passing waiter's tray and surreptitiously chugged it down in one gulp. I'd already sampled some of the Nome King's most bracing liquor to soothe my nerves before my big moment, but one more sip never hurts, does it?

I'm sure the guests would have danced all night if he'd let them, but the Nome King had more important business to take care of. It was sad, really. I would have so loved to find the man who was a perfect match for my abilities and beauty.

Of course, it was likely that that person didn't exist. If he was out there, I certainly would have met him by now.

Suddenly another memory flashed through my mind, unbidden and unwelcome.

The Other Place. Aunt Em had had a hired hand for a while who was as handsome as the day is long and who always paid me extra attention. He'd leave little gifts on my windowsill—a pretty hair ribbon, a robin's egg he'd found in the long grass, a pie still warm out of the oven—and sometimes when I caught him looking at me he'd turn bright red and look away. I'd been wildly in love with him, of course, but much too shy in those days to do anything about it.

Why was I thinking of him? At this moment? It made absolutely no sense. And yet the more I tried to swat the memory away, the stronger it became.

Tommy. He'd been called Tommy.

I wondered where he was now. Then I realized he was long dead. Time moved differently there. But before that—if he'd found some other farm girl to fall in love with and marry. If he'd ever had a family. A farm of his own. Maybe he'd moved to the big city. He had been so handsome—maybe he'd become a movie star. As the Nome King droned on, I remembered Tommy's smell—new hay and clean sweat—and the transparent blue of his eyes. I remembered how he'd always called me "Miss Dorothy" and tipped his hat when he saw me, even though I told him a thousand times that just plain Dorothy would do. I remembered—

No. I didn't want to remember. That life was over.

Tommy was beautiful and charming, but when I came back from Oz, he had joined the others in shunning me. "Miss Dorothy, you seem changed," he'd said. He'd preferred the old me, the one who had not an ounce of magic or courage. I didn't belong with him any more than I belonged with my current homicidal fiancé. At least he recognized I was royalty.

Another memory flooded in—Aunt Em baking pies in the kitchen of the old homestead. She'd made me pie after Tommy slighted me. "Nothing cures a broken heart like pie," she'd said.

"I don't want my heart. But I'll take the pie," I'd quipped. I could see Aunt Em's smile and hear her laugh and I could almost taste the pie. At the time it tasted like hope and cinnamon.

With some effort, I dragged myself back to the present, only to hear the Nome King quietly clear his throat. He was looking at me with surprise and some annoyance. I wondered when he'd stopped talking.

"My fellow citizens of Ev," the Nome King said pointedly, "I give you your future queen, the Witchslayer, the rightful ruler of Oz."

It was my cue—the moment I'd been waiting for. Immediately, all my senses sharpened; my memories vanished like smoke on the wind. This was it. This was my only chance, I knew, to escape the man who wanted to steal the fruits of all *my* hard work and claim it as his own.

Being a woman, it turns out, isn't any different in a make-believe world than it is in the real one.

I stepped forward and took off my mask. And then I looked directly at Amy. It was ironic that she was the key to my escape after trying so very hard to end me. I looked at her; the dress she'd chosen wasn't horrible. Losing the pink hair, though, was a big mistake. But it was perhaps the best I'd seen her look since that trailer dropped her in my kingdom.

Her eyes flickered with more than recognition. More than

hate. She knew what I was up to. She was smarter than I had ever given her credit for, after all. Once upon a time we were both in the Other Place wishing for some magic, excitement, and friends. And here we were now. Two tornados later. Two girls from the Other Place all dressed up at my wedding ball . . .

"Hi, Amy," I said. "Are you going to kill me now?"

And the ballroom broke out into chaos.

TWENTY

I wasn't caught entirely off guard by Dorothy's words. That small niggling part of my brain had told me to be prepared for something like this. And as soon as she spoke, I realized exactly what she was doing.

The Nome King had said there would be *one* ruler. That meant he never planned for Dorothy to survive. He just wanted to marry her to get her magic, and then he was going to kill her. Clearly she knew this—and she wanted to escape, and she wanted me to help her do it. She was trying to create a distraction for the Nome King so that *he* didn't kill *her*.

At her side, the Nome King was muttering something that sounded like a curse but was most likely a spell. A black cloud formed in the air over his head, the darkness spinning and cracking with forks of red lightning.

He held up his hands, preparing to attack, but whether he was going to go for me or Dorothy was hard to tell. My guess was me; he couldn't kill Dorothy until he'd stolen her magic. And he needed to complete the wedding ceremony to do that.

All around me, pandemonium was breaking out. People were screaming, pulling off their masks, stampeding toward the entrance to the ballroom. Diggers lashed out with whips and knives on the unarmed guests, and within minutes the air in the ballroom stunk of blood.

I had to fight against the tide of panicking guests to stay close to the dais. Where were Madison and Nox? And where was Lang? I didn't dare turn around and look. Dorothy didn't know I hadn't come to the wedding alone. If they could avoid her while I faced her down, they had a chance to get away. *Leave me here*, I thought at Nox ferociously, hoping in vain that he'd somehow added psychic powers to his résumé without telling me. *Get Madison somewhere safe. Don't try to rescue me.*

Because this was my task. It was my responsibility. All of this had happened because I hadn't been able to bring myself to kill her before.

I fought my way through the oncoming wave of people, trying to reach the dais. The Nome King hurled a bolt of red lightning at my head. I ducked and it hit the floor behind me with a sizzling hiss.

Okay, he was *definitely* targeting me first. And Dorothy was slinking toward the edge of the stage, her eyes on him.

I'd been right. This was all part of her plan—I was here to distract him while she made her escape. And the cavern must have a secret exit—the one she and the Nome King had come through. If she got away now, there was no telling if I'd have another chance.

Everywhere I looked, the Nome King's soldiers were springing into action. Dorothy had caught them off guard, but they recovered quickly. I knew if I ended up in their grip, it was game over. I could fight off a few of them, but I was horribly outnumbered. One of them came at me, his knife raised for a killing strike. I ducked and twisted, but he followed my movements effortlessly. The Nome King took training his fighters seriously.

Then again, so did the Order. This was what I was made for.

I dodged him again, circling back to get enough room to strike. He stuck by me like a leech, lunging forward again and again with his knife.

But he was favoring his right side, where a huge map of scars suggested an old, still-painful injury. I feinted to the right and saw what I was looking for—just the barest hint of a flinch as he moved to protect his vulnerable side. And that was my chance. I leapt up and spun in midair, bringing my booted foot around in a powerful kick that connected solidly with his knife hand. The blade clattered to the floor and I kicked it away, going for my own weapons.

Before I could get to them, he'd already recovered from my attack and was launching one of his own. He leapt forward, wrapping lean but incredibly strong arms around my torso and pinning my own arms to my sides.

I kicked backward with all my strength and heard a satisfying snap as my boot connected with his knee. He bellowed in pain but refused to let go, dragging me to the floor with him as he collapsed. Dorothy watched the fracas with an amused smile. The Nome King glanced at her and she froze. A frown crossed his face.

He was starting to figure out she'd planned this, too.

And then I saw Nox fighting his way toward me. "Get out of here!" I yelled at him, suddenly feeling panicky. "I'll take care of my own damn self!"

My exasperation gave me the extra surge of strength I needed and I broke the guard's grip, elbowing him in the face with a satisfying crunch. "The dais!" I screamed at Nox, pointing. "It's all that matters!" His expression faltered but, seeing that I'd broken free, he nodded at me and turned to fight his way toward where Dorothy was edging slowly but surely toward the secret exit.

The pandemonium in the ballroom was working against us, but at least it was slowing the guards down, too. A shrieking woman battering ineffectively at another man trying to tear the gold necklace from her throat lurched into the path of two guards headed in my direction. I shoved my way through the crowd and leapt onto the dais, where the Nome King stood, sneering.

"Well, well," he said. "If it isn't my old friend Miss Gumm."

He raised his hands again, preparing to throw another bolt of magic at me. If he hit me directly, I knew he would kill me. My magic was still weak, but I dug deep within myself, and managed to throw up a defensive shield just in time.

Then Lang was at my side. She hit the Nome King square in the chest with a fireball that set his velvet suit ablaze with blue and gold flames. He made a fist and punched the air and I felt the impact myself as his magical blow thudded into her jaw, snapping her head back. But she held her ground, advancing toward him. He made a fist, and she cried out, clutching at the silver bracelet around her wrist. It began to glow red and the metal seared its way into her skin. I winced at the smell of burning flesh.

"You ungrateful little traitor," he said, his voice dripping with hate. "I made you what you are. How dare you betray me?"

"You didn't make me into anything," Lang snarled through teeth gritted against the pain. She closed her eyes, screaming something I couldn't catch. As I watched in horror, her whole hand began to smoke. I realized, too late, what she was doing.

"Don't do it!" I screamed as her hand caught fire. The Nome King reached for her, but it was too late. The flesh of her hand blackened, sizzled, and peeled away, revealing charred bone and bloody gristle. The Nome King's bracelet slid off her mangled wrist and fell to the ground.

"I'm free," she said, panting. Her eyes were wild. The pain had to be unbearable. But Lang's determination wouldn't quit. "You can't hurt me anymore," she yelled. "*No one* can hurt me anymore." There was no mistaking the triumph in her voice now. She sounded exultant.

I wondered what she could have been in a different world. A world that didn't demand this kind of sacrifice. A world that didn't punish people for resisting tyranny. A world that didn't hurt you every chance it got.

It was too late for Lang. And now I would never know either.

The Nome King summoned another, enormous cloud of magic that hovered in the air above him, crackly with mystic fury.

He's going to kill her, I thought desperately. This close, there was no way he could miss.

But maybe I could still help her defend herself.

"Let me combine my magic with yours!" I screamed.

She just ignored me. The rippling nimbus over the Nome King's head glowed red-hot as the magic gathered into a single spear of jittery red light. He sent it hurtling toward her at the very second she lunged forward.

She was reaching for the knife at his belt. Her fingers closed around the handle as the bolt slammed into her body. She screamed—the most awful scream of pain I'd ever heard, and she crumpled against him.

He grabbed the front of her costume and held her aloft. I watched helplessly. "You think you can use my own weapon against me?" The Nome King cackled triumphantly, laughing at her limp form.

Lang's head lolled to the side and she looked at me. She was smiling. "Take care of Nox," she said to me. And then Langwidere buried the Nome King's knife in his chest to the hilt. Somehow she had managed to pull it from its sheath with her good hand. The metal flared with dark magic and burned into her palm, but she didn't let go.

A tremendous *boom* echoed through the cavern, knocking me to the ground with its force. Everything in the ballroom froze:

the Diggers attacking the guests, the guests fleeing the Diggers, the very air itself seemed to hold its breath. The Nome King's mouth dropped open in a round *O* of surprise. He brought one hand to his chest, looking down at the hilt protruding from it in shock.

"My own knife," he whispered. "You little traitor."

And then he toppled slowly backward and hit the ground with a thud.

I crawled forward to where Langwidere had collapsed on the dais.

Nox leapt onto the platform, with Madison close behind him He crouched over Lang's body, her breathing fast and shallow.

"How did you know that would work?" I asked her.

"I didn't." She grimaced; I realized she was trying to smile. "Glad it did."

"We have to get help," Nox said to Lang. "You're hurt. We have to get you back to the boat."

Lang's eyes were glazing over with pain.

"I'm not hurt," she whispered. "I'm dying."

"Don't say that," Nox said desperately.

She coughed weakly. "You never could handle the truth." Her eyes rolled toward me. "You're a good fighter, Amy. Now go find that bitch Dorothy and write my name with her blood."

I grabbed her hand. "I swear I will."

She smiled up at me, her eyelids closing. "And tell Melindra," she gasped, fighting for breath. "Tell her I said . . ."

But she never finished the sentence. As I watched, the rise

and fall of her chest slowed. And then it stopped.

"She's gone," Nox whispered. His eyes were brimming over with tears. I wiped away my own.

And then I looked around.

Dorothy and her little servant were gone.

We were alone.

TWENTY-ONE

"Grief later," I said, pulling Nox to his feet before he had time to let it all sink in. "We have to stop Dorothy and end this once and for all."

We raced down the narrow passage behind the Nome King's throne. I hoped that Madison was somewhere behind us, but now I could only worry about Dorothy.

We'd only been on the platform for moments; she couldn't have gotten too far. When I listened hard, I could even hear the echo of her footsteps, somewhere in the distance. We followed the twisting, turning hallway down innumerable branches and forks, and I had an odd certainty—for reasons I didn't totally understand—that we were gaining on her.

I was struck with déjà vu from the very first time I'd tried to kill her, when I'd chased her through the halls of the Emerald Palace, before the Tin Woodman came to her rescue. They say history repeats itself. I just hoped the ending was better this time.

Then the passage dead-ended at last in a large chamber, its walls covered floor to ceiling in bookshelves. Dorothy and her strange little servant—still dressed as a bush—were backed up against a shelf piled high with volumes bound in what looked an awful lot like human skin.

She'd taken a wrong turn, I realized. Now she was trapped.

There were three of us. There was one of her.

She realized her mistake at the same moment I did.

"*Dammit*," she said, rolling her eyes. "I should have made a map." She looked at my feet with a hateful expression. "I see you still have *my* shoes," she said.

"They're nobody's shoes," I said cautiously. My magic was still weak, but so was hers. If her defenses were down, plain old-fashioned hand-to-hand combat might do the trick where magic couldn't. "If anything, they belong to Lurline."

Lurline, I thought. If there was ever a good time to make a surprise appearance, now would be it. *Lurline*, I thought at my shoes. *Tell me what I need to do. Please.*

"Lur*line*," Dorothy said, rolling her eyes. "Whatever. Glinda gave them to *me*. No take-backs."

"And now you have a new pair," I pointed out. "So you don't need these." That was all it took to set her off: Dorothy threw herself at me like a little kid who'd been told Christmas had been canceled, spitting and screeching, and we fell to the floor. She raked her nails down my face, leaving long, bloody tracks, while her servant battered at my calves with a book. Nox was trying to pull Dorothy off me; Madison hit her

over the head with an inkwell. But Dorothy was like a force of
nature, unstoppable in her rage.

"Why won't you *just . . . leave . . . me . . . alone!*" she screamed,
banging my head into the floor with every word until I saw stars.
I elbowed her hard in the jaw and she gasped in pain but didn't
relax her grip.

"Lurline, tell me what to do!" I yelled.

We are made of what shapes us. Her voice echoed in my head.
The soothing power of her touch flowed through me.

My boots began to glow with silver light. Dorothy stopped
hitting me, her jaw slackening in surprise. Her outline—and
Madison's, and Nox's, and even the shrub's—began to shine
with the same silvery, angelic glow. The library around us shivered and dissolved.

And then it seemed to re-form. The air was charged with
magic. My shoes felt more alive than they had since we left Oz.

We were standing on an open, barren plain under a green-
hued sky. The Road of Yellow Brick glittered against the dusty
earth, winding its way toward the horizon. In the distance, I saw
a castle.

Overhead, storm clouds were gathering with a rumble of
thunder. I heard shrieks and howls from the sky and looked up
to see a group of winged monkeys circling through the air, spinning and diving. They were laughing, I realized. They hadn't
noticed us.

But they were looking right at us. It wasn't that they hadn't
noticed us.

They couldn't *see* us.

"I know this place," Dorothy said. Her voice sounded strange, as if something had come over her. Her face was dazed and her expression childlike as she gazed across the ghostly landscape. "I was here," she mumbled, almost to herself. "A long time ago. I was forced to work here."

Something in the way she said it startled me, and I realized that, although she was saying the words out loud, I could sense them coming before she actually spoke them. It was almost like her thoughts were flowing into mine.

It was all coming back to her. "I worked for the Wicked Witch of the West," she said. Or did she even say it?

Then I saw them both. A strangely familiar young girl in a white silk dress, her auburn hair tied back with a white bow and silver shoes on her feet. A small black dog danced nearby. Behind her loomed a one-eyed menacing figure. The girl was sweeping the dusty earth with a broom, over and over.

"She kept bees and crows and wolves," Dorothy said. "The Woodman killed them all. I didn't ask him to. Even then, he could be so cruel."

"That's Dorothy," Nox breathed, stepping close to me. "That's Dorothy when she first came to Oz and killed the Wicked Witch of the West." Of course. That's why this looked so familiar to me.

"I didn't mean to!" Dorothy—my Dorothy—cried. Her voice was still that high, strange, child's voice. Her eyes were full of tears. "I never wanted to hurt anyone! I didn't want to kill her!"

I felt a warmth in my feet and calves, and when I looked down, I saw that my boots were glowing so brightly with energy that I could barely make out their shape. The silvery magic was seeping out of them, and flowing in a shimmering stream, to where Dorothy stood, pooling around her ankles.

I didn't know why, or how, but I knew what was happening. Sort of. The shoes were connecting us to each other.

I didn't want to kill her. Dorothy's lips weren't moving anymore, but the words kept echoing in my head, as if it was a chant she was repeating to herself.

And for a brief, spinning second, I felt the ground drop out from under me as I thought of the night, long ago, on the terrace of the Emerald Palace, when I had almost killed *her*, and had stopped myself at the last minute.

The thought that had struck me in that moment so long ago came back to me.

Dorothy wasn't always like this. It wasn't until she killed the witch that she started to change.

I understood.

Before she killed the Wicked Witch of the West, Dorothy was just a little girl on a big adventure. After that, she was something else. Someone who'd taken a life needlessly. Someone who was open to evil. Not just Wickedness, but cruelty and suffering.

But what if I could change that? What if Lurline—by bringing us to this strange, frozen moment in the past—was giving me the opportunity not just to defeat Dorothy, but to undo all the damage that she had done?

If Dorothy never killed the witch, she would never become Dorothy the Witchslayer, the tyrant queen of Oz. She would never have come back to Oz a second time. All the death, the torture, and the pain that followed that would be undone as though it had never happened.

I didn't want to kill her.

That was it—Dorothy herself was the answer.

That was why I'd been brought here. Not because I was the only person who could kill Dorothy, but because I was so much like her: enough like her that I understood her, but different enough that I had chosen another way.

Everything I'd been through, everything I'd learned, every battle I'd fought, had all been part of my journey toward the truth. To knowing that another world was possible if we took responsibility for creating it.

But knowing and doing are two different things.

If we changed the past—if Dorothy Gale never returned to Oz to become a tyrant—it also meant I'd be undoing everything else, too. I'd be undoing the very thing that had brought me here, and everything that being here had accomplished.

More than that, it meant not knowing any of the friends I'd made here. It meant never knowing Nox.

Our eyes met. I could see the anguish in his face. The wheels must have been turning in his head just as they were in mine. He couldn't understand everything that was happening the way I could, but he could understand enough to know what was at stake.

I had the one thing I'd always wanted: the opportunity to

free Oz for good. But it would mean losing Nox forever. It might even mean losing myself. I wanted to shut my eyes against the pain in his face. To will my heart against the pain I felt, too.

But I couldn't. That was the whole point of everything. Dorothy would have chosen to be selfish. Now, as much as it hurt, I had to make the other choice.

"I love you," I said to Nox. "Always." Tears spilled over my cheeks as he nodded and reached his hand out toward me in a gesture of blessing. Or forgiveness. I wanted to say good-bye.

There was no time. Dorothy was wavering. She was looking up at me with a shattered, heartbroken expression, and I knew, without really knowing, that she'd just heard every thought I'd had. All the magic of Oz, and Ev—all the magic of everywhere—was flowing through our shoes, flowing so strongly between us that we were glimpsing the rawest part of each other's soul.

"Dorothy," I said urgently. "You don't have to kill her." I wasn't sure who I was talking to: Was it the grown-up Dorothy I'd come to despise so much, or the little girl standing motionless before us, who still had a chance?

But the little girl couldn't hear me. She was carrying a bucket of water. It steamed in the cool air: not with heat. With magic. Her face was set. She was looking up at the witch, her mouth twisted in a petulant scowl.

The grown-up turned her eyes in my direction, her eyes blank.

"She hurt Toto, and she put the Lion in a cage," grown-up Dorothy said. "I had to stop her."

Her expression suddenly melted from calm into anger, and when she spoke again, the seething rage in her voice shook my whole body.

"I hate her," she snarled. "She deserved to die for what she did."

"No," I said. "You know you never meant to kill anyone. All you had to do was stop her. All you *wanted* to do was stop her. That's who you were, then. Who you can still be."

Dorothy cocked her head to the side as though she was remembering something. "I never wanted to hurt anyone. Not the witches. Not Aunt Em or Uncle Henry either. I just wanted to get my way."

I'd forgotten. The Wicked Witch of the West wasn't her only victim in those early days—her family was, too. But this was the first time I'd heard her blame anyone other than Ozma for their deaths. This was the first time she had ever taken responsibility. I felt a well of hope opening up inside of me. Was I getting through to her?

"What happened to them wasn't your fault. It was an accident." There were tears in her eyes now. "They wouldn't have wanted this for you."

I looked her right in the eye.

"You can change things."

"Tin...Scare...the Lion...Toto...all their blood is on my hands." She wiped her hands on her dress as if the blood was literal.

"Dorothy..." I said.

Nox and Madison were holding their breath. I could see it in their eyes: now they understood.

She shook her head suddenly and closed her eyes. "Auntie Em would be so proud," she said bitterly.

"So make her proud now."

Dorothy blinked her tears away, hard. "What's done is done," she snapped, her face blazing. "You can't go home again. I read that on a pillow!"

I tried again. "It never had to be this way. This is your chance to change it all. You can bring them back—Em, Henry, Scare, Tin, the Lion—they'll be alive again. It will be like none of this ever happened."

Around us, Oz—its past, its present, and maybe even its future—was frozen as Dorothy struggled to make sense of who she was, and of how she'd come to this moment. I could feel her hesitation as she struggled to decide between the world she knew—the world she had come to love—and the world she thought she'd lost.

It was a feeling I understood better than I would have liked to.

"I'm strong now," she hissed. "I'm a queen. Who'd want to change that? So I killed them. It only made me stronger, didn't it?"

She was saying it all with conviction, but I knew she wasn't sure. All she needed was a push. So instead of thinking of her, I thought of myself.

"Did it?" I asked.

But she turned away from me, and I knew my words weren't reaching her anymore.

I closed my eyes and thought of Kansas.

Madison had been right. When I'd told her I put all my old hurt and pain in my rearview, didn't mean I had let go of them. I was still holding on to Salvation Amy. I was still holding on to every unkind word and thing that had happened to me along the way.

I thought of my mother. I thought of Nox, and Pete, and even Madison and Mombi: all the people who'd helped to pull me back from the edge of my own darkness, whether they'd known it or not.

I called back all the hatred I'd ever had, against people back in Kansas as well as here in Oz. I let go of all the feelings I'd had growing up in Kansas with my addict, absent mom, the resentment toward my dad for basically abandoning me, and the anger I'd felt for all the bullies and people who'd ostracized me at school. Including Madison. Especially Madison. Finally, I called up my feelings about Dorothy herself. She'd taken so much from me, and Oz. I even let go of my wrath-filled feelings for Glinda.

When I opened my eyes, I saw a ball of red fire was suspended in the air. "I forgive you," I said out loud. Like a mantra. Like a prayer. No—like a spell. The ball of fire dissipated into thin air.

I looked at Dorothy and repeated the words. "I forgive you."

I expected a scoff. But Dorothy didn't say anything. She was standing a few feet away from the girl she'd once been. A girl who was still innocent and guileless, and untainted by the blood that would soon stain her hands forever.

When she took a last step forward, the magic from our shoes rippled like she was wading through water.

Silently, and with a certain kind of gentleness, Dorothy put a hand on the little girl's shoulder. The girl looked up at her with a wide-eyed trust, as she saw herself for the first time.

That could have been me. I could have been her. Change a few things, and it would have been so easy for me to do what she had done—to become what she became. We all have a witch somewhere inside us.

As for the real witch, the Wicked Witch of the West: her face was frozen in fear, knowing what was about to happen.

Dorothy didn't let it.

She looked back at me one last time.

"Good-bye, Amy," she said. And then she took the bucket from the hands of her younger self, paused for the briefest of moments, then upended it over her own head.

The air around us held still.

Then the world fell apart.

TWENTY-TWO

I could hear Nox and Madison shouting something but everything was dark. A tiny hand clutched my own, its palm clammy with fear: Dorothy's servant, I realized. We were falling through darkness, the wind whistling around us.

Not darkness. This place was familiar. The Darklands. Something was pulling us back from the past. Some force so powerful that I could feel it like a tidal wave dragging me from shore.

Don't be afraid, Amy. I'm bringing you home.

That voice. So familiar.

"Ozma," I whispered.

A single spark sprang to life in front of me. It spread outward and took shape. Ozma hovered before me, radiant and calm. Her face was peaceful but her eyes were horribly, horribly sad.

"Oh, Amy," she said gently. "I'm so, so sorry."

"Why?" I asked, dazed. "Where are we? The Darklands?"

She smiled. "Neither here nor there, past nor present. We're in the place in between while Oz repairs itself."

"How are you—but we—" I couldn't shape the words.

"I'm a fairy," Ozma said simply. "Time is not the same for us. The world is not the same for us. I remember everything that has come before and that will come after."

I looked around me for Nox and Madison and Dorothy's servant. They were fast asleep on the ground. Only Ozma and I were conscious.

I could feel my heart splitting apart in my chest. I had done it. I'd undone everything that Dorothy had done to Oz.

And that meant the person I loved more than I'd ever loved anything in the world had no idea who I was. But how had I not forgotten him?

"You will never forget what you have been through," Ozma said quietly, almost as though she could read my mind—which she probably could. "And for that, I am so sorry. You have saved Oz, Amy, but we have asked so much of you. No one should have to sacrifice what you have sacrificed."

"Nox," I said brokenly. She nodded.

"It was a terrible thing to ask of you," she said. "But you chose well, Amy. You chose the good of all over the desires of your heart. And for that, there is one thing I can give you in return."

She bent over Nox and kissed him on the forehead. *"North, South, East, West, wind, fire, sun, earth, protect him and keep him. Protect him and keep him."*

I recognized those words: they were the blessing Gert had

spoken to me in the aftermath of my first battle. The first time I'd killed someone in Oz. The words she'd told me would keep me safe.

She'd been right. After all, I was still alive. And now Ozma was protecting Nox. I was grateful to her for that much.

Nox moaned and stirred. I wanted to reach out, push the hair out of his eyes the way I'd done a thousand times. But he didn't know who I was anymore. I was a stranger. I fought back a sob.

He opened his eyes and looked at me in incomprehension. *It's always going to be like this,* I thought. *He's never going to know what we shared.*

"Look closer," Ozma said to me, smiling. "A fairy's kiss is a powerful thing, Amy."

"Amy?" Nox said. He blinked at me, his gaze focusing. "You're alive!" he said, leaping to his feet. "I thought—"

He remembered me. Ozma's kiss hadn't been for protection. She'd given him back our history.

And now, like an idiot, I was crying again. Somehow I didn't mind. Nox threw his arms around me and I sank into his embrace. I think time might have stopped. I'm pretty sure my heart did. It was too much. Over Nox's shoulder, Ozma's smile was turning into a genuine grin.

"Amy," Nox said hoarsely, pulling me close and burying his face in my hair. "I thought I lost you. I thought you were gone."

"I thought I lost you, too," I said. I wasn't the only one crying, at least.

"There is one more gift I can give you, Amy," Ozma said. "I

can send you and Madison home at last. Whichever home you choose. Remember, if you stay in Oz, no one will know you. No one will know what you've been through or what you've done. No one but him." She nodded toward Nox. "Or I can return you to Kansas. Those who belong there," she added, glancing again in Nox's direction.

"I don't know where Kansas is," Dorothy's shrub creature said in a tiny voice.

Ozma laughed merrily. "You, my dear Munchkin, belong here in Oz. You are free at last. Free to return to your family, if you wish. Or free to see the world. Whatever you choose, my protection will follow you always."

"She's gone?" The Munchkin's face was astonished. "And I'm . . . *free?*"

"Indeed," Ozma said. "And now, Amy, I am afraid you must choose."

But I'd already chosen. I'd chosen, I realized, a long time ago. I looked at Nox, and started crying harder. "Nox," I managed to squeak out through the tears.

"That face—you never managed to build a wall instead of a window," he said, lifting my chin up.

He remembered the first compliment he'd ever given me when I was in training. "You said you liked it."

"I said you'd have to change it if you were ever going to take out Dorothy. Looks like I was wrong." He smiled, but the smile stopped before it reached his eyes. He knew what I was going to say but I had to say it.

"I have to go home," I said. "I have to go to my real home, Nox. To my mom."

"I know," he said, kissing me. "I have to let you go."

I felt a physical pain in my chest like I could barely breathe. It hurt more than anything I'd ever felt in my life. More than my mom leaving me behind over and over again.

Finally, Nox would be able to see Oz the way it had once been. As the place he'd been fighting for his entire life.

I just couldn't see it with him.

"Oz is going to be so beautiful, just like you told me it used to be."

Nox shook his head. "Not as beautiful as you." It was the most unNox thing to say. I felt myself trying not to laugh. I guess I'd changed him, too.

"You are both very brave and very strong," Ozma said. She nodded at Madison, who was still sleeping serenely. "Amy, undoing time in Oz is not the same as undoing it in your world. Both of you will carry this journey with you always."

She turned to me and Nox and rested her palms on the tops of our heads. I felt her magic moving through me, cool and cleansing as a glacier-fed stream.

"Everything that has happened before will happen again, and forever is not always forever," she said cryptically. And then she grinned. "Besides, you still have the shoes."

I looked down at my feet. She was right. I turned to her.

"Do you mean . . ." I didn't even want to say it out loud.

But she just smiled. "It's time," she said. "I'll let you say good-bye." And then she winked.

I buried my face in Nox's chest, sobbing into his shirt as he wrapped his arms tightly around me. He was still wearing the panther costume. He smelled the way he always did: sandalwood. "I love you," I said.

"I love you, too, Amy." He kissed the top of my head and then my lips. I lost myself in his kiss. The memory of being with him in Lang's hideaway. Everything we'd been through together.

Letting go of him was the hardest thing I'd ever done.

"I'm not going to say good-bye," Nox said, reaching forward to tuck a strand of my hair behind my ear. "Because this isn't good-bye."

"Someday, over the rainbow..." I said. We kissed again. But it was different from all the other kisses. It was good-bye. I felt the gravity in the kiss and it took everything in me not to give in and change my mind.

When we finally parted, he just smiled that knowing smile of his and held my gaze with his pale gray eyes.

"Thank you, Amy," Ozma said. And then in a blinding flash of silver light, Ozma and Nox and Bupu disappeared.

I blinked and my vision cleared. Madison and I were in the middle of the sidewalk in front of the drugstore in Flat Hill. The air was hot and still and no one was out on the streets. It was the middle of the afternoon.

I didn't know what day it was. I wasn't even sure what *year*. But I was home.

"What the *fuck* just happened?" Madison said, sitting up.

"Hi, Madison," I said. "Glad you're awake."

"I feel like I just got run over by a *truck*," she moaned, grabbing her head dramatically. "What happened? Where's Dorothy? Is Nox moving to Flat Hill? Are we home?"

Home. It had been a long time. And now *home* meant a lot of different things. Nox, Oz, Kansas.

But in Oz, I'd learned to finish what I started. And my mom and I weren't done. Not by a long shot. Kansas might not be home in the way it had been before Oz, but it was where I'd come from. And, like Dorothy, I had to make peace with the past before I could face the future.

Especially now that I knew I was strong enough.

"Yes, Madison. We're back in Kansas."

"Well," Madison said, looking around. "This is going to take some getting used to again."

"You're telling me," I said.

"What exactly are we going to tell people about . . . wherever we went?"

"You'll think of something," I said.

"Do we really have to go back to *high school* after all of that?"

"I don't know," I said. "I guess we could get our GEDs."

Madison sighed and kicked at a pebble. "I guess I could just tell people I was on, like, a really extended acid trip."

"Sounds about right. You ready to see your kid?"

"Oh my god," Madison said, a huge grin spreading across her face. "Tell me you remembered to bring a diaper-changing spell back with you." Then she got serious again. "Listen, Ames, I'm sorry I doubted you. And thanks. For keeping your promise."

"I would have doubted me, too," I said. "I mean, considering the circumstances."

"Yeah, there's that." She looked at me thoughtfully for a moment. "For a boyfriend-stealing trailer park ho you're pretty all right, you know that?"

"For a glitter-crusted head-cheerleading queen bitch, you're not so bad yourself," I said, laughing.

"Well," she said, taking a deep breath. "If we do go back to school, this is gonna be a hell of a senior year."

I smiled. "What can I say? There's no place like home."

Madison groaned in protest, but I was already walking down the street.

"Come on," I said. "Let's go tell these people we're alive."

Flat Hill was never going to be the same again, I thought.

But then again, neither was I.

TWENTY-THREE

I never thought of myself as a hero. Heroes sacrificed themselves for others. And for most of my life I didn't think I had anything to give. But I had saved Oz and lived to tell about it. And no one in either world—save two fairies and Nox—knew about it. That was the definition of sacrifice, right? But I wasn't so sure. What I had gotten from Oz seemed to somehow outweigh what I had given on the balance sheet. That time on the other side of the Rainbow had shaped me. Changed me. And the girl staring back at me in the mirror in Kansas wasn't the same one who had been picked up by the tornado all those months ago.

When I'd shown up at my mom's door a few days ago, I hadn't offered much of an explanation of where I'd been. After all that time in Oz, it turned out I'd only been gone from Kansas for two days. Time really did pass differently in the two places, but I never could figure out exactly how.

Mom hadn't pressed me for answers—yet. But I could tell

she was watching me carefully and wondering. Maybe she was afraid to ask.

I stepped out of the bathroom and did a dramatic hair flip. "What do you think, Mom?" I asked.

"Wow, Amy, it's ... different." She looked down at her hands. "You're different. No more pink?"

"I think I was meant to be a blonde."

I couldn't really give a damn what color my hair was anymore, but the truth was that I couldn't let go of Oz. Glamora had magically changed my hair to blond and I liked keeping a reminder with me. This morning I had chopped three inches and it now grazed my shoulders in an edgy bob instead of hanging down my back.

Mom had offered to take me to the mall for the cut and color. But I couldn't see spending the money.

"You'll be okay getting to school? Are you sure you don't want me to drive you?"

"I'll be fine, Mom. It's a two-minute walk. Besides, Madison is picking me up."

Mom frowned. For Mom, Madison would always be the girl who had disinvited the entire first grade class from my birthday party.

As if it wasn't bad enough that I had to go back to school, to add insult to irony, Mom had told me last night that my high school had temporarily moved to empty trailers in the Dusty Acres Trailer Park while the school was being rebuilt. Glamora and the Nome King-as-Assistant-Principal Strachan had caused just a little bit of damage when they had opened a portal between Kansas and Oz. You can take the girl out of the trailer park . . . but then her high school ends up holding classes there.

I slipped my feet into my boots. I wore them every day. They were silver and sparkly and Mom had never asked where I'd gotten them. What would I say if she'd asked?

My mother's words stopped me before I reached the door.

"Amy? Wherever it was that you went—I know you came back for me. To take care of me. I want you to know that I am okay. That you don't have to worry about me, darling . . ."

"Are you trying to get rid of me?" I said lightly.

"The first time you went I put up posters and I searched for you . . . this time I knew better. You weren't somewhere I could find you—I'm right, aren't I?"

I couldn't answer with words. I nodded.

"Were you happy there?"

"Mom, it was—" How did I sum up Oz? It was scary and amazing and harder and more wonderful than anything I had ever imagined. "It was . . . magical," I said finally.

"If anyone is overdue some magic . . . it's you."

"Well, I'm here now, Mom," I said, and I meant it. "I'm back." Some part of me would always be in Oz, but I was determined to find my footing here. My mother kissed me on the forehead and went off to join Jake in the kitchen, where they were making breakfast. I watched her for a few minutes as they huddled over an egg casserole. Every day she was more herself—not the woman I remembered from my youth before the pills, but something new. She seemed to have made it through the storm that we'd lived in for all those years, and she was rebuilding herself from the ground up.

I still had some work to do.

Madison was waiting outside for me with a Starbucks cup and a smile. She knew how hard it had been for me to leave Nox behind, and even though she didn't bring him up, she was helpful in her way—offering advice I was sure was ripped from one of the pages of a magazine. The articles she read were breakup ones. But I was pretty sure *Cosmo* didn't cover "How to Lose a Guy After You Saved His World and Left Him on the Other Side of the Rainbow."

Dustin was at her side, standing a little closer to her than the last time I'd seen them together. I could see them inching back together, and every touch and laugh and little joke reminded me of what I had had on the other side and lost. But I was happy for them and happy for their companionship. They were the only friends I had.

But my other classmates had not forgotten Salvation Amy, the nickname that Madison had given me before we were BFFs. People whispered and pointed as I walked past. But I shook them off. I was a different Amy.

So when I slipped into my desk in the trailer and someone tapped me on the shoulder, I didn't even bother to turn around.

The person tapped again.

This time I whipped around, prepared to return fire. But instead, I found I was staring into the only eyes I wanted to see, sitting in the desk right behind mine.

"Nox!"

Without hesitation, I climbed over my desk and into his lap. I pressed my lips to his, and the whole of Dusty Acres melted away.

Nox was laughing and kissing me and trying to talk at the same time.

"You cut your hair!" He ran his fingers through my short strands. I broke away and swatted him.

"*That's* the first thing you say to me? What are you doing here? I don't understand. Aren't you supposed to be watching over Oz? It's your home!" I was laughing and almost crying.

Nox just smiled, tucked my hair behind my ear, and filled me in: "Ozma's in charge now, and she can handle it. She's the one true ruler. And I'm the only one besides her who remembers everything that happened. Everything that Dorothy did to our home." He paused, and a tentative smile spread across his face. "But it didn't feel like home without you, Amy. Oz is safe now, and my place is with you. Wherever you are."

"Ahem." The teacher, Mrs. Labine, cleared her throat beside us. But Nox, oblivious to classroom customs—and, well, just being Nox—ignored her. "This is not the time and place for public displays of affection. In my class we sit in our *own* seats, Ms. Gumm and Mr. . . . ."

"I'm Nox. I'm new here."

And just like that Nox became a student at Dwight D. Eisenhower Senior High. There were logistics of course. Nox had to become an emancipated minor and we had to falsify some documents. The administration didn't really look that closely—no one would want to go to Dwight D. Eisenhower Senior High unless they *really* had to. And, frankly, after our assistant principal brought the school down, enrollment was kind of at an all-time low.

Nox, of course, being Nox, had come prepared for life in the Other Place. He had a stash of jewels from Ozma to pawn for cash and use to pay for an apartment. Madison and I took him to the mall and dressed him up like a real Kansas boy. Even in dark jeans and dark T-shirts, he still looked otherworldly in the best possible way.

If you thought people were whispering about me before, you should have seen the looks on Tiffany's and the others' faces when they saw me walking around with Nox by my side.

In an unlikely twist, Nox and Dustin had an instant bromance. I think Nox was just happy to have his first guy friend after years of living with all those witches and assorted creatures. Dustin—ever the jock—recruited Nox to the football team. Nox's reflexes were just as fast even without purple magic flashing from his hands. To Dustin's surprise, mine were, too, when I joined in their pickup games. My very physical training with the Order had turned me into something of an athlete. It was actually a nice way to get out my aggression. I hadn't gotten into a single fight since I'd been back.

It was books that were the challenge for Nox. I tutored him in the earthly subjects he knew nothing about. And I admit, it felt good to be the one schooling him, for a change.

The next few weeks and months progressed, but not without some hiccups. It wasn't easy for either of us to get used to a world without magic. More than once I caught Nox flicking his wrist or reaching for some shortcut spell that wasn't there for the most mundane things. Magic was like breathing for Nox, and it had become a part of me, too.

Mom was doing better every day. She'd gotten a job at the elementary school assisting kindergarteners. And Jake was hanging in there, somehow more in love with Mom every day, unlike any other boyfriend she'd ever had, including Dad. I still hadn't talked to my father, even though he had actually called during my second disappearance. Maybe one day I would return the call, but not anytime soon. Although I had learned forgiveness, and I had balled up all my hurt and pain and sent it away in a burst of fire, I had seen more of my life without him than with him. And I wasn't ready to change that yet.

I began to make plans. Not the battle plans I had gotten so used to. The kind that involve college brochures and transcripts and tests. I had never really decided what I wanted to do, except, "be anywhere but here." But now I thought about it. A lot. It was like all these new doors were open to me. I couldn't exactly put "Savior of Oz" on a résumé, but I started to wonder if there was a way to apply what I was good at and what I had learned in Oz to the real world.

But as I tried to write college-application essays, I found myself stumped because the thing I wanted most to write about was the one thing I couldn't. I saw Glamora in purple eyeshadow palettes at the mall. I saw Gert in the pond I passed on the way to school. I saw Mombi in every spider web. I saw Indigo in every bubble, and the Lion lurking behind every tree.

Sometimes I felt like I understood Dorothy more and more. It wasn't just killing the witch that changed her—it was also coming home, back to Kansas, and leaving Oz behind. She had experienced magic and power and had been surrounded by friends. She had left Technicolor for sepia-tinged black and white. And I had done the same. Even with Nox at my side, I felt myself yearning for Oz.

I saw my own restlessness reflected back at me when I looked at him sometimes. He fidgeted constantly and had trouble sitting still in the tiny desks we had at school. He was accustomed to battles, and so was I now.

But other times he seemed to just be at peace, happy to be someplace where there was no war. Prom was on the horizon, and I'm not even kidding, the theme was "Somewhere Over the Rainbow." Madison had suggested that we wear gingham for irony. But I did not want to tempt fate. And prom wasn't exactly a thing I had ever aspired to. I wasn't a prom person. Madison disagreed. She said everyone was a prom person—it was a seminal event like being born or going to the mall for the first time or One Direction breaking up.

Madison was always trying to remind me that there was magic in this world, too. We just had to work a lot harder to see it. I wasn't convinced about prom but I did see the magic. Holding Dustin Jr. (when he wasn't screaming his lungs out) and feeling him wrap his little fingers around my thumb, my mom's clean and sober laugh, getting an A-plus on my math test. And

Nox was magic. On my good days, I was magic, too.

One day after school Nox led me to a corner of the trailer park—the corner where I used to live, where the tornado that had first taken me to Oz had left behind a twisted graveyard of metal.

"What are we doing here, Nox?" I asked. I didn't need a reminder of this part of my past.

Nox ran over to the nearest intact trailer and plugged in what looked like an extension cord. The corner of the park lit up and I could see that there was a landscape painted on one of the trailers: the moving mountain range in Oz where we had shared out first kiss. Over it Nox had written in surprisingly perfect script, "Will you go to prom with me?"

Inexplicably, I started to cry. Nox took a step toward his handiwork as if contemplating turning out the lights. He didn't know what to do.

"Why are you crying? Did I do something wrong?" he asked, clearly confused. It just made me cry harder.

"Did you know the prom theme is 'Somewhere Over the Rainbow'?" I managed between sobs.

"That makes you cry?"

"Nox, do you ever wonder—what if we wake up one day and wish we had been there all along?"

"Then we go back. But I for one don't want to miss my first prom."

I leaned in to kiss him, but just as my lips met his a silver glow lit up our faces. I gasped and looked down. My boots. The boots were glowing.

"Amy," Nox breathed. "Has this ever happened before?"

I shook my head. "I thought I didn't have power here."

Nox frowned. "Maybe you don't. Maybe this is coming from somewhere else."

"But who? The only people in Oz who still remember me—besides you—are Lurline and Ozma. And they are also the only ones who would know how to use the magic in these shoes. Do you think . . .? But it couldn't possibly mean—"

"That they're calling you back?"

"They need me to return to Oz."

"What about your mom? What about your—our—life here?"

I wasn't a hero but I was no coward either—going back to Oz had something in it for me, something more than the fight itself.

"Kansas is a part of me—but so is Oz. And Ozma wouldn't contact me unless she absolutely needed to."

Nox had said home was where we were together. Dorothy had chosen Kansas and then Oz. But perhaps home wasn't so black and white. Just like Good and Wicked had turned out to be much more complicated than I ever imagined. There was magic on both sides of the rainbow. And there was no law that said that I had to choose one place over another forever.

I looked down at the shoes again.

What was it she had done? It was worth a try.

I took Nox's hand. He looked at me and nodded.

And I knocked my sparkly heels together three times.

ACKNOWLEDGMENTS

To my Munchkins: When I started writing Dorothy I didn't know any of you. Now you are a part of my story and my heart. Thank you for all the love you have shown Dorothy and the enormous gift you have given me. Every tweet, video, blog, piece of fan art, and kind word took me and Dorothy farther down our road than I ever dreamed. Amy and Dorothy both found friends and magic along the Road of Yellow Brick. Thanks to all of you, I did, too.

To Joanna Volpe, for being my champion and my friend. You fight the good fight and bring the magic. You make the impossible, possible. I am so glad to have you at my side.

To Pouya Shabazian, for understanding my commercial heart and finding places for me to pitch it.

To Team New Leaf: Jackie, Jaida, Mike, Kathleen, Mia, Chris, Hilary, and Danielle, you are rock stars and the wind beneath my pages! Thank you, thank you, thank you . . .

Many thanks to my fearless editors, Tara Weikum and Jocelyn Davies. Dorothy wouldn't be here if you didn't say yes to killing one of the most beloved characters of all time!

To Ray Shappell and Erin Fitzsimmons—for making covers so beautiful that people have to pick them up.

To Team Harper! I adore you all! You used our heart, brains, and courage to get Dorothy into the world. Margot Wood, you were one of Dorothy's first friends (and now one of mine!), and with our brilliance, you helped build her epic squad! Hugs! Ro Romanello and Stephanie Hoover, my publicity goddesses. Thanks for taking such good care of me and making it so much fun! Elizabeth Ward, you Ozian genius, thank you for metaphorically and literally painting me a Road of Yellow Brick for all to see!

And to Kate Jackson and Suzanne Murphy, thank you for keeping Dorothy on the road.

To my family and friends, I love you and thank you for being there every time I step out of Oz and back into real life. Mommy, Daddy, Andrea, Josh, Sienna. You are my heart. Bonnie Datt, you had me at Nanette Lepore, and kept me with your generosity and kindred-spirit friendship. Annie, Chris, Fiona, and Jackson Rolland, thank you for being my beloved second family and second home at least until the zombie apocalypse.

Lauren, Logan, Jasper, and Joe Dell. Laur, from J.Crew catalog to besties, you are just as generous and amazing now as you were then. Carin Greenberg, for being my oracle. Paloma Ramirez, proud of your new journey (and miss you to pieces!).

Daryn Strauss, my partner in reaching for the stars. Leslie Rider, for your razor-sharp wit chased by utter kindness.

To Sasha Alsberg, look at you all grown up! So proud of you and so glad I met you on the way to prom.

Josh Sabarra, all the advice and texts and tweets kept me going! Love you, babe!

Kami Garcia, Kass Morgan, Jennifer Armentrout, Kiera Cass, Melissa de la Cruz, Margie Stohl, and the countless other writer friends who understand and make everything better.

My Guiding Light family, Jill Lorie Hurst, Tina Sloan, Crystal Chappell, Beth Chamberlin, Alison Goodman, Jordi Vilasuso, and all the fans who still keep the light alive.

Special thanks to Crystal for rallying Team Venice. And to Sasha Mote, for being such a friend to Dorothy.

Lexi Dwyer, Lisa Tollin, Jeanne Marie Hudson, Megan Steintrager, Kristen Nelthorpe, Tom Nelthorpe, Ernesto Munoz, Mark Kennedy, Maggie Shi, Leslie Kendall Dye, Sandy and Don Goodman, Mike Wynne, Matt Wang, Seth Nagel, Kerstin Conrad, Chris Lowe, Steve McPherson, Lanie Davis, Harry and Sue Kojima, and all the other friends who know I love them but I have been on deadline for four years so you will forgive me for not thinking of you until after I sent this in.

And finally, to L. Frank Baum. I fell in love with your world when I was five. I am so honored to have gotten to borrow it for a little while.

READ MORE ABOUT LANADEL BEFORE SHE BECAME PRINCESS LANGWIDERE IN:

"Again!" Nox barked, and Lanadel gritted her teeth, preparing to repeat the knife stroke he'd just taught her for what felt like the hundredth time. She'd known training with the Order of the Wicked was going to be difficult, but she hadn't realized it was going to be *ridiculous*. She was dripping with sweat, her dark hair clinging to her neck in damp tendrils. Back home, her brothers had always given her a hard time about her wild, untamable curls that refused to stay put in a ladylike bun. They'd teased her mercilessly, pulling the loose strands like she was—

Lanadel stopped that thought cold in its tracks. Her brothers were dead, and that was why she was here. Thinking about them now wasn't going to bring them back. Their loss was so recent that every time her mind wandered she forgot they were gone. Forgot that she couldn't just go home after fighting practice, punch Beech in the shoulder on her way to fight Rowan for a loaf of their mother's fresh-baked bread . . .

Nox's fist connected squarely with her cheek, snapping her head back and sending her reeling. "Monkey's nuts!" she yelled, bringing her hand to her swelling cheek. "What the Ev did you do that for?"

"If we'd been on the battlefield instead of in the training caves, I'd have killed you," Nox said coldly, his gray eyes hard. "You can't let yourself get distracted in the middle of a fight."

Lanadel bit down on another curse. Nox was a ruthless teacher, merciless and sometimes even cruel, but he knew what he was doing. She knew he was right. And if there was anyone in Oz more stubborn than Nox, it was her—and there was no way she was going to let him see her cry.

"Right," she said, steeling herself. "Let's do it again." She was satisfied to see a flicker of surprise in Nox's eyes. She might not have his skills, but he couldn't beat her in willpower. She'd always been tenacious, but when her family died, her heart had turned as hard as the jewels that studded the walls of the Emerald City. She'd come to the Order to learn not just how to fight, but how to kill. And when she was ready, she was going to make Dorothy's minions suffer for everything they'd done to her family. She'd make sure their deaths were as slow and as painful as her family's had been. Right now, her will was the only thing keeping her from joining her brothers in whatever world Ozians went to when they died. For the first time in her life, she was alone. And since the loss of her family hadn't killed her, she was going to make their killers pay.

Lanadel gripped the hilt of the short obsidian knife Nox had given her that morning and dropped into a fighting stance. If Nox was feeling particularly nasty, he'd use magic on her, but for now he was circling her with slow, measured steps, his crouch matching her own as he searched her defenses for a weakness. He lunged toward her with lightning speed but she parried his knife strike with the ringing sound of stone on stone and he danced back, resuming his circle. *Concentrate,* she told herself. Sometimes Nox favored his left side, just barely—but just enough. There it was, just the slightest give in his step. She saw her opening and feinted to the right. When Nox went to deflect her blow, she dropped into a somersault and kicked his left leg out from under him as she jumped out of the roll. He lost his balance—but not his nerve. As he lurched forward he grabbed her shoulder, throwing her to the ground and landing on top of her. "Checkmate," he growled, his knife at her throat.

"Look down," she said. He did, and rewarded her with the briefest flash of a smile. Her own blade was pressed up against his heart.

"Not bad," he said grudgingly, rolling off her and to his feet in a single fluid motion. He extended one hand to her but she ignored it, pushing herself up on her own. Her head was ringing from Nox's earlier punch and she could feel her eye swelling shut. She'd twisted her ankle when he'd thrown her to the ground, too, though the injury was nothing a quick soak in the healing pool couldn't fix. But her training uniform was ripped in half a dozen places. She was bloody, bruised, and stinking—and Nox wasn't even out of breath. His thick, dark hair was unmussed.

He hadn't even broken a sweat. It was infuriating. As if he could read her mind, he gave her a dismissive look.

"You're getting better but you still have a long way to go," he said in his now-familiar, cool, distant tone. "You'll need to pick up the pace if you want to fight with the Order. We don't have room for weaklings."

Fury surged up in her, but she wasn't going to show him he'd gotten to her. "I've only been training for a few weeks," she said, keeping her voice even.

He shrugged. "Time isn't a luxury we have here. We're on the brink of war."

"You don't have to tell me that," she said. She hadn't told him about her family—only Gert knew that, and as far as she knew Gert had kept the information to herself.

"Apparently I do," he said coldly. "You need to work much harder than you have been if you expect to be able to be of any use to us. We're done for today; get that ankle to the pool. We meet again at sunrise tomorrow."

"Yes sir," she said sarcastically under her breath, but he was already striding away. Lanadel sighed and pulled her hair out of its totally ineffective ponytail. "You asked for this," she muttered to herself as she followed him out of the training cave and toward the healing pool.

TWO

But when she got to the pool, she wasn't alone. Another girl was there already, making half-anguished, half-ecstatic noises as she thrashed around in the warm, clear water. No one had ever bothered to explain the pool's magic to Lanadel; it just worked. You got into it injured, and you came out healed, no matter how hard a beating you'd taken in practice—but the worse you felt, the more it hurt to get better. Which was probably some kind of metaphor for real life, but Lanadel was doing everything she could not to think too much about the real world.

"Sorry," she said, embarrassed, and the other girl's eyes flew open.

"I didn't realize anyone was here!" she exclaimed. She was pretty—almost *too* pretty, with long, gold hair that swirled behind her in the water, clear green eyes, and a heart-shaped, pouting mouth. And she was totally naked. And she was totally ripped.

"N-no, it's my fault," Lanadel stammered, realizing she was

babbling as she desperately tried not to look at the other girl in the pool. Living in a house with boys, she had seen plenty of them naked without wanting to. They were completely without shame. Conversely, no one had seen her naked for as long as she could remember. Lanadel's eyes found a safe space on the surface of the water as she wondered who the naked girl was. Was she another recruit? Lanadel had never seen her before, but people came and went a lot in the caves, and she hadn't been there long.

"Oh, don't be silly," the girl exclaimed. She fluttered one hand in the water, splattering Lanadel with sparkling, crystalline droplets. "There's plenty of room, you just startled me." She looked Lanadel up and down appraisingly. "And no offense, but you look like you need the pool even more than I do."

"Yeah, uh, thanks," Lanadel said, still stumbling on her words. The village she'd grown up in had been tiny, and other than her brothers, she hadn't had friends. She didn't know much about how to act around other people, and she definitely didn't know much about how to act around other girls. Whoever this girl was, she was calm and confident and completely unflustered by the fact that she was talking to someone without her clothes on. Was Lanadel supposed to just get naked, too? Averting her eyes and blushing furiously, she pulled off her tattered training clothes and slunk into the pool, hissing in pain as the water met her bruises and cuts.

"It's the worst," the other girl said sympathetically. "Oh my god, believe me, it's just the worst. For months, honestly, until you get used to it. You're new, right?"

"Yeah," Lanadel said, still wincing. But she was still grateful the pain took her mind off of the fact that they were naked. "I've only been here a few weeks."

"The first few weeks are the hardest," the other girl said. "It gets easier, though, I promise. Pretty soon you won't even notice how much it hurts." She laughed. "I'm Melindra," the other girl added. "I've been fighting with the Order for a while now. Plenty long enough to know that"—she held up one hand, ticking her points off on her fingers with the other—"Mombi's nuts, Gert's a sweetheart, Glamora's way smarter than she looks, and Nox is an asshole." She frowned thoughtfully. "He's a hot asshole, though," she admitted. "And he doesn't flirt. Ever."

Lanadel burst into laughter for the first time since she'd turned up outside the caves, clamoring to be taught how to fight. "You tried *flirting* with him?"

"Well, obviously," Melindra said, yawning. "Once you figure out how to disarm him, there's not much else to do here. I mean, they'll teach you magic, obviously. But probably not for a bit. They make you learn to fight the hard way first." She rolled her eyes, making quotation marks with her fingers. "Because there's no telling what Dorothy will throw at us," she drawled, parroting the familiar, gruff bark of the old witch Mombi. Lanadel laughed again.

"Sounds familiar," she said.

"You'll have the whole speech memorized by the end of the week," Melindra predicted. "Duty to Oz, blah blah, bringing together all corners of the land in unity, blah blah, Wicked coming together for the first time in the history of Oz to confront this profound and unexpected new threat to our safety as a country."

It had been so thrilling when Dorothy first returned to Oz. The Wizard's era had been before Lanadel was born, but she was old enough to remember the Scarecrow's rule. The kindly fellow had been a sweet and endearing ruler, but he'd never seemed particularly effective. For a while, he'd implemented the building of schools all across Oz. Like the other kids in her village, she'd dutifully trooped along with her brothers to a little schoolhouse. She'd learned a lot of strange facts that still stuck in her brain: the annual sunfruit exports of the Kingdom of the Beasts, the tariff rate on buzzleberries from Quadling Country, and the chief dangers of traveling among the winged monkeys. But it was hard to see the point of school, and soon enough parents stopped sending their children. There was too much work to do to waste the day memorizing the names of every ruler of the Winkies.

And then something had happened in the Emerald City, and suddenly the Scarecrow wasn't king anymore and they had a new ruler called Ozma, who'd been queen all along, or something like that. News took a long time to reach Lanadel's tiny village in the far hills of Quadling Country, and her people didn't have much use for rulers; their day-to-day life was much the same no matter who sat on the throne of Oz.

But even her village knew when Dorothy returned. The girl they'd heard about in bedtime stories and legends, the Witchslayer who'd saved Oz long ago—she wasn't just real, she was back. Lanadel's family had celebrated along with everyone else. And when Dorothy became Queen of Oz—well, even better. Or so they'd thought. That was before. Before Dorothy had created those half-person, half-mechanical creatures. Before she'd begun raiding villages and towns across Oz, taking prisoners and leaving a wake of blood, chaos, and burning houses. Before those terrible things had come to Lanadel's village and—

No, she thought. *Not now.* She couldn't let herself think about what had happened to her family. It would tear her apart before she had the chance to even the scales. And the Order was her only chance at righting the balance.

The Revolutionary Order of the Wicked was mysterious— their existence had only been a rumor when she set out looking for them after . . . after what Dorothy's troops had done to her family. It had taken her long weeks of traveling and asking careful questions in inns and markets before, half starved and completely exhausted, she'd found her way to their training caves high in the Traveling Mountains. There was no map— the mountains moved too much for that. She'd had nothing to go on but half-fantastical stories: that the Wicked Witch of the West was still alive and had raised an army in order to stop the newly minted tyrant Dorothy's rampage across Oz. That Glinda was a double agent, flitting between the Emerald City and a secret location in the middle of the mountains. That the winged monkeys were evil. That the winged monkeys were good. That somewhere on the side of Mount Gillikin was the entrance to a magical warren of caverns and tunnels that led to the heart of Oz—and a huge, secret army, training in stealth until they were strong enough to go up against Dorothy's terrible forces.

By the time she reached the foothills of the Traveling Mountains, Lanadel had long since run out of food. She knew going farther into the mountains meant certain death—unless the Order was real, and unless she could find them. But she hadn't hesitated as she took the first step on the narrow, rocky path that heaved under her feet as the mountains undulated around her with deep, rumbling booms and cracks. Revenge was the only thing she had left to live for. And so far, the Order was the only hope she had of avenging her family.

"Follow the shadow of Mount Gillikin," she whispered, repeating the words an old innkeeper had told her in a sleepy hamlet in Gillikin Country. And maybe she was just delirious from starvation or exhaustion, but the innkeeper's words had taken on a literal meaning. Mount Gillikin was the highest peak in the ever-shifting range, and as the mountain moved, its long, immense shadow had taken on the shape of a giant hand beckoning her forward. She hadn't been walking for long when a huge storm descended on the mountainside, blowing snow so thick she could only see a few inches in front of her face. Half frozen and more than half starved, she had stumbled out of the storm into the meager shelter of a cleft in the rock that turned out to be the entrance to a much larger cavern. And there she had sunk to the ground, too exhausted to go any farther, and waited to die.

It was Gert, an ancient, grandmotherly witch whose sweet face belied her tremendous power, who'd found her collapsed on the floor of the cavern, and Gert who'd helped her to her feet and guided her to a tunnel at the back of the cave that led to the vast warren of tunnels and caverns where the Order's headquarters were housed. Lanadel had no idea how far the caves extended, or how many troops the Order had. In two weeks, she'd seen a handful of other people, but they were always moving quickly back and forth along the corridors of the Order's caverns and no one ever stopped to talk to her. She slept alone, in a small cave with a thin mattress on the floor, and Nox brought her her meals. She had risked her life to find the Order, but since she'd gotten here, she had lived in a weird limbo.

Gert had shown her to the cave where she slept the afternoon she arrived, and brought her a bowl of warm, nourishing broth that sparkled with an eerie green light. "Drink up," she urged. The soup fizzed in her throat as she swallowed it, and almost immediately she could feel her whole body tingling as the strength returned to her arms and legs.

She'd slept like a dead person until Gert woke her up again—she assumed the next morning, although in the windowless cavern, she had no way to tell. Gert had introduced her to gruff old Mombi and sweet, pretty Glamora, and then she'd brought Lanadel to the training cave where Nox awaited her. That first day had been brutal—and so had the day after that. But as the days passed, her muscles gradually adjusted to the constant, punishing routine of her training. She knew there were other trainees, but she hadn't met them. She hadn't met anyone at all, other than the witches.

It was as if Nox was waiting for her to do something special—demonstrate some impressive skill or undiscovered talent—before she would be allowed to do anything other than eat her meals in silence and train obsessively with him. After a few weeks, she was so lonely that she was halfway tempted to run back down the side of Mount Gillikin and seek out somewhere else to go. Except that there was nowhere else. The Order was all she had now, for better or for worse.

Melindra was the first person other than Nox, Mombi, Glamora, or Gert that she'd talked to since she arrived. And it was hard to use the word "conversation" to describe the terse interactions she had with Nox. More like he barked orders, and she followed. And Melindra was funny, friendly . . . and gorgeous.

Melindra yawned widely and dunked her head in the warm water. "What I want to know is when we get to *fight*," she said when she came back up, breaking into Lanadel's thoughts.

"You haven't been sent on any missions yet?" Lanadel didn't know what she was expecting. Everything about her life now was so new. So confusing. And so filled with pain. Every day felt like being torn in a thousand different directions—as if there were dozens of different Lanadels inside her, trying to get out.